Give Me More

Books by P.J. Mellor

PLEASURE BEACH

GIVE ME MORE

THE COWBOY
(with Vonna Harper, Nelissa Donovan and Nikki Alton)

THE FIREFIGHTER
(with Susan Lyons and Alyssa Brooks)

Published by Kensington Publishing Corporation

Give Me More

P. J. MELLOR

APHRODISIA

KENSINGTON PUBLISHING CORP.

http://www.kensingtonbooks.com

KENSINGTON BOOKS are published by

Kensington Publishing Corp.
850 Third Avenue
New York, NY 10022

All Kensington Titles, Imprints, and Distributed Lines are available at special quantity discounts for bulk purchases for sales promotions, premiums, fund-raising, and educational or institutional use.

Special book excerpts or customized printings can also be created to fit specific needs. For details, write or phone the office of the Kensington special sales manager: Kensington Publishing Corp., 850 Third Avenue, New York, NY 10022, attn: Special Sales Department, Phone: 1-800-221-2647.

Aphrodisia and the A logo are trademarks of Kensington Publishing Corp. Kensington and the K logo Reg. U.S. Pat & TM Off

ISBN-13: 978-0-7582-1441-6
ISBN-10: 0-7582-1441-3

First Trade Paperback Printing: February 2007

10 9 8 7 6 5 4 3 2 1

Printed in the United States of America

To my grandmother, Hettie Glover, the original wild woman.
I miss you, Gram!

ACKNOWLEDGMENTS

As always, thanks to my agent, the super Sha-Shana Crichton, and my editor, the guy who actually gets my humor, John Scognamiglio.

Special thanks to my PAL, Lark Howard, for her intimate knowledge of French men.

CONTENTS

Wild Thing

1

Eric gave a roar of completion and collapsed on her. Within seconds, her oxygen-deprived lungs began to protest. His chest hair tickled her nose.

Allowing him to come home with her again was a mistake on so many levels. She wedged both hands against his clammy, Aramis-scented skin and shoved.

He grunted and drooled on her neck.

"Eric," Maggie Hamilton said against his clavicle, resisting the temptation to close her teeth around the offending bone. "Get off!"

His chuckle rumbled his chest and set her teeth on edge. "Just did, babe."

Pig. "Eric, I can't breathe. Move!" What possessed her to let him come home with her? She shoved again, and he rolled off to lie, spread-eagle, next to her. She glanced at the poster of the cruise ship, docked at an exotic island port, tacked to her wall for inspiration, and then over at Eric's Mr. Happy, which looked decidedly droopy. "It's time for you to leave."

"Aw, babe, don't say that." He turned on his side, one heavy arm crushing her ribs in an effort to draw her closer.

Plop! Mr. Happy slapped against her thigh like a dead snake. She eased away from the offending member.

"Really, you should leave." She pointed the toes of one foot toward the floor, gripping the edge of the mattress for leverage.

Eric grumbled something and rolled off to stand on the other side of the bed. He scratched his butt and shuffled toward the bathroom.

"And shut the door this time, please." That was definitely something she did not want to view.

She swung to her feet and pulled on her floral silk robe, then frowned at her refection in the wardrobe mirror. Too sexy mussed.

With a quick look at the still-closed door, she rummaged in the dresser. She'd just pulled on her oversize University of Michigan sweatshirt, tugging it to her knees, when Eric walked out.

He wasn't all that bad looking, if you liked the dumb-jock persona. As he was tall and heavily muscled, his dark hair spiked and clothing rumpled, there were many woman who might find him attractive.

She looked at his heavy-lidded eyes and suppressed a shudder. Attractive only if you went for the Neanderthal look.

She didn't. Not anymore. Yet, after swearing she'd never again allow Eric into her home, let alone her bed, here he was. She had to start being more assertive.

"So, what time should I be here tomorrow to take you to the dock?" He scratched his belly through the gaping fly of his jeans. At least she hoped it was his belly. "Babe," he said, walking toward her, "I'm telling you, I think a singles cruise is a really bogus idea."

She took a step back and then sidestepped toward the open bedroom door. "Well, I don't. And you don't have to take me. I made other arrangements."

"But, babe, who's gonna kiss you good-bye?" He spread his arms, palms up in supplication.

Not you. Anyone but you. Of course, she couldn't say that. Her mother had taught her never to be rude. "Karyl said she'd take me." She ushered him toward the door.

In a flash, he turned and closed his arms around her. He smelled of aftershave, beer and sex. On him, not a winning combination.

Barreling her arms to break his embrace, she stepped back and reached to open the door. "I'll see you in a few weeks."

"Babe! How long is this damn cruise?"

Not nearly long enough. But she couldn't say that either. "I'm not really sure," she lied. "I'll call you when I get back." *Yeah, why don't you hold your breath on that one.*

His beard-stubbled face leaned close to her, intent clear in his bloodshot, mud-brown eyes.

A quick sidestep took her out of target range. She pushed him out the door and closed it.

He pounded on the solid imitation wood. "Babe!" *Bang, bang.* "Open the door!" *Bang, bang, bang.* Aren't you even gonna kiss me good-bye?"

"No!" she yelled, sliding the chain home.

"But, babe!" His voice carried through the door.

She strode to the bathroom and stripped and then stood under the tepid spray, waiting for the hot water.

"Babe," she growled in a mocking voice, grabbing the shampoo and squirting a liberal amount into her palm.

She lathered her short hair with a vengeance, determined to wash away every trace of Eric. Shampoo foam ran everywhere. It oozed down her face, slithered over her shoulders, slid over her hips and sluiced down both legs to tickle her toes. Way too much shampoo.

"I'm never going to get this rinsed out." She rinsed until her arms ached. Her hair still felt slick to her questing fingers.

"Babe," she growled again, twisting off the controls and jerking a towel from the duct-taped towel bar.

Then reality hit her . . . Eric didn't remember her name.

After stripping the sheets and starting the washer, she remade the bed and fell in. Exhausted, she should've been instantly in dreamland. But no. Instead she tossed and turned. Her back began aching. Did she remember to run the dishwasher?

With a sigh, she tossed back the covers and stomped into the tiny kitchen. Her dishwasher had two cycles—on and off. While it appeared to be off, steam oozing from the top told her she'd turned it on.

Back in bed, comfort and, therefore, sleep eluded her. Maybe she should invest in a new mattress when she came home. Did she remember to pack her red dress?

Feet again met carpet, neatly sidestepping the brick Eric had used months ago to "temporarily" fix the leg of her bed.

Grunting with effort, she dragged over her heavy suitcase and plopped it onto the bed. There it was. The red dress was right on top.

The sound of her suitcase zipper closing filled the silent apartment. She dragged it back to the closet.

"I wonder if I can fit in an extra bikini? It shouldn't take up too much space."

On tiptoe, she felt along the top shelf of her closet. No bikini, but she found a box she didn't remember having up there.

Pulling it down, she walked closer to the light.

She gasped, then glanced guiltily around.

"No one's here, dummy." She stroked a finger down the amazingly realistic plastic. Then she gave the bulbous tip a little squeeze. Wow. It even felt semireal.

Mystery Lover Model 4099. A present from Karyl—for

Maggie's birthday last year—the vibrator had caused raucous laughter and comments from her friends when she'd opened it. She'd never even tried it out.

She glanced around and then checked the locks on her door, just to make sure.

Walking slowly back to her bed, she untied her robe, her gaze never leaving the gleaming phallus where it lay nestled in purple velvet, surrounded by an impressive assortment of flavored body gels.

"Let's try raspberry." She opened the tiny pot and dipped in the tip of her little finger; then she sucked off the sweet concoction. Not bad.

Dipping her index finger this time, she slathered the gel all around the top of the vibrator and then swirled her tongue around it until every speck of gel disappeared.

Next she finger painted the entire length of the plastic shaft, squeezing her legs together to calm the sudden restlessness she felt.

Dropping her robe, she climbed on her bed to lie on her back, the vibrator held high above her.

"Open the hangar," she said on a giggle, remembering childhood games. "Vvroom." She guided her private missile in a gliding circle to her open mouth, taking as much in as she could without gagging.

After a while, the ache between her legs became harder to ignore.

The wet tip of the vibrator cooled her skin where she dragged it between her bare breasts and down her abdomen until she reached the point that wept her need.

A few circles around her clitoris had her moving on the sheets wadded against her back.

No point in letting the gel go to waste.

She held the vibrator between her thighs and reached for another little pot. Strawberry.

She coated the entire shaft, swirling her tongue and fingertip around the top, imagining herself on her singles cruise, a hot island breeze bathing her bare skin while she licked and sucked one of the many lovers who existed solely for her sexual gratification.

It wasn't enough. How did she turn the dumb thing on? It was allegedly the top-of-the-line of vibrators—Karyl spared no expense when it came to embarrassing her.

The phone rang. Maggie screamed, automatically squeezing the vibrator.

Slick with gel, it shot from her fist like it was coming out of a rocket launcher and scored a direct hit on her grandmother's china lamp, plunging the room into darkness.

The phone rang again.

With a last look at the remains of her lamp, Maggie reached for the cordless phone on the floor.

"What took so long?" Karyl's voice echoed from the speaker. "Oh, don't tell me you actually took pity on that throwback and let him spend the night!"

"No, of course not." Maggie glanced around the room as if her friend could actually see the contrary evidence—which was no doubt on her bathroom floor somewhere. Eric never could seem to hit the trash can.

Karyl let out an exaggerated, relieved sigh. "Thank you, Lord. So . . . what are you doing? I know you're all packed. Mags? You sound like you're breathing hard. What's going on?"

"What makes you think anything's going on?" She gave a feeble laugh.

"Because I've known you since kindergarten, and I know when you're hiding something. Now . . . what?"

"Vibrator," Maggie managed to mumble.

"What? Is there something wrong with your refrigerator? I can't hear you. Are you talking into the wrong end of the phone again?"

"I said," she almost shouted, "I was just fooling around with the vibrator you gave me."

"You were?"

"Don't sound so pleased. I can't even figure out how to turn the dumb thing on." She gave a bark of laughter. "Story of my life." She walked to pick up the "dumb thing" and returned to sit on the side of the mattress.

"Mags, it's state of the art. There isn't a switch."

"But how do you—"

"See the little fake testicles at the base?"

Maggie's eyes widened. "I wouldn't exactly call them little." She ran her palm over them in an idle caress, tracing the flowing script of the gold ML at the base with her fingertip.

Karyl laughed. "Whatever. When you're using it, you, um, sort of grip the balls and squeeze them together. The tighter you squeeze, the stronger the vibration."

Maggie gave an experimental squeeze. The vibrator emanated a low buzzing sound, vibrating the hand holding the shaft. "Oh!" She gave a shriek of laughter and dropped it to the floor.

"I'll let you experiment for a while," Karyl said, a smile in her voice. "I'll be there tomorrow morning by no later than eight. You already printed up your boarding pass and everything you need, didn't you?"

"Yes, I—"

"Great! See you tomorrow." Karyl hung up.

Maggie pressed the OFF button and laid the phone on the nightstand, then picked up the vibrator.

It wouldn't hurt to try it. After all, it had been a gift. It would be rude never to use it.

The rounded tip teased her opening. She looked down and wondered how it would ever fit.

The gel was cool against her labia but quickly warmed as it came in contact with her internal heat. She stretched to accommodate the girth of the vibrator.

To her surprise, it slid in to the hilt quite smoothly. Maybe the gel helped. She tightened her internal muscles. ML—or Mel, as she nicknamed it—slid back out to her waiting hand. Bereft, she glided Mel back in. In. Out. In. Out.

Close. She was so close.

Panting, she reached down a shaking hand and squeezed the rubber testicles.

And screamed when the foreign object within seemed to take on a life of its own.

When she was able to relax a bit, the vibration worked its magic, setting off tingles deep within. Her muscles began to vibrate. Internal lubrication made Mel slippery. She squeezed the testicles in her fist, unable to gasp more than shallow pants of air. Her heart thundered, pounding as though it would rip from her chest.

Her next scream had nothing to do with surprise as wave after wave of pleasure washed over her, drowning her in sensation.

2

Maggie awoke to sun streaming in through her open blinds, Mel still clutched in her hand.

Make that stuck to her hand. Ick. She peeled her personal device from her palm and sat up. The covers must have been somewhere on the floor.

Next she noticed she was naked. And sticky. She ran her tongue over her furry, strawberry-flavored teeth and winced.

She glanced at Mel, lying innocuously on the messy sheet. Who knew?

At that moment, her alarm clock chose to blast the room with oldies, making Maggie realize she had a headache. *What was in that strawberry body gel?* she wondered as she dragged herself into the shower.

By the time Karyl knocked on the door at seven fifty-five, Maggie was dressed and ready to go, a cleaned and shined Mel tucked neatly into the inside pocket of her bulging suitcase. After last night, she realized she didn't need an extra bikini. Mel was a necessity.

"Well, I can see by the glow on your cheeks that you liked

my gift," Karyl said with a grin, her green eyes sparkling through her always overlong bangs. Karyl was the only white woman Maggie knew with Tina Turner hair. On her, though, it looked good. "Did you get any sleep?"

Maggie sniffed and tried not to grin. "Of course. Let's go."

"Wait, I have a bon-voyage gift for you." Karyl presented a flat gold box tied with confetti-colored strings. "Quick! Open it, and say, 'Thank you, Karyl,' so we can go."

"I can't believe you did this! Thank you so much!"

"Mags? You haven't opened it yet." Karyl had a knowing grin.

"Oh." It took a moment for Maggie's shaky fingers to remove the million or so strings and shove the top off the box. "Oh! Karyl! I can't believe you bought this!"

"Why not?" Karyl grinned. "I got sick of watching you drool all over the window every time we went by the shop. Believe me, my motivation was strictly selfish. Do you know how embarrassing it is to watch you covet something for so long?"

Maggie held up the scarf, admiring the way the sunlight shone through the gossamer, off-white silk that sparkled from the tiny gold and silver threads. She wrapped it around her shoulders and struck a pose. "How do I look?"

"Fabulous, dahling!" Karyl accepted her grateful hug. She handed her a bulging purple bag. "I also brought a few items left over from my Boudoir Buddy party. You can check them out once you get out to sea. Now, get this stuff packed so we can vamoose!"

The BumbleBee was a disappointment, as cruise ships go. Docked between liners of monstrous proportions, it looked like the love child of the larger vessels.

Maggie glanced at the ticket information clutched in her hand. Yes, her ship was, indeed, the BumbleBee. She supposed she should have known a cruise line with a name like Cruises R

Us wouldn't have the largest of cruise ships. She took heart in the fact that her ship was equipped with all the amenities—not that she would know the difference.

A couple walked up the gangplank, arm in arm. Maggie glared at them. Didn't they know it was a singles cruise? How stupid could they be, taking a singles cruise together?

She grimaced and shook her head, then followed them. A smallish man stood at the top, directing the passengers to check in.

She dismissed him with a casual once-over. It should be a requirement, on a singles cruise, to employ only attractive people. It only made sense, businesswise. Maybe, after the cruise, she would contact the corporate office and offer her services. Heaven knew the fledgling cruise line needed better PR.

The toothy clerk at the check-in desk seemed excited about Maggie being assigned to the Tarzan and Jane's Lair stateroom.

Maggie frowned, negotiating the stairs while trying not to knock a fellow passenger to his or her death with her suitcase. According to the clerk, unlike most cruise ships, all the Bumble-Bee's rooms were on the upper floors.

Maggie thought of the name of her room and said a little prayer for it not to mean her singles cruise was a blind-dating type of cruise. She inserted her card key and pushed open the scuffed, once-white door.

"Oh, my." She looked at what appeared to be a tiny jungle, composed entirely of dust-encrusted, plastic foliage. A flip of what she thought was the light switch activated the pièce de résistance—jungle sounds. Very loud jungle sounds. So loud, in fact, she doubted she'd be able to converse on her cell phone. Or sleep. And where was the dang light?

She dragged in her suitcase and shut the door, throwing the bolt home. Always a good idea for women traveling alone. Patting the wall, she made cautious progress. Light became secondary. Now that her initial shock had subsided, she noticed light streaming in from a small skylight in the middle of the room as well as spilling from an open doorway on the far wall. She could see fine. But the jungle noise reverberating in her head had to stop.

Surely there had to be a volume control somewhere. Not finding one, she flipped off the switch. The control broke off in her hand.

The cacophony blared on.

A step into the room brought a definite burn to her nose. She sneezed. Her ankles itched where the dusty plants brushed against them. Everywhere, plastic plants surrounded her, their leaves furry with who knew how many years of accumulated dust. She sneezed again. Her eyes began to tear. And Karyl had made fun of her for bringing her fresh-air machine. Without it, her dust allergies would run rampant.

Finally she found the bed. At least, she thought it was the bed, since it had what appeared to be camouflage-printed sheets and pillowcases. The bed itself eerily resembled a giant coconut shell. A very tall coconut shell. She'd have to take a running start and leap into it. Maybe she could have them bring up a stool.

She giggled. The room was so hokey, it was laughable.

The gurgle of water, now rising above the call of the wild, drew her attention as she finished unpacking.

"Must be the in-suite spa they mentioned on their Web site." She smoothed her hand over her new, beautiful scarf, carefully folded it and laid it in the top drawer of the chest of drawers disguised as a steamer trunk. She swatted at a particularly aggressive swath of mosquito netting and walked toward the sound.

There it was. Pitiful. Touted as a grotto for two, she had to ask, two what? She doubted she could fit in there without folding her knees to her chest. A glance at the trickling "waterfall" told her where she'd be showering. A peek behind the surrounding plastic leaves revealed a tiny sink and toilet.

She flipped open her cell and punched a button.

"Karyl, you are not going to believe this."

3

Maggie sniffed and wiped her nose with the tissue stuck in the belt of her once-white slacks and tried to rinse the grime from the washcloth. Sweat trickled between her breasts, making her wish she had never invested in the new instant-cleavage-enhancer model. A lot of good it did her.

Hunched over the miniscule sink, she rubbed at the dust-streaked terry held under a flow of water one step above trickle status. When it became obvious that most of the dust was embedded for eternity, she twisted the little pointed knobs to turn off the water and made her way back into the living quarters to resume her cleaning, careful to avoid poking her eye out on the colorful beak of a stuffed bird next to the "grotto."

An hour later, she stretched and rubbed the small of her back while she looked around at her progress. All one and a half plastic bushes of backbreaking progress.

"This won't do."

She walked to the wooden box housing the phone and called the concierge.

* * *

Ten long minutes later, a timid knock sounded. She fought her way through the vinyl, slid back the bolt and opened the door.

The small man from the deck stood all but quivering in the hall, his clipboard clutched to his scrawny chest.

"Ms. Hamilton?" he called above the jungle sounds, "I'm Otto, the purser. Front desk said you had a complaint?"

"Yes, Otto, I certainly do!" she shouted back and motioned him inside. "Come in."

Just when she wondered if she'd have to resort to dragging him bodily into her suite, he stepped across the threshold.

She waved her hand in the direction of her personal jungle. "I'm afraid this just won't do. I feel like I need a machete to even find my bed! Plus, I'm very allergic to dust." She pointed at one particularly fuzzy example, in case he failed to notice. "And the noise is, well, you can hear for yourself. I need to change rooms."

The poor man seemed to cower. "I—I'm afraid that's just not possible, M—Ms. Hamilton. All the other books are roomed." He stepped back, his knuckles white where he gripped his clipboard. "I mean, all the other rooms are booked." He reached back and opened the door, his intent on escape clear.

"Wait!" She lunged toward him, eliciting a startled whimper from the man. "Please. I'll take anything." She sneezed and focused her teary eyes on him. "Please. The dust is killing me."

His lips disappeared into a tight line. He stood a bit taller. "I'll speak to the cruise director, but I doubt he can do anything."

He hurried out and closed the door with a snap before she could think of an argument.

"Great," she murmured, swiping at a particularly obnoxious split-leaf elephant ear that had been whacking her head in the air-conditioned breeze. "Just how I wanted to spend my first day at sea."

* * *

She'd just dragged out her portable air cleaner and located a plug—no easy feat, given the decor—when a knock echoed in the little jungle.

She crawled out from under yet another fake palm and got to her feet, brushing the dust bunnies from her white slacks as she walked toward the door. It no longer mattered that her door did not have a peephole. Jack the Ripper could be on the other side and if he offered her a clean room, she'd gladly follow him anywhere.

Her pile of dust-gray cleaning rags caught her attention. Keeping up appearances was a necessity. In a swooping motion, she bent to scoop them up as she walked by. Her bare foot hit a wet spot on the edge of the grotto. Her mind registered the cool, slick feel of the porcelain "beach" a nanosecond before she slid with a scream and a splash into the churning water.

The woman's scream from behind the locked door made Drew's blood run cold. Even the ridiculous jungle sounds couldn't drown out her distress. It was bad enough to be assigned to the honeymoon cruises for his final season. He'd be damned if one of his last cruises would lose a bride.

Hands shaking, he fumbled with his set of master keys before he found the right one and got the door unlocked.

He saw her immediately.

She sat chest deep in the grotto, little islands of what looked like dirty washcloths floating around her. One small hand covered her left eye and forehead.

"Are you okay, ma'am?" He pocketed his keys and moved to the edge of the water.

She didn't blink. "My eye hurts," she said, the husky quality of her voice slipping down his spine like a seductive fingernail. Great. Finally his libido kicks in, and it's with a newlywed woman.

"What happened?" He scanned the room for her husband,

ready to personally throw the bastard from the ship. Men who abused women were lower than a snake's armpits, as far as he was concerned.

"I slipped and fell into the water."

Sure, you did. He reached out a hand to help her stand on what he knew to be a less than skid-free tub bottom. "I've got you. Just take small steps, and then I'll help you over the rim. Do you need to see a doctor?"

She shook her head, her short curls sticking to her skull. Wet, her hair looked almost translucent, so he'd bet she was a blonde.

The silk shirt sticking to her like a second skin most likely was yellow. He tried to avert his eyes from the scrap-of-nothing bra revealed by the wet fabric but couldn't seem to drag his gaze away from the tempting sight. Lordy, it was enough to make a grown man weep.

Once-white pants clung to world-class legs, leaving little to the imagination. Why were all the good ones married?

Her hand felt tiny within his grasp. He resisted the urge to pull her close. Barely. Damn, what was wrong with him? Maybe he'd been out to sea too long. He was definitely drowning in the clear turquoise of her bloodshot eyes. Why did women stay with bastards who made them cry?

Wow. Maggie looked up—way up—into the blue eyes of easily the most handsome man she'd ever seen. *Now, this is more like it.* Tan, with golden-brown hair and mile-wide shoulders, dressed in a white uniform shirt and Bermuda shorts, he looked good enough to eat.

Dang. She realized she was holding his hand like some starstruck teenager. She dropped it and took a step back.

Unfortunately she was a bit too close to the edge of the grotto.

Arms flailing as she fell backward, she grabbed for the first thing her hands came in contact with . . . his shirt.

With a huge splash, they landed chest to chest, heads banging together. Maggie tasted blood at the same time she realized she was held underwater by the weight of the man. Shoving him aside, she broke the surface and gasped for air, trudging toward the water's edge.

"Did you have to land on me?" Sputtering and coughing, she turned on him.

He lay facedown in the water.

"Shit!" She plowed against the force of the jets and grasped the back of his uniform collar to haul him above the surface of the water.

Her arm around his chest, she dragged him to the edge of the whirlpool, grunting with effort.

Good thing she was a lifeguard.

Beneath her palm, his heart beat a strong rhythm. He was breathing. Breathing was good.

"Let's get you out of these nasty wet clothes," she whispered, flicking open one gold button after another. She'd sworn to be more aggressive on her cruise, and fate had dropped the hunk in her arms. True, he was unconscious, but that wouldn't last for long. Who was she to buck fate? Unfortunately the man's forehead was rapidly growing a nasty goose egg. Before her eyes, it darkened to a deep cherry red right before the skin split from the immediate swelling.

Having her way with him would obviously have to wait.

With a grunt, she rolled him to his side and thumped his back. He coughed a few times and wheezed as he struggled to sit up.

Shoot. Mouth-to-mouth would not be needed.

"Are you okay?" His voice was croaky. He cleared his throat and looked at her through sinfully thick, blond-tipped lashes. The once-over from his baby blues had her sitting back on her heels in an effort not to squirm.

He traced the tender skin next to her eye where she'd bumped her head in the first fall, leaving a trail of fire.

Forcing back a wince, she reached out to touch the now huge bump on his forehead. It was hot.

His breath hissed. He leaned back a bit. "Ow." He probed the bump. "I really whacked my head." He glanced up. "Are you sure you're okay?"

"Fine." More than a whisper seemed inappropriate, for some reason.

He broke whatever connection they had and stood, helping her to her feet. "Thanks for dragging me out of the water."

He scanned the room. "Where's your husband, Mrs. Hamilton?"

"Ah, it's Miss. Or Ms." Her skin burned with his scrutiny. "I mean, I'm not married."

"Excuse me?" She couldn't have said what he thought he'd just heard. He wasn't that lucky.

"I said I'm not married." She frowned and brushed at her wet, see-through pant leg before meeting his gaze. "Wouldn't that defeat the purpose?"

"What purpose would that be?" Somehow his shirt was un-buttoned, so he began working the sharp buttons through the wet fabric. No need to get excited, despite her claim. Newlyweds often forgot they were married at first. Probably a tough acclimation.

"The purpose of the cruise, of course."

The woman sounded annoyed and looked a little agitated. Maybe it was best to humor her. "I suppose different people take cruises for different reasons." Although why a single person would take a honeymoon cruise was beyond him.

He gave her another once-over. She sure was a looker, he'd give her that.

She flashed a little lopsided smile that sent heat zipping through him.

Too bad she was married. And lied about it. Not to mention the fact she was more than a little wacky.

He turned toward the door. Best to cut his losses and get on with his day.

"Wait!" She grabbed his arm, the warmth of her palm doing funny things to his heart rate. "I don't even know your name."

He glanced at her hand and then back to her red-rimmed eyes. Their clear color seemed incongruous with the almost-painful-looking redness surrounding them.

"Drew. Drew Connor." He extricated his arm and offered his hand. "Cruise director."

She slipped her hand into his in what felt like an oddly intimate gesture.

Get a grip, Connor! The woman is just returning your handshake.

"Maggie Hamilton." She shrugged and removed the temptation of her hand. "But I guess you already know that."

"Ms. Hamilton?" He tilted her chin with his finger tip.

"Maggie," she said on a breath. "Call me Maggie."

"Maggie." Despite his best intentions, he leaned closer. "Think hard. You're not really single, are you?"

Her brow wrinkled. She stepped out of his reach and heaved a sigh. "Why are you having such an issue with my marital status?" She threw up her hands and strode to the side of the bed before turning on him. "Don't you think I would know it if I'd married someone? What? Do you think I'd forget something like that?"

Maybe she was telling the truth.

Fists on hips—very shapely hips, he might add—she glared at him. "Why are you grinning like that?"

He took a step toward her.

"Mr. Connor—"

"Drew." He took another step.

"Drew." She held up her hand. "Okay, you can stop right there, *Drew*." He took another step. "Why are you looking at me like that?"

He closed the distance. Practically chest to chest, he felt the heat. He knew she felt it, too.

"You're really single, aren't you?" He raised her limp left hand and surveyed her ringless finger.

"I—" She swallowed and looked up at him with her incredible eyes. "I already told you that."

Damn, this was stupid on so many levels.

He put his arms around her, half prepared to be kicked or slapped.

She reacted by encircling his neck with her arms.

Okay. Let's think about all the reasons why this is a bad idea.

He pulled her closer.

One: it's against company policy.

He leaned down, feeling the exciting warmth of her breath against his lips.

Two: even if she isn't married, she should be off-limits, due to reason one. Plus, if she isn't married, why is she on a honeymoon cruise? Maybe she's an escaped criminal. Maybe she's the female equivalent of a gigolo, who preys on married men.

The last idea fueled his excitement. He ground his already rock-hard erection against her.

She smiled and ground right back, eliciting a moan he hoped sounded more like a growl. Growls were more manly.

Three: stop reacting with your body, and listen to your mind, stupid! You don't even know this woman. This isn't some singles bar. You're going to get caught.

He glanced down at her. The heat from their wet clothes practically made steam. Her incredible eyes were heavy lidded. She licked her lips, and he was a goner.

Four: time to score.

* * *

Maggie looked up at the man holding her in his arms and felt her knees go weak. If he didn't kiss her soon, she might just climb up his hard body and have her way with him right here, right now.

"Kiss me," she said on a breath, his mouth poised mere millimeters from her own.

"Oh, darlin', I plan on it, I definitely plan on it." His husky whisper vibrated her lips an instant before settling in for the duration.

Whew! The guy sure knew how to kiss. She wouldn't be surprised if she had steam coming out of her ears.

He nibbled the edge of her lip before swooping in for another toe-curling, bone-melting kiss.

Her knees threatened to buckle. She couldn't take a deep breath, even through her nose.

He shifted position slightly, deepening the kiss she swore couldn't get deeper. Who needed to breathe, anyway?

"Our clothes . . ." she finally managed to whisper against his lips.

"What about them?" He nuzzled her neck.

"They're wet." Her teeth closed around his earlobe.

He shuddered. "Well, we'll just have to get out of them," he returned.

His hands bracketed her waist, pushing the wet silk of her top ever upward while he continued to feast on her lips and neck. He paused a moment at the front clasp of her intensifier bra before popping it open with a flick of his wrist.

She held her breath. Would he notice the disparity in size once he palmed her actual flesh?

Then his hands cupped her, and she released a sigh. Who cared? As long as he kept doing what he was doing.

Her top came up and over her head, his mouth scarcely leaving hers.

Breaking contact, he knelt at her bare feet, peeling the wet linen down her hips and then balancing her while she stepped out of the sodden fabric.

A hot trail of kisses tracked his progress up her body until they again stood chest to chest. Well, actually more like chest to abdomen, since he was a good foot taller.

His mouth once again took possession of hers while he slipped her bra straps from her shoulders and down her arms.

She rubbed her pebbled nipples against his firm chest, loving the friction.

In response, his hips bucked against her while he deepened the kiss, all but lifting her from her feet.

She wrapped her arms around his neck, swallowing a tiny gasp of excitement at the feel of his fingers hooking in the sides of her thong. The wet string dragged along the skin of her hips and then rolled beneath her buttocks to scrape down her thighs. When it fell to her knees, she was forced to break the kiss and step out.

Somewhat of a klutz under normal circumstances, she didn't want to risk tripping on her own underwear during what might easily be the most awesome sexual encounter of her life to date.

His gaze left a trail of fire down to her toes and back up again. Beneath her palm, his heart pounded, his breath coming in harsh drags of air.

"This is nuts," he said on a breath. "Tell me to stop." He nibbled the edge of her lip. "Are you sure this is what you want?"

She nodded. Karyl wanted her to walk on the wild side. Maggie glanced at her personal jungle. It was about as wild as she was going to get. "I want to do something wild to celebrate my first cruise." She hoped her smile was more assured than she felt. "Let's make love in the water."

His eyes widened; then a slow grin revealed a set of blinding white teeth and a lethal dimple. "Anything the lady wants. . . ."

He made short work of stripping—dang, she didn't get a chance to check him out—and then scooped her up in his arms and stepped into the grotto.

She gripped his shoulders to keep from drifting away from the delicious heat of his hard body.

"Wait." He reached for a boulder at the edge of the waterfall. It opened. He pulled out what looked like a small foam Boogie Board and positioned it at her back.

"Lie back, relax," he instructed. "Let me do all the work."

It was difficult, but she managed to somewhat relax while Drew caressed her legs from ankle to thigh. With each pass of his hands, her muscles grew more pliant.

He stepped into the vee of her legs.

Warm water lapped at the juncture of her thighs. She resisted the urge to clamp them together and squirm.

"So pretty," he said in a low, husky voice, his breath telling her he was oh-so-close to her most private place. "So smooth. Soft." His lips whispered over her, causing her to arch in a silent plea.

Water sloshed in her ears, but she was beyond caring.

He licked and suckled while his fingers played with her flesh, spread before him like a sexual smorgasbord.

Good thing she'd indulged in a Brazilian wax, she thought, and swallowed a giggle when Drew lapped at her then flicked her nub with the tip of his tongue.

Her muscles twitched before taking on the consistency of wet spaghetti. She clamped her legs around his head, anchoring him in place.

Shudders rippled through her. Arching her back, she gasped in her effort not to scream.

It worked. Unfortunately the action plunged her head beneath the water, and she managed to suck in about a gallon of water.

Great. Attempts to cough were moot, with her head still

below the surface of the water. Her body twitched. Whether it was from the earth-shattering release or impending death was a toss-up.

Just her luck. The most powerful orgasm of her life was obviously going to be her last.

4

With a gasping wheeze, Maggie broke through the water, clutching Drew's shoulders to remain above the churning bubbles while she coughed. Dang, choking on water was bad enough, but if she lost her lunch, the mood would definitely take a downward swing.

"Maggie? Are you okay?" Drew's concerned voice echoed within his chest against her ear. "Can I get you anything?"

How about another good tongue lashing followed by a heart-tripping orgasm? Of course, she'd been brought up not to say things like that, so she settled for "Huh?" Okay, sparkling repartee it was not, but her brain cells were waterlogged.

He held her away from his sexy heat and bent to look in her eyes. "I said are you okay?" He kept steadying hands on her shoulders until her feet were under her. "Look, about what just happened. I don't normally do stuff like that, and, well, I'd appreciate it if you wouldn't do something—"

"Do something? Like what?" Had he read her mind?

"Like report me. This is my last season, and I'd hate to be fired. I—"

Wait. This could work. He thinks I have the power to get him fired. Okay, Karyl, you wanted me to walk on the wild side. Let's go for it! "Well, I should hope you don't go around stripping unsuspecting women—"

"I don't!" His eyes begged her understanding. "Really, I don't. In fact, I've never even had any sort of personal contact with a passenger in the last five years."

"Well, Drew, baby, that's about to change." She stepped closer, determined to prove her moxy. "Because I plan to be very up close and personal with you." She trailed the tip of her finger from his chest to navel and then lower, below the water, to find him hard.

Loosely fisting her hand around his arousal, she dragged it down his length and back a couple of times. His indrawn breath had her biting back a smile. The cruise was one of her best ideas to date. She stretched her fingers beyond his base and stroked his testicles as she leaned close to whisper, "Do you want to . . . you know?"

In response, he bucked his hips, his hardness sliding in and out of her hand.

"Do you like this?" Emboldened, she straddled his rigid length and let her aching folds take up where her hand left off.

He growled in response.

Excitement had her all but dancing on the tub floor. Control was a powerful aphrodisiac. "Would you consider being my sex slave in exchange for my silence?"

He went still, and for a moment she worried she'd pushed too hard, gone too far too fast.

He bent to stare into her eyes. A slow smile lighted his face. "Your wish is my command," he replied in a husky whisper.

The heat in his gaze told her she was playing with matches, but she realized she was willing to burn in the sexual fire they ignited.

She backed against the tub. Best to cool things a bit or risk spontaneous combustion. "Then let's play . . . um, sexy house-cleaning. Have you ever played that?" He shook his head. Neither had she, but that didn't mean she couldn't make things up as she went along.

Hopping out of the grotto, she reached for a towel and motioned him to stand before her. When he'd complied, she knelt at his feet and began to lick and dry every drop of moisture from his knees upward, paying special attention to the jutting part begging for her attention.

Other than his breathing and monster erection, he appeared to be unaffected. She, on the other hand, was all but foaming at the mouth for him to reciprocate.

Drew stood practically vibrating with pent-up sexual frustration. Hands clenched at his sides, he watched the rise and fall of Maggie's pert breasts in a vain effort to not look at her hungry little mouth practically devouring his cock. Just as he thought he could stand no more, she stopped and sat back on her heels.

The view made his dick twitch.

Her moist lips curled into a smile. "First rule is you have to talk dirty to me." She glanced up through her lashes. "It turns me on."

Feeling pretty turned on himself at the moment, he said, "No problem. What do you want me to say?"

"Anything you want." She stood, dragging her hand up his body, threatening to make him burst into flames.

He pulled her into his arms and held tight, allowing her to feel his heat, his need.

And that's exactly what it was, he realized. A need. A primal, aching need. For her. And if it meant his job, so be it. If he got fired, it was going to be for a damn good reason.

He took nibbling kisses up her neck, reveling in the taste and smell of her.

"In that case," he said against the shell of her ear, "I want to fuck your brains out."

She giggled, her breasts shimmying against his chest, setting off tremors deep within. "Sounds like a plan, but first . . . you have to do your chores."

"Chores? You mean like bathe you? Give you a thorough massage? Or something more . . . interesting?" He took a fortifying breath. Dirty she wanted, dirty she'd get. "Like suck your tits till you scream, and eat your pussy?"

Her smile had him so damned near to coming, he had to tamp down his excitement.

"Oh, you'll earn the opportunity to do all those things . . . and more."

She picked up a few of the gray washcloths and dipped them in the water and then wrung them out. The action caused her tits to jiggle.

Sexual housecleaning. He could definitely get into that.

He cleared his throat. "Okay. What do I need to do first?"

She pointed to a big elephant ear. "Wash the dust off, and your reward will be on the other side."

Less than three minutes later, the leaf was shining. He eagerly pushed it aside and saw her.

Perched on a rock, she'd drawn little hearts around each of her raspberry-colored nipples with some kind of goo.

"Good job!" She shot a sultry look and cupped her bare breasts, offering them up to him. "You deserve a snack."

The sight had him salivating . . . until she coughed and he looked up at her face.

5

Red, her eyelids were all but swelled shut. The tender skin below her left eye had a distinct purple tinge.

He suspected he didn't look much better.

His sympathetic nature chose that time to raise its ugly head and devour the flames of desire. What was he thinking? The woman was injured. Not to mention a guest on the cruise, not his personal sex toy.

He knelt before her, drawing tender circles around her breasts while his mouth salivated with the desire to lick the gel from her nipples.

"Darlin', I'd like nothing better than to claim my reward. But . . . I think maybe you should see the ship's doctor." Before she could protest, he placed the tip of his finger on her pouting lips. "That was a pretty nasty fall you took earlier, and your cough doesn't sound very good either."

"I'm fine," she insisted in a croaky voice. "It's just an allergic reaction to all the dust. Once I get it all cleaned and my air cleaner does its thing, I'll be okay."

He leaned closer, noticing the increase in her breathing.

Just a quick taste, he promised, and then he'd see she got medical attention.

Bracing his arms on each side of her hips, he dipped his head and flicked the tip of his tongue over a distended nipple. It puckered prettily. Strawberry, he noted while bathing her hot skin with his tongue until he had licked and sucked all the sweet goo from her.

He rose to stand with her in his arms, feeling a slight buzz of a headache from the sweet concoction. Or maybe it was the hot babe in his arms causing the feeling of light-headedness.

Cautious steps took him to her bed, where he placed her on the butt-ugly camouflage sheets. He pulled the top sheet over her to resist temptation.

She reached for him. He stepped back but grasped her hand in both of his. He bent and brushed her lips, knowing he dared not deepen the kiss.

"Rest," he said against her mouth. "I'm going to go check in and get some medicine. If you won't see a doctor, will you at least let me take care of you?"

All the ways he'd like to take care of her sprang to mind— along with another part of his anatomy.

She sighed and closed her eyes with a nod. "Hurry back."

"You don't need to tell me twice." He kissed her forehead and both eyelids. "You get some rest. I'll be back before you know it."

Stepping into his uniform, he checked the pager all Bumble-Bee personnel wore. Damn. Three. Two from the captain. Better see what he wanted first.

A quick glance back at Maggie confirmed she rested as he stepped into the hallway and secured her door.

By the time the door clicked behind Drew, Maggie was out of the bed and headed toward the bathroom.

Less than twenty minutes later, she lay where he left her, but with a few improvements. After washing out some lingerie and hanging them on the cute little butterfly clips from her goody bag, she'd showered and slathered flavored body lotion all over. Then reapplied her makeup, doing her best to disguise her impending black eye.

Next to her coconut bed, she'd set the stage. Flavored body frosting and assorted sex toys she'd discovered in the bag Karyl had handed her—demo items and more favors from Karyl's Boudoir Buddy party—lined the edge of the bed within easy reach.

She coughed and wondered if she should have popped an allergy pill, immediately dismissing the idea. The pills made her sleepy, and she didn't intend to miss a second of her first out-to-sea wild adventure.

The sheets, despite their garish design, felt soft and sensuous against her bare, lotion-slicked skin. The shape of the giant coconut held her in a cocoon of warmth. Her muscles began to relax.

Maybe she'd just rest while she waited for Drew to return.

She awoke aroused. Within a nanosecond she identified the source of the arousal.

Drew dragged a wedge of fresh pineapple up the inside of one leg and then the other, each time stopping before things got really interesting.

He climbed onto the bed beside her, his skin hot against hers, and continued his torture by pineapple, circling each breast, then lapping the juice before it could travel down her rib cage.

Outlining her mouth, he licked away the juice before settling his mouth on hers. He tasted sweet, the juice cool against her tongue.

Finally he broke the kiss and, the tip of his nose against hers, met her gaze with his incredible baby blues.

"Hi." Pineapple-scented breath fanned her face.

She took the pineapple from him and touched it to the cleft in his chin, sucking the juice from the indention.

He growled but held her in place when she would have shimmied beneath him for a more intimate alignment. "I can't stay long. The captain just about ripped me a new one for abandoning my post for so long this morning."

Maggie ran her hand across the smooth expanse of his back, cupped his firm buttocks with her palms. "Then why are you naked?"

His sexy mouth curved into a sly smile. "Just wanted to see how observant you are—and to feel your hot body against mine, even for a little while. Need to have something to remember you by while I'm working."

What to do? Her womb screamed its frustration. She'd wanted to have sex with Drew practically from the moment she'd seen him. For some reason, she knew if he left without her having him, she might never have the chance again.

"Then we need a little less talking and a lot more action," she said with a smile as she neatly flipped him to his back and straddled him.

Beneath her wet sex, his erection throbbed, telling her he was not unaffected. His warm hands bracketed her waist but made no move to push her away. That was a good sign, wasn't it?

Pushing her lips into an exaggerated pout, she said, "You disappoint me, Drew. Have you forgotten our deal so soon?" Her hand closed around the nearest party item. Sparing a quick glance, she hid her frown.

Maggie wasn't exactly certain of her ability to use the flavored gel clutched in her fist. Putting it on her nipples hadn't done all that much earlier. Maybe it would be more successful on Drew's nipples. Did guys like that as much?

Only one way to find out.

The seductive smile felt stiff, but she leaned forward and swiped each flat button with the tip of her tongue. Pleased to see that her hand shook only a little—maybe Drew would think it was because she was so turned on—she carefully circled each pebbled tip with a thin band of purple gel.

Immediately the scent of grapes wafted to her. Yuck. She'd never been a fan of grape jelly.

Holding her breath, she lapped the area clean, pleased to hear his altered breathing.

"Maggie," he said through clenched teeth, "I really can't stay long enough to play right now. I need—aw, hell, I need you!" He looked around, a sort of desperate look on his face. "I didn't bring anything. Do you have any?"

Before she could ask, "Any what?" understanding dawned.

With a smile—yes, she was finally going to have mutually satisfying sex!—she reached into Karyl's bag of tricks and pulled out a string of multicolored condom packages.

Drew jerked them from her hand and ripped one open with his teeth. In less than the time it took to take a deep breath, he'd flipped her over and plunged into her.

Her eyes widened at the sudden intrusion, but her body was more than ready and willing to accommodate him.

"Next time," he said on a grunt, "next time we'll take it slow and easy." He leaned down to take her nipple lightly between his teeth and gave a gentle tug.

She felt it womb deep. It set off tingling between her legs, causing her to gyrate against him in an almost desperate attempt at satisfaction.

Drew groaned and increased the tempo. "Oh, baby, that feels so—"

Maggie froze and tried to shove him off. "Don't call me baby!" She squirmed far enough to sever their connection and pushed herself the rest of the way out from under him.

Now standing next to the bed, breath heaving with the exertion, her gaze took in the magnificent body sprawled on her bed, his iron-hard, impressive erection still sheathed in Day-Glo orange, and wondered if she'd overreacted a tad.

After all, it would be a waste not to use the condom. Especially after he went to all the trouble of opening it and putting it on. It might even be construed as rude.

But, dang, she hated to be called babe or baby. So much.

Drew started to sit up, and she realized she needed damage control, or yet another opportunity to complete the sex act would pass her by.

"It's just . . ." She placed her palms on his warm shoulders and pushed him back on the sheet. "When you call me baby, it makes me feel, well, anonymous. Yes, that's exactly it. Anonymous, an anonymous vagina, like any vagina will do." She climbed up to straddle him again. "And that makes me sad. I want to be sure, beyond a doubt, that you know exactly *whose* vagina you're in." She smiled down at him. "Now, where were we before I so rudely interrupted?"

Drew smiled back at her, his teeth gleaming in the dimness of the room. "I was about to tell you, *Maggie*, how much I want to fuck you and how sorry I am it has to be a quickie." He pulled her down for a lingering kiss and then palmed her breasts. "But," he whispered, "I plan to come back tonight and make up for it." He flicked the hardening tips of her nipples with the pads of his thumbs, causing her breath to hitch. "If that's okay with you?"

Grinning, she sat back until she'd taken him deep within, relishing the fullness. With a little shimmy, she said, "I guess. As long as you remember our deal? You're supposed to talk dirty—"

"Damn, woman! Your mouth is driving me crazy. If I wasn't so desperate to fuck your brains out, I'd stick my cock in that sassy mouth and get off watching you give me head." He arched his back, driving himself deeper. "But for right now, I'm just going to have to fuck you hard and fast and hope to hell you come as fast as I do."

He reversed their positions and pounded into her. Conversation disintegrated to a series of grunts.

She didn't mind, relishing the intimate sound of flesh slapping against flesh, the combined smell of lotion, grapes and sex in the air.

In fact, she was so intrigued by the smell and sounds of the act that her orgasm took her by surprise.

Her breath lodged in her throat, every muscle tightened and tingled; her heart tripped. She was drowning, reveling in the sensation. Her uterus contracted so violently it made her whole abdomen ache. So wiped out by her body's response, she could only lie there while Drew kissed his way off her body and pulled the sheet over her nudity.

Drew watched Maggie's eyes drift shut, wanting nothing more than to crawl back in her bed and give her an instant replay. But he knew it wouldn't be instant, and he really had to get back to work.

It took all his willpower to turn and stride into the bathroom to do a quick cleanup and dress.

He smiled at the brightly colored condom and wondered if they glowed in the dark. Might be kind of fun.

Cold water did nothing to wipe the stupid grin off his face.

"Damn," he whispered, looking at his reflection in the mirror above the little sink. "I look like a guy who just had his clock cleaned." Anyone—well, any guy—who saw him would know exactly what put the cat-that-ate-the-canary grin on his face. He stifled a laugh. What he ate was so much sweeter than canary. And he planned to eat it again and again for as long as he could during the cruise.

Reflected in the mirror, Maggie's string panties caught his attention. He turned and blinked. What were they hanging on? A step took him closer and he picked up the little pink cylinder.

A purple padded clip held a pair of barely there white lace panties. From the other end of the cylinder dangled a soft-gel purple butterfly. He racked his mind in an effort to remember where he'd seen the two little cylinders before. Then he touched the dial on the bottom and the cylinder began to vibrate in his hand.

He swallowed a bark of laughter. Who knew his little Maggie had a wild side?

Back in the stateroom, he stopped next to the bed. Maggie hadn't moved. Drawing back the sheet, he placed a soft kiss on each delectable nipple.

She gave a soft moan and shifted beneath the sheet.

Judging by his instant physical reaction, he knew he had to leave. Gently covering temptation, he walked to the door. He'd come back sometime during his shift to tell her where to meet him for dinner.

With a final glance at the wild woman sleeping so innocently in the big bed, he made a final adjustment and let himself out.

The end of his shift couldn't come soon enough. And not only because he'd broken his long dry spell.

He'd never used nipple clamps.

6

Something nudged Maggie awake. She stretched, relishing the inner aches she hadn't felt in a long time. The action pulled the sheet from her breasts, bathing the puckering tips in the cooler air of the stateroom. She smiled, enjoying the sensation.

"I'm not sure I trust that smile," a male voice said close to her ear.

With a shriek, she clutched the sheet to her chest and scrambled to a sitting position; then she relaxed when she recognized her intruder.

"Drew," she said, willing her heart to resume beating.

"Sorry to startle you," he said with a grin that said he wasn't all that sorry as he tugged the sheet from her grasp. He leaned forward and licked each nipple before sitting back on the side of the bed. "I love your breasts."

"Really?" The money for the instant-cleavage bra had been wasted. Who knew?

"Yep." He tapped the tip of her nose. "I'd love to crawl back in bed with you, and if you don't cover up that bodacious body, that's exactly what I'll do."

She let the sheet slip to her waist.

He groaned. "Maggie, I mean it." He primly pulled the sheet back up and tucked it beneath her. "I don't have time to do anything but frustrate us both. I just wanted to come back to get that jungle beat quieted and invite you to have dinner with me tonight. At eight. There's dancing after dinner."

"Are you allowed to dance with the passengers?" She tried not to squirm at the fire in his eyes brought on by her innocent question.

"Are you kidding? It's required. Lucky for you, everyone is paired up—"

"Already?" Wow, while she'd been cleaning and sleeping, the gusto had passed her by?

"What?" He shook his head. "Never mind." He waggled his eyebrows and grinned. "My point was we'll be *stuck* dancing with each other. I guess we'll just have to come up with something to amuse ourselves." He leaned in to brush a kiss across her lips. "See you at eight."

Stunned. Before she could think of an appropriate answer, he was gone.

Precisely at eight, Maggie entered the dining room. The tables, with their starched white linen cloths, reminded her of little islands, the colorfully dressed diners their surrounding sea.

Smoothing the skirt of her blue silk sundress, her gorgeous new scarf tied in a jaunty bow at her neck, she glanced around, more than a little anxious to find Drew amid the roomful of strangers.

A tall man in a blinding white uniform caught her attention when he walked toward her. Drew. She gave a little inward sigh. The sight made her mouth water—and not for food. His uniform was impressive, but knowing what was beneath it had her impatient for the first part of their evening to be completed.

Drew smiled, his teeth a flash of white in his tanned face, his hand touching her elbow to guide her to his table. Along the way, several passengers greeted him. In response, he nodded or mumbled a pleasantry but kept walking.

At their table, he introduced her to three other couples. Boy, he hadn't been kidding when he said everyone had already hooked up.

She glanced at Drew and said a silent prayer of thanks. Not only was he by far the most handsome man on the cruise, he appeared to be the only one who was unattached. Good thing she had staked her claim early.

Her smile faltered. She *had* staked her claim, hadn't she?

Everyone gaped at her, no doubt due to her added color, thanks to her up-close-and-personal experience in the grotto.

She touched the swelling by her eye as she claimed a seat next to a man with a bad comb-over and smiled. "You should see the other guy." Unfortunately she was the only one who laughed. Tough crowd.

After an awkward silence, Drew cleared his throat. "So, how is everyone enjoying the cruise? Let's start, while we wait for the appetizers, by saying a little bit about ourselves to break the ice."

The comb-over directly to her left, Oliver, droned on about the island they were married on.

What? Married?

"Excuse me. Did you say married? You and Sue are married?" While not especially attractive or a sparkling wit, even Oliver would have to be a special kind of stupid to take a singles cruise on his honeymoon.

Sue, who wasn't all that attractive either, nodded and flashed a sappy smile at Oliver. "Three whole days."

Maggie managed a weak smile. *Gag me.* What were they thinking?

Gamely, she turned to the other closest couple, Dave and Debbie. "Can you believe they're married?" She smiled and rolled her eyes. "So what about you two? What's the story with you?" She'd noticed Dave at check-in. Tall, athletic looking. Good hair and teeth, which was becoming more and more important in her search for Mr. Right. And a great butt. Also a desirable quality. Maybe she should have made a move. Who knew Deb would snap him up so quickly?

Unfortunately the way he grinned down at the ever-present Debbie said he was going down for the count. Scratch good old Dave off her list of potential victims, er, candidates.

Yeah, it was a good thing she'd found Drew when she did. He was so hot she had no doubt he wouldn't have been single for more than a day. All the ways she wanted to use him— rather, cement their fledgling relationship—sprang to mind.

"So, where did you two get married?" Oliver asked, looking down the table at the third couple, Beth and Micah.

"Oh, we've been married a year already," Micah answered. "We never had a honeymoon, so—"

"Then why did you choose *this* cruise?" Maggie knew she interrupted but couldn't contain her curiosity another second. How weird was it to be at a table with not one but three couples? It was a singles cruise, for Pete's sake! Had no one else read the brochure?

Six sets of eyes stared at her.

"Um . . . because it's a honeymoon cruise?" Oliver ventured a guess.

Maggie snorted her laughter, "Yeah, right!" She looked around the table. No one appeared to be sharing her humor. Her gaze sought Drew. His look did nothing to reassure her as she took a bite of her now tasteless meal.

He leaned close and whispered, "It *is* a honeymoon cruise, Maggie. That's why I kept asking if you were married. I—"

The last bite of roast duck lodged in her throat.

Drew was on his feet immediately, thumping her on the back.

Debbie advised her to drink some water.

Sue said that wouldn't help; instead, she should put Maggie's hands over her head.

Maggie glared at Sue. If Sue didn't shut up, Maggie would put her hands around Sue's throat and squeeze.

Wheezing in air, she finally stopped her coughing fit. Drew, still at her side, continued to rub her back.

"Are you okay?" His warm breath fanned her ear.

Are you insane? Of course I'm not okay! Instead she managed to rasp out, "I need to get out of here."

He helped her up. "I'm going to take her outside for some air. Please, go ahead with your meal."

On the deck, she whirled to face him. "A *honeymoon* cruise? Are you kidding? It has to be a joke." She glanced around the deserted deck. "Are we on hidden camera or something?"

Drew managed a feeble smile. " 'Fraid not."

"But—but it can't be a honeymoon cruise!" Memories of all her sacrifices and saving flashed through her mind. "I did my registration myself. I signed up for the singles cruise. The *Fun in the Sun* package! There has to be some mistake!" However, one look at his solemn face told her there was no mistake. And if there was, it was hers. Her shoulders slumped. "Why does stuff like this keep happening to me?" Did she wear a sign that said LOSER? "Turn the boat around. I want a refund."

He clamped his lips together as though he were biting back a smile. "It's a ship."

"I don't care! It has a reverse, doesn't it?"

"Maggie, we're already at sea. You may as well relax and enjoy the cruise." He tilted up her face with the tip of his finger and said in a low voice, "You have to admit, it hasn't been all bad. I mean, we've had some fun." He pulled her into his embrace and smiled down at her. "We could enjoy each other's company for the next three days and four nights. Besides, I'd appreciate having you around."

"What's the big deal? I'm just another passenger." She made a halfhearted effort to disengage his embrace.

He bent his knees to look into her eyes. "Maggie, believe me, you're not 'just another passenger.' I already told you I've never—and I mean *never*—had any sort of personal contact with a passenger. Until you."

When she didn't respond, just blinked her incredible eyes— okay, her incredible *eye*, because the other was still swollen almost shut—he had to act.

No way were those pretty pink nipple clamps going to continue doing laundry duty tonight.

7

He pulled Maggie tight against him, letting her feel his erection. To ensure his intentions, he ground his hips against her, swallowing his sigh of relief when she ground right back, an impish grin on her oh-so-kissable lips.

The first strains of music drifted out to them.

He leaned to kiss the tip of her nose. "Let's dance. I want to make every other guy in the room jealous while I hold you so close they'll be trying to decide if we're making love on the dance floor." He waltzed her toward the dining room entrance. "Then I want to take you back to your room and"—he remembered their deal and swallowed before completing his sentence—"and fuck you in ways that are probably illegal in several states."

A look of surprise flashed across her face. It was difficult to tell in the dimness, but he thought she might be blushing.

Good. He hoped she was embarrassed. He was.

He opened the door for her, the air-conditioned breeze cooling the heated tips of his ears.

They danced silently to several songs before the band

switched gears. Heaving a silent prayer of thanks, he pulled her into his arms and tried not to groan at the contact of her firm breasts against his eager chest.

Too soon, the song ended.

Maggie broke contact, stepping back. "I'm really thirsty. Where's the bar?"

Drew raised his hand, summoning a waiter. Within seconds they had fruity rum drinks in their hands. Shocked, he watched Maggie drain hers in record time.

"Another?" he asked, signaling their waiter.

"Please." She smiled.

He watched the pink tip of her tongue swipe the last of the fruity concoction from her lips, wishing he could do the same. Unfortunately in public it would be suicide, jobwise.

A few sips later, she'd once again drained her glass.

"Maybe you should take it easy on those drinks. I know the bartender on duty. He tends to be generous with the rum."

"Oh, pooh!" She swatted at something and then grinned up at him, her good eye shining. "Less dance! You can tango, can't you?" Standing a bit unsteadily, she began undulating to the beat and then fell to the side.

He caught her and returned her to an upright position. Maybe dancing was a good idea. It might sober her up.

"Sure, I can tango," he assured her with a smile. "It's a job requirement."

But he'd never tangoed quite like they tangoed.

Maggie threw herself into the dance. Literally. He had to catch her to prevent her from doing a face plant on the dance floor. In his arms, she became boneless. It was like dancing with a gyrating statue of Jell-O.

To free up both his hands, Drew tossed back another drink and set it on the tray belonging to a passing waiter.

Maggie rubbed against him, all but purring. Personally he felt more like roaring. Or howling at the moon. Or both.

He dipped her and then panicked when her short curls all but touched the hardwood floor. He pulled her back up for a sweeping turn.

"You're a very good dancer, Drew," she whispered, sending renewed desire ripping through his body. "Among other things." Her giggle ended on a hiccup.

"You're not too shabby either." It was true. Even in her altered state, she followed his every move as if they were connected. Connected. Bad analogy, if the fit of his dress trousers was any indication.

"I need another drink," Maggie said to their waiter as he walked by. "Make it a double!" she called to his back.

"They don't make those drinks in doubles, Mag." Drew executed a series of hip turns and steps to divert her attention.

"S'okay. He can just give me two." Plucking a rose from the vase of a nearby table, she placed it between her teeth and batted her eyelashes as they danced dramatically across the floor.

Drew noticed the other dancers had stepped back. Whether it was in homage to their dancing or to stay out of their way was a toss-up. He found he didn't care.

He was having the time of his life.

Too many drinks to count later, Maggie jumped from her chair and dragged Drew back out onto the dance floor. Her lips were numb, but the restless feeling had to be assuaged.

Or else she might do something really naughty, like strip herself and Drew bare and have her wicked way with him right out there on the dance floor. Hmmm. Naked ballroom dancing. It definitely appealed. She glanced at the other couples at their table. True, naked ballroom dancing was right up there on her list of fantasies, but not with an audience.

A slow ballad played, giving her an excellent excuse to cozy up to Drew's hard body. Beneath his jacket, she slid her hands around to discreetly palm his butt. *Buns of steel, and all mine.*

"Excuse me? What did you say?" His breath fanned her ear.

Oh, no, did I actually say the buns thing out loud? She licked her lips and smiled up at him. "How 'bout another drink?"

"They just announced last call." He shrugged and pulled her closer, his erection evident, even through all the layers of their respective clothing.

Bumping and rubbing against him, she felt his heart thundering against her ear.

"Is it hot in here?" Her nipples ached beneath the thin layer of silk. And between her legs was a growing ache only Drew could relieve.

Their eyes met.

Drew swallowed. "Sure is. And it's getting hotter every second."

Now swaying more than dancing in order to attain maximum rub, they locked together, staring eye to eye, breathing accelerated.

"Let's go back to my room and get naked," she suggested with a little shimmy against his hard chest. "Maybe a dip in the grotto will help cool us off."

His nostrils flared, firm lips flattened. "I doubt it. But it's worth a shot." He glanced around at the dwindling passengers. "I have to stay until they close." He nuzzled her hair, further increasing her heart rate. "Stay with me."

"No problem." She snuggled against him and felt the rhythmic sway of his body, following blindly. Was it possible to dance in your sleep?

No doubt about it, she had to get some physical gratification. Soon.

Her gaze swept the room, empty except for a few couples at the bar. Did she dare make a move?

One look at Drew's smoldering gaze told her: she dared.

All it took was a slight readjustment and her breasts were

freed from the sundress bodice. A flick of a few middle buttons on Drew's shirt provided enough skin for perfect alignment.

He pulled her closer still. Breast to breast—well, okay, breast to upper abdomen—was a lovely way to dance. It amazed her to think of all she'd been missing over the years.

Her hand slid between them to discreetly unzip Drew's trousers.

"Maggie," his voice warned in her ear, "behave."

The warning was obviously for show because she noted that his abdominal muscles contracted for easier access. So . . . she accessed.

Drew's breath hitched when Maggie's hot hand cupped his rampant erection. Now what? He glanced down and was somewhat relieved to see that his coat hid her activities. Her hard nipples rubbing against his skin sent him into overdrive. Just when he thought he might survive the evening and remain employed, she unzipped him and slipped her hand beneath his boxers. Concentrate. He had to concentrate on not thrusting into her soft hand. If anyone knew what they were doing out there, he would definitely lose his job.

The song ended, and the band began packing up.

In Maggie's hand, his cock throbbed with each beat of his excited heart.

To his horror, she began to step away. He jerked her flush against his body.

"We can't just walk away!" He nodded toward the band and cleanup crew. At her confused look he explained, "We're exposed, Maggie. If we don't want the whole world to know what we've been doing out here, we need to dance to your room."

"Won't that look a little weird?" To his disappointment, she tucked her delicious breasts back into her dress. "There." She grinned up at him. "Now to get you, um, back where you belong."

It was a stretch, but his boxers more or less covered him. They weren't so lucky with his pants. Maggie pushed and shoved, generally making him harder with her attempts.

"Stop," he hissed in her ear. "You're making it worse!"

"But I—"

"Unless you want me to come in your hand, please stop rubbing me like that."

"Oh." She raised her eyebrows and gave a little smile. "Dance?"

"Dance." He nodded and moved toward the nearest door.

On the deck, he twirled with her, humming as they danced down the deck toward the elevator.

As soon as they stepped into the elevator, Maggie had a brilliant idea. She hoped.

Snuggling up to Drew, preventing him from pushing the button, she said, "Let's have sex in the elevator."

He heaved a sigh and held her away from him, nodding toward the security camera mounted in the back corner. "I don't want my coworkers to know me that well."

"Can't you turn it off?" She cupped him again and rubbed his length, his back to the spying camera.

He shook his head. "No. All I can do is lock the elevator. But with the camera running, there's no point."

"Lock it." Wow, her brilliant ideas just kept coming.

"I told you—"

"Lock it." She hiccupped. "I have an idea."

Shrugging, he reached past her and inserted his card key into the shining brass panel, then pushed the lock button. "Now what?"

She stood, calculating distance. Yes, it would definitely work.

Directing him, she slipped beneath his arm and wedged back against the corner beneath the surveillance camera. A glance up confirmed they were well out of the camera's range, with maybe a foot to spare. "Sound?" she asked, pointing up at the camera.

He shook his head.

"Good, then let's take care of your zipper problem." In one swift move, she pushed down his boxers and pants. Dropping to her knees, she took his length into her mouth and tried to remember the technique in the magazine she'd read while she'd had her hair highlighted.

Drew gripped the brass handrails on either side of Maggie and closed his eyes. Watching her hot mouth devour him would push him over the edge almost before they began.

The muscles in his legs began to quiver. He locked his knees and tried not to thrust like a wild man.

She petted his balls and ran her velvety hot tongue up and down his length before once again attempting to swallow him whole.

He clenched his jaw so hard he wouldn't have been surprised to crack his molars.

Damn! He ached to reciprocate. But all he could reach was the top of her head. He ran his hands through and around her tousled curls. It wasn't enough. Not nearly enough.

The thought of all the things he'd do to her once they gained her room caused his hips to pump faster.

8

Realization slammed into Drew as Maggie gagged. He took a hasty step back to rectify the situation. And, with his pants and underwear tangled at his ankles, stumbled and landed flat on his back on the plush red carpet of the elevator floor.

Maggie scrambled to her feet, intent clear in her good eye.

He had no recourse. He raised his foot to stop her from coming to him. The action, with his pants still around his ankles, caused him to roll into a curve like a sex-starved armadillo.

"Camera," he ground out while struggling to pull his boxers up over his tent-pole erection.

"What can I do to help?" She cast a nervous glance up at the offending black box.

Was that a tear glistening?

Crying was never a good sign. He racked his brain for a way to salvage a situation that had disaster written all over it.

"Stay right there. There's no reason for us both to be caught with our pants down."

She frowned. "My pants aren't down. I'm wearing a dress."

"It was a metaphor, Maggie." He got to his feet and glared over his shoulder at the camera while jerking up his pants.

"But I feel so awful!" Head hanging, she mumbled, "I can't do anything right."

Disaster was beginning to morph into capital letters.

He had to do something. Now.

"Show me your tits," he said in a choked voice. She'd told him she liked him to talk dirty, but now that he'd gotten to know her, it was more difficult.

Color blossomed in her cheeks—well, her cheek, since the other one was pretty colorful already. Just when he decided to tell her to forget it, she slipped the bodice down, exposing her breasts.

Damn, he loved her breasts. He'd always been a leg man, but there was just something about her breasts that had him salivating and hard as a rock. Not large by any standards, they were just right. They fit perfectly into the palm of his hand. And his mouth. Bad thought, when he was trying to stuff his eager cock back into his pants.

"Okay, cover up before I say, 'Fuck the camera,' and come over there." At the widening of her eye, he said, "You have no idea how much I want you. Right now. Right here." He chuckled and shook his head, more than a little relieved when he finally convinced his zipper to close. "But I also need to keep my job." He smirked. "Assuming my full-frontal display just now didn't already jeopardize it."

Turning back to the panel, he unlocked the elevator and pushed the button to resume their ascent. "If no one else gets on the elevator, stay back there until we get to your floor. And no matter what, do not turn and look at the camera. Just walk straight out of here."

"What if someone else gets on before our floor?" Her voice

sounded small and uncertain. It was all he could do to stay facing forward.

"Then we try to blend with the crowd and get off wherever they do. If we have to, we can use the stairs the rest of the way."

Drew dared not look back at Maggie until they were a safe distance down the hall. "Give me your key." He put out his hand and finally looked at her.

Then he almost swallowed his tongue.

Sometime during their ride, or maybe as they walked down the hall, Maggie had done something with the top of her dress. It was gone. In its place was the sparkling scarf she'd worn around her neck. She'd fashioned it into some kind of strapless halter-looking thing tied between her breasts.

"You're killing me, you know." His gaze took in every inch of the sheer top, its metallic threads playing peekaboo with her nipples.

"You don't like it?" She grinned and did a slow turn.

The back was virtually nonexistent, so sheer was the scarf. As she turned back to face him, he realized she could most likely wear the thing in public, given the way the sheer fabric bunched in strategic places. And the bow helped hide the crucial areas from the casual observer.

Of course, he was no casual observer and saw it only as a giant bow wrapping up a delectable present he was itching to unwrap.

As soon as the door clicked shut behind them, he threw the bolt home and pulled her into his arms. The passionate kiss that followed precluded conversation.

Finally he broke the kiss and looked down at her. "What happened to the top of your dress?"

"It's still here. I tucked it into the skirt."

"Very clever." Grinding his erection against her, he said on a growl, "Lose it."

She didn't have to be told twice. After waiting a lifetime to be this wild, this free, she wasn't going to waste a second of it.

Hooking her fingers in the sides of the silk, she shimmied it over her hips and let it fall to pool at her feet, allowing Drew time to admire the view she made in nothing but her scarf and purple thong panties with her high-heeled blue sandals. If the expression on his face—and the bulge in the front of his trousers—was any indication, he admired it very much.

Her nipples puckered beneath his scrutiny, rasping against the metallic threads running through the softer silk. Dampness in her thong made her want to squirm.

He stepped forward and hooked his fingers beneath the string on each side of her panties, pulling her close while he kissed her.

Deepening the kiss, he hauled her up by the string, the action pulling the thong high into her flesh.

To her surprise, it was not unpleasant.

The kiss continued, teeth clicking as he walked, holding her off her feet high against his chest. Somewhere along the way, her shoes fell off with a soft thud on the bamboo floor.

The cool edge of her coconut-shell bed touched the back of her calves a second before she felt the softness of her sheets against her bottom.

Breaking the kiss, Drew rose to tower over her. He glanced down and licked his lips and then spread her legs as far as they would go, his gaze riveted to the damp flesh exposed by the miniscule panties.

He reached down to push the thong to one side, running the tip of his finger over her weeping folds. "So pretty," he whispered.

Should she say thank you? What exactly was the protocol in a situation like this? For that matter, how many drinks had she sucked down tonight? She squinted her good eye and found

that Drew looked more than a little fuzzy around the edges.
Also, her lips were numb.

Her mind cleared some of its fog and shifted back to her
partner when he slipped one finger into her and wiggled it before slowly gliding it in and out.

Her hips arched off the bed. Just when she thought she might
scream her frustration, he withdrew, causing her to whimper at
the loss.

His hand stopped her from removing the thong.

She wasn't sure she totally trusted his smile, but she was
more than eager to see what he had in mind.

She didn't have to wait long.

He pushed the thong to the other side and dragged his
tongue along the edge of her labia, taking little forays beneath
the sodden silk. When she groaned, he shifted his attention to
the other side, so close yet so far from the spot that wept for
him.

She moaned, lolling back on the bed, enjoying the sensations
racing through her blood, along with the generous amount of
alcohol she'd consumed.

Time blurred, along with her vision.

When his mouth left her, it was like waking from a delicious
dream.

Straightening her panties, he placed a hot kiss on her silk-
covered mound and then pushed his way up onto the bed with
her.

When did he take off his clothes?

He petted her through the scarf and then took a silk-covered
nipple into his mouth and suckled, the action causing renewed
dampness to surge between her legs.

Was it possible to have an orgasm just from someone sucking your breasts? Then there was the way he had of swirling his
tongue around the aureole, causing the wet silk to take on a life

of its own, pulling at her, shooting arrows of arousal to her core.

She fumbled with the knot the scarf bow had become.

"Shhh. Wait." His hot hand covered her cool, trembling ones. "Let me. I'll be right back."

He stood, his erection boldly announcing his carnal intention . . . thank goodness!

Reclined across the bed, her legs spread in wantonness, eyes closed, Maggie enjoyed the feel of the breeze from the air-conditioning across the damp silk.

In a flash, he was back, murmuring against her flushed skin as he kissed his way from her feet upward.

Woohoo! It felt good. Why was it so difficult to open her eyes? No matter. She didn't need to see to feel the wondrous things Drew was doing to her.

And she just knew it was going to do nothing but get better.

She smiled what she hoped was a sexy smile when she felt the sodden silk being untied and tugged from her body. Naked. She wanted to be naked.

"Don't worry. I want you naked, too," Drew said against her belly button.

Uh-oh. Must've voiced her thoughts again. *Note to self: don't let thoughts fall out of mouth.*

It seemed to take forever, but he finally managed to peel her thong down her legs and off her feet.

She felt like laughing with the exhilaration of being so free. The air blew across her heated skin, caressing every inch of exposed skin—and it was *all* exposed. Better yet, she thrilled to the idea.

Who knew walking on the wild side could be so liberating, so fun, so—

"Oouch!" Wide awake now, she jackknifed to a sitting position from the excruciating pain originating at both nipples and shooting through her extremities. "What the hell are you doing?"

Drew lay half on top of her, blocking her retreat. "Don't yell at me. They're *your* nipple clamps! I thought you were into that kind of thing."

"Nipple clamps? Why the hell would I have nipple clamps?" She glanced down at the pink torture devices hanging from her nipples like obscene trapeze artists and wished the alcohol had numbed more than her brain. Wait. They were beginning to look familiar. "Those aren't nipple clamps! They're lingerie grippers."

Drew's smile was grim. He reached out and slid a little black switch on the base close to the dangling butterflies she'd thought were so cute. Butterflies of death.

At first the vibration felt like jolts of electricity zapping her nipples. But before she could scream, the sensation changed. Wow. Maybe they really were nipple clamps.

But they still hurt.

Biting back a scream, she deftly removed the clamps and pushed Drew to his back, straddling him, his hot erection thumping her backside.

Maybe it was the alcohol talking, but suddenly she felt very X-rated. Scooting back, she allowed his penis to drag up the center of her until she was close enough to lick the darkened tip.

Then she deftly attached a clamp to each sac and turned on the vibration in one move.

With a roar, Drew jerked to a sitting position, almost toppling her from the bed.

In hindsight, maybe not such a great idea.

"I'm sorry. I shouldn't have done that." Her giggle took a little away from the sincerity of her apology. "Here, let me take them off."

He slapped her hands away. "No! Let me."

After making several faces, he managed to disengage the vibrating clamps and dropped them to the mattress. They lay, making an innocuous buzzing sound against the sheet.

His erection was noticeably . . . less erect.

Oops. She prayed she hadn't done any damage. Unless she relied on Mel, Drew was her only sexual release for the next three nights and four days.

His heated gaze met hers. She stole a peek. Yes! A comeback was in the works.

"You know, there are other uses for those things." He fondled a nipple and then placed a gentle kiss on the tip of each one. "More pleasurable uses." He licked her now erect nipples and then reached for the vibrators of death.

"Drew, I don't think—" She scooted toward the opposite end of the big bed.

"Shhh! I won't hurt you." His hand closed around her ankle, dragging her back to him.

The movement caused her legs to spread, and the way he eyed her crotch made her both uneasy and turned on at the same time.

Maybe alcohol turned her into a nympho.

9

"Watch this." Drew picked up a clamp and stopped the vibrating then worked until he disengaged the evil clamp claw. He flipped over the device and removed the pretty lavender gel butterfly and then installed it on the business end of the pink barrel. A flick of his thumb had the little butterfly wings fluttering.

His hand petted her until she'd somewhat relaxed against the sheets again. Positioning himself between her legs, he proceeded to lick and suck her vulva until she was a puddle of need. At that point, he could have done anything to her.

The low hum barely registered.

Drew spread his fingers, holding her open to his ministrations, and then touched her sensitized skin with the fluttering wings of the butterfly.

"Relax," he whispered when she struggled to sit up. He moved the busy little wings up and down, setting off all kinds of tingling.

Then he allowed the butterfly to alight on her already aching nub.

Jolts of pleasure zinged through her. Her heart did a back-flip, her breath lodged. Every nerve ending stood on alert as a riptide of pleasure washed over her, gushing over the butterfly and Drew's hand.

Collapsing against the sheets, gasping for breath, it was a moment before she could form a coherent thought, much less a sentence.

"I h—h—hope it's w—waterproof."

"Sure is," he assured, gathering her in his arms and scooping up her boneless body.

Seconds later, they were submersed in the churning water of the grotto, Maggie astride Drew's lap, his monster erection jutting up between them.

Gazes locked, he used one buzzing butterfly on her nipples while his other hand was busy between her legs with the other butterfly, giving a repeat performance.

Detached yet feeling every flutter of the pliant gel, Maggie watched as he pleasured her. Her nipples pebbled into hard, almost painful points, jutting against the soft wings. Each flutter sent a fission of sensation to her womb. Between her wide-spread legs, the little purple wings vibrated in a breathtaking pulse, disappearing occasionally.

She lost count of the number of orgasms. Pleasure was such a simple word for the things she'd experienced.

Drew set the pink passion vibrators on the sand of the grotto and gripped her waist, intent evident in his clear blue eyes.

While she'd love to impale herself and do the wild monkey dance with him, she wanted him to feel at least part of the pleasure he'd given her.

She reached past his shoulder and grabbed a butterfly. It hummed merrily as she circled each male nipple, pausing every once in a while to whip the wings against her own.

She and Drew watched the butterfly hover nearer the tip of

his erection. They held their breath at the first tentative flutters against the engorged head.

Within seconds, they were both panting, frantic for each other.

Impaled now, Maggie began her wild ride. Drew dragged a butterfly across her nipples occasionally and then reached between them to let it flutter against her nub. Each time, the effect was a mind-blowing orgasm.

By the time he shouted his completion, she was limp from repeated pleasuring and more than ready to sleep.

Drew, evidently, had his second wind.

Lying bonelessly on her bed, she watched a light bobbing toward her. She squinted. It looked like a giant firefly coming toward the bed.

It was Drew, wearing nothing but a glow-in-the-dark yellow condom and a smile.

Part of her exhaustion washed away in the renewed surge of lust.

She grinned up at him. "I think I read these are also flavored." Her hand closed around him, drawing him nearer.

An experimental swipe of her tongue registered little but a vaguely sweet taste. She ran her tongue up and down his yellow-encased shaft. Pineapple? Swirling her tongue around and over the bulbous tip, she decided it was definitely pineapple and . . . something else. Drawing him deep into her mouth, realization dawned: piña colada.

Drew watched as Maggie's hungry mouth covered most of his glow-in-the-dark erection, the remaining section giving her face an eerie yellow sheen.

When she began her rhythmic suckling, he was torn between watching the light show between his legs and the havoc she created higher up in his heart.

Havoc won.

Pulling free of her suction, he flipped her over onto her stomach, raised her hips and plunged into her wet heat. He paused, emotion constricting his chest. *Mine.*

Maggie wiggled her hips, her ass rubbing against him in an inflammatory way.

His thoughts headed south, his only goal to give and receive pleasure.

He pulled her up onto her hands and knees, pounding into her. Primal gratification surged with each of her lust-filled, reciprocating grunts. Curling over her, he reached beneath to cup her jiggling breasts. Lord, he loved the way they responded to his touch, their pebbled tips jutting into his palm. Feeling them echo the force of his thrusts made him increase his tempo.

Beneath him, Maggie squirmed, wild with her need. She grabbed one of his big hands, pushing it from her breast to between her legs. Close, she was so close to another record-breaking orgasm.

Drew straightened from her. She whimpered her distress.

She shouldn't have worried, she realized, because he didn't break the connection.

His warm hand bracketed her ribs, gently pulling her to a semistanding position. With her on her knees, he continued to thrust from behind while pleasuring her breasts and clitoris with his talented hands.

She'd never done it in that position but it was a fast and easy acclimation.

With Drew's hot body pounding into her from the back and his busy hands on her front, her climax hovered.

Then he squeezed her nub between his thumb and forefinger in time with his thrusts.

Her gasp rapidly turned into a throaty scream. An earth-shattering release thundered through her, all but stopping her heart.

Immediately Drew lowered her to the soft mattress, its sheets abrading her sensory-overloaded nipples while she quivered in the aftermath. He stroked his hand down her left leg and eased it upward until he'd turned her onto her back without withdrawing from her needy body.

They grinned at each other.

He continued stroking both legs until her ankles rested on his shoulders; all the while, he was performing little, inflaming, circular thrusts. Once she was positioned for maximum reception, he slid his hands up her back, gripping her shoulders.

He placed nibbling kisses along her jaw and down her neck, obviously in no hurry to continue. His mouth closed over her earlobe, and he sucked gently, two, three times, then resumed his exploration. All the while, his hips flexed in an almost involuntary internal caress.

He dragged his tongue along her jaw and then circled her mouth before settling his lips on hers. But they didn't linger. Instead he brushed her lips with the lightest of kisses, driving her mad with desire.

Finally, feeling restless and needy, she grabbed his hair and pulled him to her mouth.

With a groan, he fell into her kiss. His tongue swept her mouth in a replay of the way it had swept into her vagina earlier. The thought made her hot.

With her legs raised to his shoulders, though, she couldn't pull him closer to deepen the kiss with full-body contact.

He broke the kiss just when she was getting into it. But she couldn't complain, because he kissed his way to her breast.

Oh, yeah. So enraptured by the hot suction at her breasts and the corresponding wet restlessness between her legs, she had to remind herself to breathe. Now the position made sense.

Just when she teetered on the brink of another orgasm, he stopped. Cool air bathed her wet nipples. Darn. But he still had the hot hip action going, so, again, she couldn't complain too much.

Then he tightened his grip on her shoulders and began hard, deep thrusts, and she couldn't complain at all.

Drew lay panting, Maggie draped across him, and knew if he died right then, he'd die a happy man. Definitely a satisfied man.

Maggie's breathing told him she'd drifted off already. He drew his fingertip along the side of her breast and was rewarded by the flexing of her hips in her sleep. Damn, she was responsive. He toyed with a nipple, watching it pebble in the feeble predawn light.

His cock stirred. Maggie wasn't the only responsive one.

He knew better than to think it was love. But he also knew he'd never been so turned on in his life as he was by just thinking of or looking at Maggie. How would he survive the cruise with his job—and heart—intact? He knew he sure as hell couldn't stay away from her. Not an option. His entire body went on high alert when she just walked into a room.

He pulled the sheet over them and snuggled closer, determined to ignore his hard-on and get a little sleep.

His hard-on had other ideas.

Evidently, so did Maggie, because she squirmed her naked, lush behind against his growing arousal when he tried to spoon her, her moist pussy kissing the engorged tip.

He ground his teeth. He would not take advantage of a sleeping woman.

Then the sleeping woman guided his hand to knead her breast before pushing it downward to feel her dampness. And she sighed.

The sigh pushed him over the edge. Who could sleep when

their hand was on warm pussy and the bed partner obviously liked it?

He could do it. He could lie next to her and pleasure her with his hands without seeking gratification. After all, she deserved it for allowing him to do the things he'd done with her. If he were the blushing type, he'd be beet red when he thought of all the ways he'd had her.

Almost groaning with frustration, he slid his finger along her slickness.

In response, she made a sound somewhere between a moan and a sigh and pushed his hand lower, spreading her legs to accommodate him.

He circled her opening with his fingertip, loving the way she wiggled against him and purred. He'd never made a woman actually purr. He dipped into her warmth, luxuriating in the wetness he found.

Her hips bucked against his iron erection while she sought gratification from his fingers, now two-deep in her heat.

He bumped against her, the feel of the smooth skin of her butt making him impossibly harder.

Whether she moved or he did, in the next instant his cock was deeply imbedded in her willing flesh. Holding her spoon fashion, they thrust faster and harder.

Gratification was underrated.

10

Maggie stretched and grinned. What a night. The thought brought instant arousal, and she reached for Drew, her own personal stud muffin.

The sheets were cold. She knew instantly he was gone. No point in calling for him.

Dragging herself out of bed, she grabbed the scarf and wrapped it around her nudity as she padded toward the bathroom, enjoying the friction against her skin.

A note on the bathroom mirror perked her up.

*Mag—I had breakfast duty. See you on the Leedo deck.
To help me keep my job, please wear something less revealing than last night—how about a turtleneck?* ☺
Love, D

Love? Did that mean he thought he loved her? She ran the idea around in her head and realized she wouldn't mind. Wait. Did that mean she loved him? Already?

She shook her head. No, it was too soon. What she had—

and she suspected Drew had as well—was a good hard case of lust. *Hard* being the operative word. She giggled at the thought. After washing the scarf and hanging it to dry, she took a quick shower.

Today was the first day of her wild adventure at sea. If last night was a preview, she could hardly wait.

"If that's it, sir, I'm needed on deck." Drew stood with his hand poised above the doorknob. Despite his captain's tirade of the last—he stole a glance at the clock—twenty minutes, his thoughts had been on Maggie. Would she be looking for him?

"—are you listening to me, Connor?" Captain Murray leaned forward, hands tented on the shining top of his pristine mahogany desk. "I understand you're looking forward to the end of this season and your time on the BumbleBee, but you still have responsibilities." He pointed to the exhibitionistic scene freeze-framed on the monitor. "Dropping your pants and masturbating on the elevator floor is not one of them. What were you thinking, son?"

Drew bit down on his lip, thankful no one noticed Maggie's exit from the elevator due to his scene on the floor. That didn't mean he could tell the captain what he'd been thinking—it would lead to real trouble.

"I don't know, sir," he finally answered. "Maybe I had too much to drink." He shrugged and turned the knob. "I don't really remember much."

"Dismissed." Murray's balding head shone as he returned to his paperwork.

Heaving a sigh of relief, Drew double-timed it to the breakfast buffet and surveyed the morning crowd. Not seeing Maggie, he did a quick inspection of the serving tables lining the deck, nodding here and there to passengers.

Finally Maggie walked up to the table closest to him and picked up a heavy white plate, giving him a bird's-eye view of her cleavage. Good Lord, didn't the woman own anything with a higher neckline?

A breeze chose that moment to flutter the brightly printed wrap skirt, tantalizing him with glimpses of her smooth leg clear up to her hip. Was she wearing panties?

"Wow. What a spread!" She speared several slices of pineapple and then shot a meaningful glance his way.

He swallowed past the knot in his throat. It didn't take a rocket scientist to know what she was thinking. And anyone walking by could see the obvious effect she was having on his body.

Slices of watermelon and cantaloupe joined pineapple, along with several plump strawberries and a generous dollop of whipped cream.

He averted his gaze as thoughts of all the ways he'd like to enjoy the fruit—with Maggie's body as the serving plate— flashed through his mind. Running his finger around his collar did nothing for the sudden constriction of his clothing.

"Are these mimosas?" She held up a fluted glass.

He nodded. "I have to go check on . . . stuff. I'll see you later."

Like a shot, he walked away from her, almost barreling into an elderly couple on their way to another buffet table.

Mumbling his apologies, he checked with the steward and then hightailed it back to his quarters for a cold shower.

Maggie absently licked whipped cream from a strawberry while she watched Drew make his getaway. And that's exactly what it seemed like to her. For some reason, he wanted to escape. From her.

Sadness washed over her. Had she done something wrong, been too needy? Maybe she should cut her losses and steer clear of him.

Wait. It was her vacation, bought and paid for by her hard

work and persistence. How dare he ruin it for her? After all, she'd determined to take a walk on the wild side during the cruise. Sure, she'd goofed up by evidently transposing the numbers and ending up on a honeymoon cruise instead of the singles cruise. But that didn't mean she couldn't walk on the wild side—and Drew was the only victim, er, candidate to walk with her.

Decision made, she located his room by bribing the steward and set off after her query. She was going to have fun in the sun, damnit, and Drew had better not try to muck it up for her!

Drew stepped from his miniscule shower and wrapped a towel around his hips. Who could be knocking on his door? He hadn't had time to mess up today.

Raking his dripping hair from his face, he threw open the door.

Maggie stood, hands fisted on hips, looking none too hospitable.

"Are you avoiding me?" She shoved past him, the high heels of her sandals clicking on the tile as she walked into his tiny room, filling it with her sweet scent. Beneath his towel, his cock stirred.

He swallowed. "Of course not. I just, well, I had some stuff to do. Like I said."

Her blond eyebrow quirked. "Stuff? Like take a shower? You didn't already do that before you put on your uniform this morning?" She glanced around. "This is really a small room. Don't you get claustrophobic?"

If he ignored her—and his growing erection—she'd just stay longer. If they were going to have sex, and he suspected by the way she eyed his towel it was a distinct possibility, they may as well get to it.

There was a chance no one saw her come in. The sooner he got her out of his room, the better.

Oh, who the hell was he kidding? He was panting after her like a dog in heat.

"Are you wearing underwear?" He took a few steps and was practically chest to chest with her. He ran his finger along the edge of her sky-blue, stretchy top.

She made no move to stop him or remove temptation. Beneath his fingertip, her heartbeat increased.

"It has a built-in bra," she said in a breathy voice.

"It's not doing its job." He jiggled one plump breast and then delved in his hand to cup her warm weight, dragging his thumb across the hard tip of her nipple.

The way her breath caught made his erection twitch.

"I need to check it out." When she again raised a brow, he explained, "It's my duty, part of my job, to make sure things work like they're supposed to." He pulled the top up and over her head and then tossed it on the wooden chair in the corner.

The sight of her breasts, their hard nipples puckering in the air-conditioned breeze, sent his heart into double-time. He slid his hands up her ribs to cup both breasts, thumbs rubbing a lazy rhythm across the tips.

She shifted, obviously aroused.

He gently squeezed each pebbled tip. She gasped.

Immediately contrite, he asked, "Are you sore from the clamps last night?"

She shook her head, her curls sweeping the tips of his own hard nipples. "Turned on."

He grinned down at her. "Yeah? I can fix that." Ever so slowly, he tugged the tie on the side of her waist until the bow holding her skirt around her delectable body gave way. "I feel like I'm unwrapping another present." And he was. In more ways than one. What was the petite woman standing there allowing him to undress her in the bright light of day doing to him?

Finally—finally—the tropical print parted and slid to the floor.

Damn. Standing before him, in nothing but a pair of pink thong panties and high-heeled sandals, she took his breath away.

Something shifted in her gaze. She pressed her hot little body closer and walked him backward until the edge of the chair pressed against the back of his legs. She swept her top off the chair, jerked the towel from him and pushed him to sit.

They both eyed his jutting erection.

*Tsk*ing, she shook her head and stepped out of her panties. "I think we need to take care of that first, don't you?"

She grabbed her handbag from the end of the bed, reached in and pulled out a clear plastic container of fruit from the buffet. Extracting a plump strawberry, she bit off the tip and then trickled the cool juice over the head of his penis.

It must have made steam because the pungent smell of ripe strawberries filled the room. The juice blazed a tingling trail to his scrotum.

Maggie's hot tongue followed, lapping up every drip.

Experiencing altered breathing, all he could do was watch, vibrating with arousal and the thought of what she might do next.

She didn't disappoint.

Running her teeth lightly around the bulbous head, she flicked the tip with the point of her tongue.

His biceps bulged when he increased his grip on the edge of the chair.

Just when he thought he could stand no more, she placed a loud, sucking kiss on the tip, stood, and ate the remains of the strawberry with gusto.

He tracked the sway of her hips as she sauntered back to the bed. Naked, the high heels magnified her every step.

Another berry in her hand, she cast a smoldering glance through her lashes.

His heart tripped when she sat on the end of his bed and spread her legs.

Maggie watched Drew devour her with his eyes. It wasn't enough. She'd vowed to walk on the wild side, and, dangit, that's exactly what she would do. So what if his hot gaze made her tremble, her flesh weep. *I can do this—I am woman, hear me roar.*

Before her bravado deserted her, she ran her tongue suggestively around the plump strawberry, acutely aware of the tiny seeds against her tongue. Its smell wafted around her. Maintaining eye contact, she took a deep breath and pushed the fruit as far as it would go into her vagina.

Drew's eyes widened. His shaft wiggled.

"Want a strawberry?" Her voice was barely a whisper. What if he thought she was a weirdo and threw her out, strawberry pussy and all?

An eternity, but probably only seconds, later, he knelt between her legs, his hands petting her from her ankles up to the inside of her quivering thighs, the pads of his thumbs barely brushing the distended folds. His hot breath bathed her trembling flesh.

Her breath caught at the first touch of his tongue when he ran it around and around in slow motion. The circles diminished when the strawberry shifted within from the movement of his tongue.

The seeds she'd noticed earlier abraded her opening, only to be salved by the warm velvet of his tongue.

But instead of flicking the fruit from her body, he played with it, taking little nips and sipping the resulting juice, driving her wild.

It was a short drive.

With her feet on his shoulders, she bucked, begging him with her body to take her.

Shameless, she knew he could do anything with her, to her, and she'd gladly comply as long as he continued giving her such rapturous pleasure.

His mouth closed over her engorged nub.

Her breath stopped halfway between a pant and a gasp.

To her delight, he moved his jaw back and forth, the edges on his teeth spreading bliss throughout her body.

She teetered on the edge of what promised to be the orgasm to end all orgasms.

He sucked the pulsing nub in rhythm to the movement of the finger he'd inserted next to the strawberry.

It was too much and yet not enough. The rubbing of the fruit against the slick walls, the counterpoint of his finger deep within, moving with every rhythmic pull on the ridiculously sensitive bud. Her senses were on erotic overload. Wave after wave of ecstasy slammed into her.

She screamed.

The door to Drew's room flew open, banging against the wall. The ceiling light flashed on.

"What in blue blazes are you doing to that woman, Connor?"

11

_____

Drew jumped to his feet, fumbling with the bedspread in a belated attempt to cover their nudity.

"Sir! Captain Murray, sir, I—"

"My God," Murray interrupted, a look of disgust on his craggy face. His gaze was riveted to the bed. "Connor, is that blood? What are you, some kind of animal?"

"No!" Drew shook his head, color darkening his cheeks—possibly both sets, if the full-body flush he had going was any indication. "It's strawberries! Sir."

The captain sniffed the air, still pungent with crushed berries, his facial expression softening a bit. "I'm going to take a walk down the corridor." He walked toward the door and looked back. "Young lady, I expect to find you gone when I return." His gaze landed on Drew. "Mr. Connor, I also expect you to be cleaned up and dressed for duty. We'll discuss this incident when I get back."

The door closed with a snap.

Maggie and Drew looked at each other.

* * *

She began to pull the soiled bedspread around her. "If you'll just hand me my things, I'll dress and get out of your way," she said, avoiding eye contact.

His warm hand on her shoulder stopped her before she could escape to the bathroom.

"Maggie, I'm sorry." He rubbed her skin with the pad of his thumb.

She wished she could erase the last two minutes and go back to where they'd been when they were so rudely interrupted. Of course, that's what got them into trouble in the first place.

"I'm the one who should be sorry," she finally managed to say around the lump of self-loathing in her throat. "If I hadn't followed you down here like some pathetic, needy—"

"—sinfully attractive, sexy, hot woman, my wildest fantasy come true," he finished for her, drawing her into his embrace, placing his forehead against hers. "I'd have been able to resist you if you'd been all the things you said. But this." He skimmed his hand under the spread along her skin from hip to breast, where he tweaked a nipple. "No red-blooded male with a heartbeat could resist this." He brushed a kiss across her slack mouth and then gave her buttocks a quick squeeze. "Now, you'd better throw on your clothes and make tracks if you don't want to run into Captain Murray again."

Paused by the bathroom door, she had to ask. "Do you think he'll fire you?"

Drew exhaled and shook his head. "Nah, I doubt it. This is my last cruise season anyway. Firing me would serve no purpose and would leave him shorthanded." He grinned, his teeth a slash of white. "But that doesn't mean he won't chew me out and make me wish he *would* fire me."

She stepped into her panties and skirt, pulling on her top as she exited the bathroom.

Drew stood by the chair, holding her sandals. He motioned for her to sit down and then placed her shoes on her feet after kissing each toe and running his tongue under the arches of her feet.

She clamped her legs together in an effort not to squirm. Toe sex. What he did could only be construed as toe sex. Or maybe toe foreplay? Whatever it was, it certainly got her hot and bothered.

"Well, I'd better get out of here." She stood, only to be stopped again by his hot hands.

Dipping his palms into her halter, he released her breasts from their confinement and kissed them with plenty of suction and tongue action before placing them back in the built-in bra. "I miss you already," he said, his hungry gaze on her cleavage. He glanced up at her and grinned. "I'll miss you, too."

"Gee, thanks. I think." Snatching her purse from where it had toppled to the floor, she opened the door and peeked out. "The coast is clear. I'm making a run for it. See you later?"

He nodded. "But probably not until dinner. I'm sure I'll have to do some kind of penance for what went on here today."

With a nod, she left.

Mere minutes later, Drew opened the door to Captain Murray.

The captain strode to the chair and sat, motioning Drew to do the same.

"I want this room shipshape ASAP, Mr. Connor. Then I want you to report to the navigator. You will work there the rest of the day. Ray can fill in for you. We make land by sixteen hundred. The passengers who wish may disembark for a brief shopping trip, returning by no later than nineteen hundred for the usual dining and dancing as we shove off. You will escort them unless your playmate decides to disembark, in which case you will stay aboard. Do I make myself clear?"

"Yes, sir." If Drew said more, he'd end up digging in deeper. Which wouldn't do him or Maggie any good.

Murray nodded and stood. "You need to steer clear of that girl, son. You've had a fine and distinguished record with the BumbleBee. I know you'll want to leave with it intact."

"Yes, sir."

"Fine, fine. I thought we'd reach an understanding. Report to the nav room, Connor." He paused by the door. "And steer clear of icebergs, if you get my drift."

The door shut. Drew's shoulders slumped. Damn. He'd planned to find ways to see Maggie during the day and keep her busy all night.

"The best laid plans . . ." he mumbled, pulling a clean uniform off its hanger.

And speaking of laid . . . He smiled. He would be getting laid tonight. Regardless of what his captain thought.

Maggie cast a nervous glance at the cute guy taking Drew's place on the excursion and swallowed her disappointment. She'd really wanted to explore the tiny island with Drew and then go back onboard for another night of wild sex in her jungle.

"Oh! I'm so sorry!" She steadied the elderly couple she had almost pushed into the shallow water in her hurry to exit the skiff onto the dock.

The woman smiled at her and clasped the old man's bony arm. "No worries, sweetie. You run along and have fun. We're just happy to finally be together." She leaned toward Maggie and whispered, "We were engaged for forty-three years! I was beginning to think we'd never get married." She beamed at her groom. "And it was everything I'd dreamed it would be."

Thanks for that word picture. "Well, congratulations!" Maggie gushed instead. "May I ask why you were engaged for so long?"

The man harrumphed. "Her old bat of a mother! She didn't approve. Had to wait until she croaked."

"Oh." Maggie stole a glance at the woman, relieved to see

she didn't seem bothered by her husband's declaration. "Well, you're together now, that's what counts. I'll see you on the boat in a few hours."

Wow, forty-three years, she mused, heading toward a souvenir shop close to the dock. Would she ever love someone enough to wait for them, no matter how long it took? Admittedly, she didn't wait well, but she hoped to find a love like that.

Drew's smiling face flashed in her mind. Had she found a possible candidate for Mr. Right? As Mr. Right Now, he certainly filled all her criteria. And a few other things. She grinned and asked to see a sequined purse that would go great with her scarf. The bag wasn't very big, but it would hold the essentials, like lipstick, breath mints. Condoms.

The thought had her tingling in places that should not be tingling when she had no way of satisfying them. At least right now. She thought of Drew walking to her clad in a glowing piña-colada condom and experienced her first hot flash.

Maybe she'd need a bigger bag, after all.

Drew ran to meet Ray as he hobbled up the gangplank.

"Stephenson, what the hell happened?" he asked, grasping the other man's arm and taking some of his weight.

Ray grimaced and shrugged. "I was helping a couple of passengers with their bags. Before I could shut the door of the taxi, it drove off—right over my foot!"

Drew scanned the returning passengers. No Maggie. "Did you get everyone back?"

Ray shook his head and lowered himself onto a deck chair. "I think everyone is here except the hot little blonde. Did you see her? The shorts and peekaboo top she wore just about made me drool." He sighed as though the memory was better than Drew wanted to hear. "Man, when she bent over to pick up her shopping bag to go souvenir shopping . . . well, I sure could've given her something to take with her—"

Drew gave a halfhearted laugh. "Whoa! I don't want to get you in trouble! Too much info."

Ray lifted his sunglasses and stared up at Drew. "Hey, man, I heard about the reaming you got from Murray. Was she worth it? You know . . ." He made a crude hand gesture.

Drew shoved his fists in the pockets of his shorts to keep from knocking the guy's teeth out. "I don't want to talk about it," he said around clenched teeth.

Ray nodded his understanding. "Got it. Trouble with a capital T, huh?"

"Something like that."

"Murray assigned me to your table tonight," Ray said, standing and flexing his leg. "Sure hope I'm up to entertaining Miss Hot Pants. See ya."

Drew vibrated with rage as he watched the man limp away. Any "entertaining" of Maggie Hamilton would be done by *Drew Connor*. He glanced around the almost deserted deck.

And speaking of Maggie . . . where the hell was she?

Maggie strolled toward the dock, licking a watermelon ice. She shifted her purchases and glanced at her watch. Yikes! She was late meeting the others.

Picking up her pace, she hurried along the dock until she slammed into a hard chest. A hard chest covered in a starched white shirt. A white uniform shirt.

The glare from the sun prevented her from seeing the face of the man steadying her, but the voice she'd know anywhere.

"Where the hell have you been?" Drew snapped. "The skiff already took everyone back to the ship. We're about to set sail. C'mon."

He gripped her elbow and hustled her to the little boat waiting to ferry them to the BumbleBee.

Hopping down into the boat, he grasped her waist and

hoisted her none-too-gently to the platform seat and then took off with a roar of full throttle toward the waiting cruise liner.

On the way, she had to grip the seat to keep from being tossed overboard. Periodically she heard Drew's voice rise and caught a word here and there. Because he seemed to be yelling at her, she was glad his tirade was being drowned out by the engine and water.

Assured the boat would be properly stored, Drew helped Maggie from the skiff onto the gangplank, not stopping until they reached the deck.

"Get to your room, and get ready for dinner," he ordered, "while I go make sure everything is secure." He turned her in the general direction. "Go!"

After securing the skiff, Drew radioed the information to the bridge. The engines started up, the ship creaking in its effort to get under way.

The idea of not being seated by Maggie or dancing with her settled like a fist in his gut. He plopped into the first deck chair he came across to think about how he could get around the captain's orders.

"Mr. Connor!" Captain Murray's bellow shook Drew from his thoughts. "What in Sam Hill is going on in your head?" He stalked in Drew's direction.

Having nowhere to hide, Drew stood. "Sir?"

"The Cunninghams! Remember them? A little old couple about this high?" He held his hand at shoulder height. "They're missing! And do you want to guess where they are?" Before Drew could hazard a guess, Murray blustered, "I'll tell you where they are!" He pointed aft. "They're back there! You left them on the island! Just had a ship-to-shore call. Do you have any idea how this will look on our record? We'll be damn lucky not to get sued!"

Drew winced. Damn. He'd been so concerned about Maggie, he hadn't even thought to check for other stragglers.

The captain turned on his heel and stalked away, calling over his shoulder, "I've given orders to go back for them. We'll be coming about as soon as we reach deeper water. I consider it your responsibility to go pick them up."

Of course he did. Everything was Drew's responsibility. The end of the season couldn't come fast enough, as far as he was concerned.

Would he see Maggie after the cruise ended? He knew what he wanted but wasn't too sure of her feelings. Maybe he'd been a shipboard fling. Something to slake her lust for a few days away from reality.

What a grim thought.

Ways he'd like to slake her lust—and his, while he was at it—crossed his mind.

Would Maggie object to being tied up and drizzled in honey?

If so, she could always tie him up. He was an equal-opportunity sex fiend.

12

Maggie paced her room. Where was Drew when she needed him? Sure, he had duties. After all, it was his job. When the ship had returned to the island, she saw him taking the skiff and then returning a few minutes later with the old couple she had met that afternoon.

After a leisurely but lonely bath, she'd generously applied the lotion he seemed to love so much. When it became apparent he would not be licking it off, she dressed in one of her most demure sundresses.

A glance in the mirror confirmed her worst fear: she looked like a librarian. Or a nun. Dressed in the navy, high-cut, sleeveless dress with the white collar, it could go either way.

And without Drew, she didn't care. Sometime during the day, she'd come to a major realization: she wanted to attract only Drew.

Hopefully it was only temporary insanity.

Meanwhile, the hottie who'd taken her to the island was filling in for Drew at dinner. She had to eat. Maybe it was a test of the true depth of her feelings for Drew. The only thing to do was meet the challenge.

Shoving her feet into strappy white sandals, she set off toward the elevator.

It wasn't until she was seated at the table, forcing a smile for her fellow diners, that it hit her.

She wore no underwear.

Drew watched Maggie join the rest of the passengers at the table; her back looked stiff. Damn, he wished he could see her face. At the head of the table, Ray kept glancing at her, a smarmy smile on his clean-shaven face. What was going on?

"Turn around, Maggie. Let me know you're all right," Drew said under his breath from his hiding place by the service door.

It looked like she merely picked at her dinner, and she skipped dessert altogether.

A hand clamped his shoulder.

"I'm proud of you, son," Captain Murray said close to his side. "You kept your word. A rarity these days." He patted Drew's back. "Fix a plate, and take it back to your quarters. You deserve it. Call it a night."

"And tomorrow?" He had to know.

The captain chuckled. "Well, we'll let tomorrow take care of itself. Far as I'm concerned, you can resume your duties." He pulled him aside and lowered his voice. "Hell, we've all been ruled by our dick heads every once in a while. I got a look at what had yours standing at attention. A definite prime piece of ass." He winked. "Just don't let it happen again." With a farewell slap on the back, he was gone before Drew had a chance to punch him.

Drew glanced out again in time to see Maggie picking her way through the after-dinner crowd, headed toward the exit. He didn't like the way Ray's gaze followed her.

Was that all Maggie was to him, a "prime piece of ass"?

Maybe, maybe not. But regardless of that, she was *his* piece of ass. At least for the duration of the cruise.

And he'd be damned if he'd spend their last night without her.

13

Maggie stepped from the shower and briskly toweled off. Slathering on her scented lotion, she decided to put the incident in Drew's room out of her mind.

Embarrassment heated her cheeks again at the thought of the captain seeing her butt naked, spread-eagle on Drew's bed.

She flipped the switch to fill the stateroom with jungle sounds and then walked to the coconut bed and lay down to wait. Drew would come to her. She just knew he would.

He'd better. Mel was still packed in her suitcase.

Just when she was ready to give up hope, a soft knock sounded on her door. He let himself in by the time she got off the bed.

They rushed into each other's arms.

Lifting her from her feet, he practically devoured her with his kiss. Too soon, his lips left hers to trail kisses down her neck.

"I thought today would never end!" He nuzzled her hair, his hands moving in an elongated caress up and down her back, bunching the sheer nightie along the way.

"Me, either," she whispered, planting frantic kisses any-where she could reach.

"I don't care if they fire me, I want you. Now!"

Maggie stiffened and stepped back, stopping him with her hand when he attempted to close the distance.

"They'd actually fire you because of me?" How could she enjoy what time they had left with something like that hanging over her head?

"It doesn't matter. All that matters is—"

"Yes, it does!" She stepped away again. "Drew, I don't want to be the cause of you losing your job."

Fists on hips, he met her gaze. "Maggie, I swear, it's no big deal. This was my last season anyway. I told you I plan to take the bar and go into my grandfather's law practice. So—"

"So? So I think we should avoid each other for the rest of the cruise." She stalked to the bureau and pulled out a small pad and pen. After scribbling her address and phone number, she walked back and handed it to him. "Give me a call when you get back to Houston." Blinking back tears, she had to force out the next words. "Maybe we can go out sometime." *See where it goes, if we still spontaneously combust whenever we touch.* Of course, if she said that, she'd crumble and end up begging him never to leave her. And that wouldn't do.

The muscle in his jaw clenched. "Go out sometime? That's it?"

It took every ounce of acting ability she could muster, but she shrugged in what she hoped was a nonchalant manner. "What did you expect, Drew? A declaration of undying love? We've known each other only two days!"

"And nights," he reminded her in a low voice that sent goose bumps skittering over her body.

"Yes, and nights." She sighed, more determined than ever. It was for the best. "We had mind-blowing sex." She touched his arm, bracing for the zip of current she always felt touching him.

"It was great. But that's all it was . . . sex." Her laugh sounded feeble to her own ears. "If you feel like a repeat, when you get to Houston, look me up."

"And if I don't?"

Wincing inwardly at the pain the thought inspired, she managed another shrug. "Then it would just prove that what we had really wasn't worth risking your job for, wouldn't it?"

Muscle in his jaw still flexing, he nodded and brushed a kiss across her cheek. "Have a good life, Maggie Hamilton. Enjoy the rest of your cruise."

Back straight, shoulders stiff, he let himself out of Tarzan and Jane's Lair.

Gulping to keep from calling to him, begging him to come back, she made her way to the bed, where she curled into the fetal position and cried for all she'd lost. Possibly for all she never really had.

It was pitch dark when she sat up again, cried out and hungry. Digging an apple from the complimentary fruit basket, she grabbed her cell phone and headed out to the deck where she'd get better reception.

She was a woman on a mission.

14

Pogo-Doo was a tiny island, by any standards. But it had the distinction of having a deep ship channel, allowing the smaller cruise liners to dock close enough for passengers to disembark for sightseeing without the need of a skiff.

Squinting against the sunshine, Maggie headed down the stairs to the dock on unsteady legs. She'd left a note for Drew in her room, along with money and instructions with the purser to deliver her bags to her apartment at the end of the cruise.

A glance at her watch confirmed she had a few hours until she needed to make her way to the other side of the island to catch the commuter plane.

Refusing to glance back at the ship, she set her shoulders and headed toward the interior of the island. Anywhere was fine, as long as she didn't have to look at Drew.

"What's this?" Drew stomped toward Henry, waving Maggie's note in his fist. "Do you know where Ms. Hamilton went?"

"Y—yes, sir." He handed Drew his note and check. "She said she was taking an alternate route home."

"Like hell she is!"

A few minutes later, he let himself into Captain Murray's office without knocking.

"I quit!" He threw the crumpled note on the smooth desk.

The captain removed his reading glasses and placed them in their case, then leaned back in his executive chair and regarded Drew for so long Drew had to force himself not to shuffle his feet.

"You can't quit," the captain finally said. "You signed a contract. Your ass is ours until the end of the season."

"I want out." Drew placed his palms on the cool surface of the desk and leaned down. "This was my last cruise."

"You're out when I say you're out, son. And not a minute sooner." The captain straightened his pens. "Don't worry. There'll be other young ladies to catch your eye on the next trip—it's our dance aerobics cruise. Very popular with sweet young things." He chuckled. "Lots of fresh meat to choose from."

"I don't want fresh meat! Damnit, I want Maggie! And if I have to break my contract and go after her, that's exactly what I'll do."

"So," the captain said, tenting his fingers and leaning back, the leather of his chair creaking. "You fancy yourself in love, then?"

Drew frowned. Love? Was what he felt for Maggie love? Maybe. But he'd never find out if he didn't spend more time with her or even see her for the next two months.

"I don't know," he finally said. "That's what I need to find out."

"Mr. Connor, I don't see the problem. You can spend the day with her—assuming you don't neglect the other passengers—before we dock in Galveston."

Drew shoved the note across the desk. "The problem is she got off the ship and plans to fly back. I need permission to go find her. Sir," he added in a last-ditch effort to suck up.

It must have worked.

"Permission granted . . . as long as you don't do it to the exclusion of the other passengers."

Drew glanced at his watch and swallowed a growl of frustration. A little more than forty minutes left, and he'd still not found Maggie. Where could one small woman hide on an island with less than two hundred inhabitants?

Steps slow with defeat, he decided to search the little dockside restaurant one more time on his way back to the ship.

"Monsieur?" A very tall, male-model type approached him. "Table for one?" he asked in heavily accented English.

Drew shook his head, still perusing the tables. "I'm looking for a woman."

The waiter raised his eyebrows.

"No," Drew hurried to assure him, "not just any woman, an American. Blond. Pretty—very pretty. About so high." He held his hand at midchest height.

"Oui," the waiter said and nodded, pushing Drew in the direction of the bar. "Is she the one?" He pointed toward the back corner.

It took a moment for Drew's eyes to adjust; then he saw her.

Huddled over an umbrella drink in the far back corner, Maggie sniffed and wiped her eyes with a napkin. Dressed entirely in white, with her scarf loosely draped around her neck, she looked like an angel. A lonely angel.

He couldn't leave her. Not here, not now. Possibly not ever.

Something broke free, allowing him to take the first good, deep breath of air he'd had all morning.

Quick steps took him to her side. "Maggie! I've been looking all over the island for you. It's time to go back to the ship."

He'd decided, if he found her, to pretend he knew nothing of her plans to abandon ship.

She sniffed and turned watery eyes to him. The bruising around her eye and cheek had faded to a nasty-looking yellowy-green stain.

"I'm not going back that way. I'm flying."

"I wasn't aware you were rich," he said, hoping to goad her into leaving with him. "Why else would you blow money on a plane when you have a perfectly good cruise ship already paid for? I even had the dust all cleaned for you."

Her eyes filled again. "That was you?" she asked in a choked voice.

He nodded, feeling pretty choked up himself.

The blast from the BumbleBee's horn vibrated the floor of the bar.

He glanced over his shoulder and then back. "We really need to get going, Mag."

Instead of agreeing, the confusing woman stood there, crying and shaking her head.

"I don't have time for this." He bent and scooped her off her feet, carrying her over his shoulder out of the restaurant. The waiter gave a little salute as they went by.

Onboard, Drew held Maggie until they had the gangplank drawn up. In silence, they watched the water increase between the dock and ship.

Maggie turned teary eyes up to him. "Why didn't you just let me go? We agreed—"

"We agreed to nothing, Maggie!" He gripped her shoulders, forcing her to look at him. "I couldn't let you go. And I don't think you wanted me to, either, did you?"

Her lips trembled, but she shook her head.

"Ah, Mag." He pulled her into his arms, loving the intimate way she snuggled against his heart. "I don't know anything about relationships or love."

She leaned back, eyes wide, and looked up at him.

"Don't panic," he said quickly. "I just meant I don't want this—whatever it is we have—to end. I'll be in Houston for a few days before the next cruise. I'd like to spend it with you, okay?"

Okay? Was it okay? She wanted to squeal and jump into his arms. But that might make her look too needy. Instead she nodded again.

She didn't want what they had to end either. It may be too early for love, but she was definitely in deep lust. If a few days were all they had, she'd take it.

"And," Drew continued, petting her back and drawing her close again, "like I said, this is my last season. I'll be back in Houston permanently in about two months. How about making a date for then to explore whatever this is?"

Love, I think this may be love. Hot damn, I may have found Mr. Right!

"I'd like that," she said, leaning in to his kiss as the ship gathered steam.

A sea breeze caught her scarf, flapping it against her back, whipping it against the side of her face. A few seconds later, the scarf joined the breeze in a dance, floating across the water toward the dock like a giant butterfly.

"My scarf!" Her hurried reach was a second too late.

"I'll buy you another one," Drew said against her neck. "After the inventive way you used it, I'll make sure to buy you another one!"

She looped her arms around his neck and snuggled closer. "Deal. Now . . . where were we?" Her mouth captured his.

In the grand scheme of things, she realized, the scarf was insignificant. Nonetheless, she breathed a silent sigh of relief when she saw the fluttering silk land on a waitress clearing a table at the dockside restaurant.

She wished the waitress good luck with her new, beautiful scarf. It had been a gift to her; she'd enjoyed it. Now she was gifting someone else with the scarf.

Drew closed his hand over her breast, and she purred. After all, she had the best gift of all, right there in her arms.

Hold Me, Thrill Me

1

Ryan Holmes watched the departing cruise ship with murder in her heart. Damn. What she wouldn't give to be onboard on her way back to the States to kill Bill.

She pocketed the change from the table. Honeymooners were notoriously bad tippers. Another glance at the Bumble-Bee as it chugged toward open waters proved even more painful.

A couple stood by the railing, lost in what looked to be a very passionate kiss.

Once upon a time, Ryan believed in happily ever after. Until Bill.

While she watched, the woman's scarf caught the ocean breeze and drifted toward the shore. In what seemed like a heartbeat, said scarf laminated itself against Ryan's surprised face.

In the background, dishes clattered. Ryan peeled the scarf from her face in time to see the tail end of the ship pass out of sight.

She glanced down at the soft, insubstantial piece in her hand. Waning afternoon sun cast it in a glow, reflecting from the tiny threads of silver and gold shot through the thin, off-white silk. It smelled faintly of some exotic perfume.

Ryan clutched the scarf to her uniform shirt and blinked back tears. Hope swelled her chest. Her life was about to change, she just knew it.

"*Pardon.*" A deep voice interrupted her thoughts.

She glanced back to see the incredibly hot French waiter, Jean Bogart, striding toward her, and wished, not for the first time, that she'd studied more in her high school French classes.

"*Oui?*" It sure would help if the guy spoke English, like a normal person.

"*Ça va?*"

"*Bien.*" Of course she was all right. It was just a scarf. She tied it around her hips, picked up the napkins and slung them into the bin of the bus cart. A shadow fell across the table.

"Would you like *prendre un verre?*" For such a gorgeous specimen, Jean looked nervous, towering above her.

Verre. Drink. He had asked her to go for a drink! At least, she hoped he was asking her to go for a drink. For all she knew, he could be asking her to pour him one. Or to varnish something. Darn French. Why did it have to be such a confusing language?

Jean continued to look expectantly at her, so she assumed he waited for an answer.

"*Oui*, I'd like that." At least, she thought that's what she said. He smiled, so she must've been successful.

"*Bien.*" He continued to smile as he backed away.

It wasn't until he turned that she could take a deep breath. No doubt about it, the guy was drop-dead gorgeous. Not that she was interested.

After Bill, she'd considered becoming a lesbian, until she found she really wasn't attracted to women. Other than that, she'd have switched in a minute. Maybe.

She sighed. The Frenchman really had a fine butt on him.

Tight and firm, it moved smoothly within the thin uniform trousers, just begging to be squeezed.

Not that she was remotely interested; she was just noticing.

The rest of the evening passed in an uneventful blur. A few native islanders came for their nightly songfest and more than a few drinks. A couple strolled in, arm in arm, and had some wine. Jean was their waiter. Ryan marveled at the woman's ability to keep her eyes on her escort instead of the yummy piece of beefcake hovering over their table. Moonlight glistened from his shiny golden-brown hair, causing Ryan to sigh before resuming her work.

All too soon, it was closing time. Within minutes after last call, only the staff remained.

Amid the sounds of tables being cleared, liquor being restocked and money being counted, Ryan added up her orders and separated her tips. Shoving the surprisingly hefty roll of bills into her backpack, she headed toward Roman's office to turn in her till.

Roman Holiday had an unfortunate name, but within seconds you forgot it in the presence of easily one of the most irritating men on the face of the earth.

"Did you count it?" Roman asked around the slimy-looking cigar hanging out of the side of his mouth.

"No, Roman, I wanted it to be a surprise." She plunked the bank bag onto the scarred desktop and stepped back. "Of course I counted it."

"And correctly filled out the deposit form this time?"

"Yes," she said through clenched teeth.

"And it's all there?"

"Would I turn it in if it wasn't?"

He grinned, exposing small tobacco-stained teeth. His beady black eyes reminded her of a ferret. An ugly ferret.

She suppressed a shudder when he gave her his nightly once-over. It was yet one more reason to hate the job.

"If it's short . . . I could look the other way, with the right encouragement." He shifted the smelly cigar to the other side of his mouth.

Oh, yeah, that's it, baby, bowl me over with your slimy come-hither look. "No need," she replied.

His smile fell. "If you'd get off of your high horse, you could do much better around here, you know. Loosen up! You're lucky I keep you around, what with the way you treat customers and everybody else."

"I'm the best damn waiter you have, and you know it."

"More money if you tended bar," he reminded her. "Especially if you'd loosen up and wear something, er, revealing." He shrugged and leaned over the receipts and cash. "For that matter, it would help your tips, too."

"I do okay." She shifted from one foot to the other while the little worm clicked away on his calculator and counted her money. "Finished?"

He nodded and let out a sound somewhere between a grunt and a burp. She didn't know or care which. One more day in this hellhole to mark off her calendar.

"Hear anything yet?" Sam, the bartender, shone the bar while he carried on his conversation with Jean.

Jean nodded, reaching behind the bar for a sweating bottle of beer. He popped the top before he answered. "Yes. The company is firm. Their offer is good for only thirty days."

Sam shook his head. "You have a bitch of a deadline, my friend."

Jean took a deep swig from the bottle and wiped his mouth on the back of his hand. "*Oui.*"

"Did you go to the embassy?"

Jean nodded. "They said their hands were tied. Not enough time for a visa. My only hope is a green card. If I do not find a way into the United States, and *vite*, it's over." After all his education, all his experience designing surfboards, to have the job of a lifetime slip through his fingers was beyond agony.

Sam tossed his rag aside. "You'll come up with something. You always do."

Jean waited by the door, watching Ryan pretend to tolerate that warthog Roman. How women put up with him was a mystery.

Choosing to ignore the slug, he concentrated on Ryan. She stood with her back ramrod straight, shoulders stiff, her body language shouting her repulsion. Of course, pigs like Roman were inept at reading the finer things like body language. They were coarse and common. Women, especially women like Ryan, should never have to deal with such lowlife.

His cock stirred within his low-slung uniform pants while he studied the finer points of Ryan's ass, shown to perfection by her own thin uniform.

He'd been attracted to her from first sight, but since she'd tied the incredibly sexy scarf around her hips . . . *mon dieu!* All he could think about tonight was getting her naked.

She turned, staring out across the harbor, the light from Roman's desk casting her in profile. Her normally perky brown ponytail sagged, its ribbon dangling onto one shoulder. Her nose was pert, perfect for her small oval face.

But it was her lips that drove him to distraction. They looked ripe and juicy. He salivated just thinking about them. Several times each shift, he'd caught her worrying the edge of them with her teeth and had to look away to keep from groaning in frustration.

His perusal continued down the slender column of her neck to the next point of interest. Her breasts. Full and firm looking, they would easily spill over his hands.

Inviting her out was most likely a mistake. But she was his only candidate, and he was desperate.

He needed a wife. An American wife.

2

Jean set two more drinks on their table and smiled his bone-melting smile at her.

Her lips were already numb, but she gamely picked up her drink, did a little salute and downed the fiery liquid. Jean did the same and then motioned for more.

"No, please," she said, frowning at her slurred words. "I really should be going." She hiccuped and felt a full-body flush of heat streak over her when she stood.

She shook off his hand and staggered out into the street.

"*Attention, tu vas te faire écraser!*" Jean grabbed her shirt and hauled her back against his hard chest just as a car whizzed by within inches of her toes.

She sagged against him. "*Merci!*" She looked back over her shoulder, their gazes locked and she wondered what it would be like to kiss him.

Maybe their language barrier would be an advantage. She thought of Bill's profanity during their inadequate lovemaking and decided a silent partner would definitely be preferable.

Jean pulled her up and around to face him and rattled off

something in French, but her brain was beyond the capabilities of translating. It was an effort to even keep her eyes open. While she stood there, trying not to sway, he leaned down and kissed her.

Blind. I've gone blind. I should've listened to my mother— oh, wait. It's Jean's head. Why is he kissing me? More important, why am I analyzing it instead of kissing him back?

She slid her arms up around his neck, clasping his silky hair in both fists, and became an active participant.

His lips were warm and pliant against hers. At least, she thought they were, but with the numb-lip thing going on, it was sort of hard to tell. Oh, yeah, his tongue was definitely warm and tasted pleasantly of the liquor they'd consumed.

Whatever aftershave he wore absolutely made her mouth water. She'd noticed it several times since they started working together. Now, kissing him, having his arms wrapped around her, the scent wafted up to intoxicate her even more.

He walked them backward until they stood in the shadows, her back against the sun-warmed stone of the bar. His hard length pressed against her abdomen while his hands slid beneath her now untucked shirt to dip into her bra. He fingered her nipples before giving them a light pinch. Warmth gushed between her legs. Had it not been for his solid length pressing her against the wall, she'd have slid to the sidewalk in a puddle of need.

He spoke more incoherent French against her ear. She thought it had something to do with sex, so she nodded.

He released her and attempted to smooth her top down, then held her close as they walked at a fast clip down the deserted street. Due to the disparity in height, she found herself trotting to keep up.

Each step abraded her sensitized breasts, now free of the confines of her bra cups. The dampness between her legs was also becoming uncomfortable. Wherever they were going, she hoped they got there soon. Until tonight, she hadn't realized how horny she'd become. She wanted sex. Needed sex.

Jean rounded the corner and pushed open a door, stepping in and closing it behind them.

Ryan knew immediately it was Jean's place—the air was permeated with his scent. She dragged in a great lungful. It had the immediate effect of an orgasm.

During the time her eyes tried to adjust to the darkness and make out the furnishings, Jean evidently was stripping. When he turned to her, weak moonlight reflected from his bare skin. *Oh, wow.*

Within seconds, she stood as naked as he, wondering what to do next.

Luckily Jean was the innovative sort. Lifting her from her feet, he took her nipple into his greedy mouth. She felt his suckling all the way to her toes and wrapped her legs around his bare torso.

He staggered. Her back hit something hard and cold. Metal clanged on the floor.

Then hard heat, gloriously hard heat, filled her. Jean growled as he surged into her.

She threw back her head and laughed.

Hot damn, the draught was over. She was finally having sex.

Jean thrust into Ryan, holding her against the wall of his kitchen. In the distance, he heard pans crashing to the floor. He didn't care. All that mattered was salving the incredible ache he felt to bury himself deep within the hot, wet center of her. To plunge into her welcoming wetness over and over again.

Around his throbbing cock, her internal muscles contracted, signaling her climax, milking him of his. Too soon. It was going to be over too soon.

He tried thinking of something—anything—else, even Roman, but to no avail. She jerked and bit his shoulder. His heart stumbled. He took one final, deep plunge with a triumphant shout then shuddered his release.

As the afterglow waned, Ryan became aware of the cold surface of the countertop on her bare behind. Against her back, something sharp poked at her ribs. But her chest was toasty warm, protected by Jean's big, hot body. She squeezed her legs, which were still wrapped around him, tighter while she did a little shimmy with her hips.

He groaned and planted nibbling kisses on her neck.

Grumbling something, he clasped her legs and slid them down his hips, severed their connection and stepped back.

Cool air bathed her wetness. Noticing the direction of Jean's gaze, she clamped her thighs together.

He forked his hand through his mussed chin-length hair and avoided eye contact.

Wow, this is awkward. Shielding her breasts with her forearm, she visually searched the floor for her clothes.

She eased one foot toward the floor, but the counter was higher than she estimated. Her toes connected with nothing but air. She leaned forward a bit more. Too far.

With a half shriek, half squeak, she hit the tiled floor.

Pain radiated through her kneecaps up to her hips. Her elbows and wrists echoed the sensation.

Well, that was graceful, Ryan, she thought. *Nothing like calling attention to your naked, cloddy self.*

"Ry-an! Are you all right?" Jean bent to help her to her feet.

She loved the way her name rolled off his tongue. The way his gaze raked her body from head to toe and back again wasn't too shabby either.

She scooped her clothes from the floor and then clutched them in front of her while she looked around for her panties.

Perusing the room, she finally noticed Jean leaning negligently against the island. Her sheer thong dangled from one long finger. His smoldering gaze heated every millimeter of her bare skin.

"Thanks," she managed to squeak out, grabbing the panties. "Where's the bathroom?"

He compressed his lips then pointed toward the next room.

Jean watched Ryan hurry toward the bathroom and snickered. She'd asked where she could go swimming, but he assumed she meant the bathroom. Her *français* was laughable, but he admired her courage. He supposed he should admit he spoke English, but French was so much easier. And it was fun to listen to her attempts. Eventually he'd confess. After they were married.

The thought of sleeping with Ryan every night made him hard. How long would it take to get her out of his system?

Where was she? He walked to the doorway of his room. From there, he could see her, perched on the edge of his bathtub, regarding her knee. She'd put on her scrap of underpants. Beneath her arm, the soft flesh of her breasts pushed against the top of her leg with her movement, creating pillows of temptation.

"Ry-an." He approached her slowly, giving her time to turn him away.

She gave a weak smile, hugging her legs in such a way as to obscure his view. Foolish American women and their false modesty. Images of her spread before him flashed through his mind, adding to his arousal.

Still naked, he walked toward her, daring her to deny their chemistry. Daring her to look away.

She just stared up at him, eyes wide, hunger evident.

He reached around her to fill the tub. The sound of running water echoed from the tiled walls.

The small light above the sink cast them in an intimate glow.

While the tub filled, he reached down to trace her breast with the tip of his finger. Arousal leaped at the feel of such smooth skin beneath his fingertip.

Instead of shrinking back as he'd half expected she would, she arched toward his palm.

He reached for her hand and placed it on his erection, then continued toying with her nipples, which were beading to hard points under his touch.

She moved her fingers, at first timid, barely moving along his engorged length. He tweaked her nipples. She gasped and squeezed his turgid flesh and then began stroking base to tip.

His hand shook when he turned off the water.

The only sound in the little room was the drip of the faucet in the bathwater and their ragged breathing.

"Poor baby," he said against the reddened skin of her knee. He planted a soft kiss on both knees and then lifted her high against his chest to give her a tender kiss.

Slowly severing the connection of their lips, he bent to strip down her panties, then lowered her into the water.

"This will make you feel better," he said, reaching for the scented soap his sister gave him last Christmas.

Ryan leaned back and tried to relax against the cold enamel of the claw-foot tub. Having Jean play with her nipples had her aching again. She watched his long fingers caress the soap until bubbles covered his hands and part of his forearms.

He leaned over the tub, his hair falling to tickle her nose while he feasted on her lips. His soapy hands covered both breasts, massaging the soap in concentric circles, occasionally flicking her nipples with his thumbs.

She squirmed in the warm water and pushed her breasts higher into his grasp.

He trailed one slick hand down her stomach, swirled soap

around her belly button and then slid beneath the water to tease her opening, sliding his finger along her slit. Massaging her aching nub.

Despite her arousal, her eyelids drooped. Floating on sensation, she relaxed and felt her body move with the rhythm of the water.

Jean's soap-slicked hands continued to caress every inch of her. Between each toe, until she began to writhe. What was happening to her? Every place he touched became an instant erogenous zone.

His hands slid back up her legs at the speed of a slug. By the time they reached their destination, she was more than ready, eagerly spreading her legs.

Beside the tub, Jean's breathing was erratic. She peeked through her lashes. His hot gaze devoured her while he lathered his hands again.

Her heart skipped a beat when he generously lathered her bare folds, pushing apart her lips.

"Relax," he crooned. "You will like what I'm about to do."

His slick finger slid into her. Deep. Very deep. It felt wondrous. Different.

She opened her eyes and looked down.

Between her pale thighs, his arm and big hand looked even more tan. But what held her fascination was what slid in and out of her slick opening. Was it some sort of dildo?

She touched her nubbin, then slid her finger to her opening. Slick. Extremely slick.

Soap. He was sliding an elongated bar of soap in and out of her. But it was such a turn-on, she leaned back and enjoyed it.

Jean watched Ryan's eyes widen when she realized he was fucking her with soap and worried he'd gone too far too fast. But when she relaxed against the tub, knees wide apart, and began fondling her clit while he slid the soap in and out of her, he began to shake with need. His heated, rock-hard cock touched the cool side of the enamel tub with each movement, further tormenting him.

But he wanted to do this for her. To her. So hot, so responsive, her body was meant to be loved.

Eyes glazed, nipples hard, she arched, her breathing signaling her impending climax.

He dropped the soap, using his finger to help rinse out the soapy residue. Faster, harder, her hips moving in perfect counterpoint.

She gasped and arched out of the water. Around his finger, muscles clenched, gripping him in their passion.

While she shuddered in the throes of her powerful release, he climbed in with her. Water sloshed over the edge of the old tub, making splashing sounds on the tile floor. He was beyond caring.

He leaned to take a nipple in his mouth, sucking and then gently nipping the tip before grasping her waist and guiding her to his lap.

Her eyes opened wide when he slid her onto his shaft, but one buck of his hips had her moaning and wrapping her arms and legs around him. She melted into him, settling in for the ride.

So primed, he was wild for her. It was over almost before it began. Just when he could hold off no longer, she stiffened and clutched his neck, her inner muscles convulsing around him, milking him.

They cried out their completion within seconds of each other.

He shifted to lean against a side of the tub that did not have faucets and stroked her back, murmuring nonsensical things in her hair.

A thought hit him like a thunderbolt. He wanted to do something he'd never done with another woman.

He wanted to spend the night with her.

3

Ryan hung limply from Jean's arms as he toweled her dry and then carried her to bed. At least, she assumed that's where they were headed and breathed a sigh of contentment when she felt the cool sheets beneath the bare skin of her back.

"Ry-an, look at me, *ma petite*," Jean said against her hair. He held up a crockery-looking jar. "I have body crème to protect your delicate skin, *si tu veux*."

He scooped a good-sized glob with his fingers and set the jar on the bed next to her.

It smelled sweet, like honey and flowers.

Whoa! And cold! Her breath lodged in her chest when the icy lump landed on her back. Within seconds, she relaxed. No one had ever given her a massage. She could get used to it.

Suddenly fire streaked across her back with each swipe of his strong hands.

Gasping, she rolled over. Before she could speak, he began a thorough massage up her legs to her breasts, where he paid special attention to getting the cream completely absorbed into her skin.

His touch was gentle, but she felt like she would burst into flames any minute now.

She grabbed his wrists, coincidentally holding his hands cupped over her breasts. He took advantage of his position to rub the pads of his thumbs over her distended nipples.

She moaned and then swallowed and looked up at him. "That's hot."

"*Oui*," he agreed with a leering grin.

She stopped the movement by gripping his hands. "No, I mean, well, yes, it's hot, but I meant temperaturewise."

Understanding obviously dawned. He laughed and tweaked her nipples.

"*Oui, c'est chaud.*" He nodded. "It warms with your body heat. Did you not like it?" He demonstrated by circling her breasts, smoothing the cream along her rib cage.

In response, or maybe a little bit of retaliation, she dipped her fingers into the pot and swirled the concoction around his flat nipples and then licked and sucked it off. Sweet. Definitely had honey in it. Beneath her tongue, his heart pounded. She smiled against his skin. Served him right.

He flipped her back onto the sheet. Within a nanosecond, he'd slathered cream over her breast and enthusiastically sucked it off.

She grinned and watched him draw a line down her abdomen. Jean was obviously a fast learner.

He nudged her legs apart with his chin, blindly reaching for the crock. She obliged and slid it within easy reach.

The cream iced her folds and then immediately set them on fire. With a gasp, she arched off the bed and would have fallen had his strong hands not anchored her to the mattress.

She sighed at the cool smoothness of Jean's tongue as he licked her clean and then blew across the wet skin.

She shifted, spreading her legs wider to accommodate his broad shoulders.

His thumbs gently parted her while the tip of his tongue traced every petal.

She moved restlessly and tried to remember when someone had last been this up close and personal. The answer: never.

Jean tickled her clitoris with his tongue, and warmth filled her. Then he closed his mouth over it and sucked.

Every part of her centered on the one tiny nub receiving such lavish attention. Every nerve ending stood on alert.

The orgasm hit her with the force of a two-by-four. Had she not been lying down already, she surely would have fainted from the force of it.

Pleasure paralyzed her lungs, drowning her in sensation.

Every nerve ending quivered, then fainted dead away.

Ryan awoke a few minutes or a few hours later, Jean's iron erection clamped possessively in her hand. She looked up to find him smiling down at her, a definite gleam in his eyes.

"Do you plan to do anything with that, or are you just going to hold it?" In French, even that sounded sexy.

Still feeling the effect of the alcohol they'd consumed, she didn't trust her somewhat shaky grasp of the French language.

After all, showing was always better than telling.

The crock was still almost full, which surprised her. Cool, the body cream had the consistency of peanut butter. Creamy peanut butter, of course.

Thoughts of peanut butter made her stomach growl. She moaned, hoping to cover the telltale sound.

Taking a generous dollop, she slathered it over his erection and down, around and over his clean-shaven sack.

She paused and checked out the new territory. Testicles sans hair were much sexier, she decided. She ran her fingertip over and around one, eliciting a groan from Jean.

Placing an apologetic kiss on each sack for her delay, she proceeded to lick the cream from them. The skin seemed as soft as that covering his penis. Why was it guys did basically nothing for soft skin yet had it pretty much all over their bodies, while women spent thousands on creams and lotions? Not to mention pedicures and waxing and such.

Jean shifted restlessly on the sheet, his hands clutching her hair, drawing her attention back to the fact that she had a gorgeous male laid out before her, totally nude and incredibly aroused. A girl would have to be a special kind of stupid to ignore something like that.

Swirling around her tongue and then dragging it from the base of his shaft to the tip had them both squirming. On her knees, she took him in her mouth, careful not to let him bump against her molars. She'd left a mark on Bill that way.

She paused. Too bad she hadn't bitten it off.

Jean's gentle pressure on her head reminded her she was lucky to be rid of Bill the Boring. Even luckier to finally be having sex again. Luckier still to be having it with the recent object of her lust.

His hips began bucking. She sucked harder while circling him with her tongue, bringing him to the brink before leaving him to trail kisses up his long—also hairless, she noted—legs.

She kissed her way up his torso and gave each erect nipple a love bite before lowering onto his monstrous erection. Had they not already had sex, she'd have worried about her ability to take him. Instead she confidently took him in, inch by inch, until they were pelvis to pelvis.

He thrust up, big hands cupping her breasts in obvious possession. She liked it. It felt good. Right. Like she belonged there.

He ground against her, touching something deep within.

Tucking her knees tight to his hips, she began her wild ride.

Jean loved the feel of Ryan's generous breasts in his hands. He gave a slight squeeze, noting that they were definitely more than a handful. If he continued holding them, he'd come before he intended. With great reluctance, he let go, trailing his hands in a restless caress all over Ryan's body. And what a body it was. A body made for sex.

He swiveled his hips in a move created to drive her wild. It worked. Her hips began pumping at a furious rate. Her internal muscles clutched him tightly again and again. Gritting his teeth, he gripped her hips and pounded into her as hard and deep as humanly possible.

She screamed, shuddered and collapsed on his chest, her hot breath coming in short gasps.

We're not done, ma chérie, he thought, rolling her to her back.

Half asleep, her eyes widened with his renewed thrusts. Arms locked, he ground into her, moving in tight circles.

Her response was immediate. She locked her smooth legs around his hips and met him thrust for thrust.

Within seconds she began contracting again. The look of surprise on her face would have made him laugh, had he not been so intent on bringing her to another orgasm.

The muscles in her legs began to ripple against his hip. Her back arched as her pussy all but sucked him in.

He was determined to hear her scream.

She whimpered when he withdrew, but she remained lying like a rag doll—an X-rated rag doll—on the sheet, eyes closed, a half smile on her lips.

He flipped her to her stomach with more force than necessary. He wanted her awake and willing.

Shoving apart her legs, he thrust back into her wetness, loving the surprised catch in her breath.

She was definitely awake, grinding her hot little ass against him as though trying to get closer still.

While he loved the tactile feel of her back against his chest, he wanted more.

He got his knees beneath him and pushed up. Her hips came with him, because he was still buried deeply within, but the upper half of her body remained on the bed.

Leaning, he stroked her belly. Ever responsive, she didn't let him down. Within seconds she'd lifted to give him access to her breasts. Once there, all it took was a gentle push to get her to her hands and knees.

He pounded into her, spurred on by the sight of her breasts wiggling with each thrust.

He wanted more.

Ryan perked up when Jean slid into her from the rear, and she squirmed against the sheet. As she was still well lubricated, it felt marvelous, decadent even, to have him sliding in and out while she was so relaxed. Within seconds the sheets began abrading the tips of her still tender breasts.

Jean reached beneath her to caress her nipples. A slight pressure had her eagerly on her hands and knees.

He picked up the pace. Now she was so wet it was amazing he didn't slip right out.

His hips slapped against her harder, the tip of his penis prodding her uterus.

She spread her legs a little wider, hoping to keep her boobs from hitting her in the face with each thrust.

Jean, bless his heart, obliged by reached around to hold her while tweaking her erect nipples. Moisture gushed. And when he slid his hand lower to play with her nub, a jolt zipped through her entire body.

She wouldn't have been surprised to see electricity arch from her nipples.

She screamed.

Jean felt her orgasm right before she screamed. With a smile, he allowed the release he'd been fighting free rein and collapsed, careful to keep his full weight from crushing her.

Wide awake now, Ryan snuggled to Jean's side beneath the lightweight blanket and sheet, her head on his shoulder. She loved the way he continued to kiss her cheek, her hair—any-where his lips touched—and held her close.

"Jean?"

"Hmmm?"

"Are you awake?"

"Ah-hmmm." He rubbed his jaw against her hair and gave her a little one-armed hug.

"That was . . . incredible."

He chuckled and brought his other hand around to toy with her exposed nipple. "*Oui*."

"Is it always like that . . . for you?" Please don't let her be another notch on his bedpost.

He placed a soft, lingering kiss on her lips and then met her gaze, his blue eyes sincere. At least, they seemed sincere to her, but what did she know? "*Non*."

"So . . . you, well, like me?"

He grinned and kissed the tip of her nose. "Very much."

She settled back down on his shoulder and tried not to smile like a dork while he continued to play with her nipple.

"Would you be interested in helping me do something?"

"Anything." He turned to lean down and flick her nipple with his tongue. "Name it," he whispered, his breath hot against her breast.

"Go back to the States with me." Ahhh—he took her nipple between his teeth and gave a little tug. It was difficult to think when he did stuff like that.

"But of course," he said, sliding his hand beneath the covers to find her weeping sex. "Anything you desire." He slid a finger into her.

She squirmed and tried to remember her train of thought. Difficult to do with Jean moving his finger in her like that.

"Great," she finally managed to say, "because I need you to go back with me and help me kill my ex-boyfriend."

4

Jean stilled. Had the wild American said what he thought she'd said? Given her translation abilities, she may not have meant what she said.

"*Pardon? Je n'ai pas compris ce que vous avez dit.*" At her confused look, he longed to translate, *I do not understand what you said.* Instead he waited.

She chewed on her lower lip, drawing his attention to her kiss-swollen mouth.

"*Tuer?*" She made little stabbing motions with her hand.

He had understood correctly. "*Copain?*"

She nodded.

Great. Not only did she want to kill her boyfriend by knife, she seemed to expect him to help.

"*Cette nuit?*" How did he get himself mixed up in this?

To his relief, she shook her head, her silky hair snagging his attention from the grim conversation.

"*Non!* Not tonight. Later. Much later." She snuggled closer, the warm pillows of her breasts burning into his side.

The sheet covering his lap moved.

"First," she said, placing a soft kiss above his heart, "I have to save enough money to go back to the States." She wiped her eye on the edge of the sheet, her voice suspiciously thick. "Bill the Bilious not only left me here, he took all my money, credit cards and what jewelry I had."

"The pig!" he felt obliged to say.

With Ryan running her hand beneath the cover, up and down the length of his leg from thigh to groin and back, it was difficult to follow her words.

She shuddered. "You have no idea."

He pulled her closer to his heat. "He did more?"

She nodded. "Much more." She turned glistening eyes up to him, causing his heart to lurch. "He not only stole my money, he robbed me of my dignity." Just when he thought she would not continue, she said in a low voice, "He charged people to watch him violate me."

"*Quoi!*" Outrage surged through him, bringing him wide awake.

What. Did he want to know what exactly Bill subjected her to? Or was he merely expressing shock? Well . . . she could sure shock him.

She swallowed. Jean was not only hot and sexy as hell, he was a superstud when it came to sex—combined with being a gentle lover. He deserved to know her tainted past.

"We came here on a working vacation. In hindsight, Bill was probably already planning to dump me." She took a deep breath. Dang, it was hard to talk about the sordid mess her life had been back then. "I got a job right away at Roman's, but Bill couldn't find work. At least, that's what he said. I was such a pushover! I actually believed his tears and felt sorry for him, handing him my money so he could buy clothes to job search." She sighed. "One night we'd been drinking more than usual, and Bill wanted me to, um, do some stuff with him."

"Stuff?"

Nodding, she continued. "Yeah. Long story short, we had rowdy sex in the living room of the little flat we rented . . . with the drapes open." Swallowing hard, she said, "It wasn't until I heard the applause that I realized we'd been entertaining a crowd. Bill convinced me it was an accident. Then . . ."

"Then?" He wasn't sure he wanted to hear what else her despicable ex had done, but, on some level, he knew she needed to tell him.

"He didn't hurt me. Not really." She sniffed and hid her face against his shoulder and then whispered, "He'd use things on me. Kitchen appliances, tools." Appliances? Tools? Perhaps she'd mistranslated. "Always careful to stop before he actually hurt me or left any marks."

She clung to him now. His heart lurched, causing an ache within his chest.

Her tears burned hot trails along his ribs.

Growling his anger and frustration, he clutched her tighter. "Son of a bitch! Were he here, I'd kill him myself!"

In reply, she petted his shoulder, calming him with her light touch.

"Shhh," she whispered, her breath still smelling faintly of the alcohol they'd consumed earlier. "I only told you because, well, I was worried you might have heard about it, and I wanted you to know I'm not like that. Not really."

"I hadn't heard." Turning to his side, he pulled her flush against his body. "And it wouldn't have mattered anyway."

"I hoped you'd say you didn't care," she said, lapsing into English. "Because tonight is the best night I've had in, well, I can't remember when. Heck, maybe when you think about what I've done, you'll decide you don't want anything to do with me." She nibbled the edge of his lip.

In response, his cock pulsed against her belly.

"I know you can't understand me, but I'm too tired to remember French." She shrugged and licked his chin. "Maybe it's for the best. I just know I've been hot for you for weeks. I remember the first time you came in, how I wanted to push you down on a table and have my way with you." Her hand closed over his erection. "I don't know what's happening to me. It's like I can't get enough of you." Her fingers trailed up and down his length. "I've never wanted anyone to, you know," she whispered. She confessed, "I guess you have that effect on me."

He carefully maintained the blank look he'd perfected around her. But below the sheet, his penis wanted to jump for joy.

"You haven't got the slightest idea what I'm saying, do you?" She grinned up at him and twirled her fingers around his balls, setting off goose bumps. "Maybe that's a good thing. I can tell you I'd like to play French chef with you, covering your penis in whipped cream and sucking it off. I could tell you how turned on I was tonight when my bottom was on the cold countertop and your hot hardness was buried deep inside me. I never wanted it to end."

The hard tips of her breasts dragged slowly across his chest, threatening to short-circuit his brain. Maintaining controlled breathing, he concentrated on her words. He wanted to hear what she had to say.

"With you, there is no limit to what I want to do and have done to me." Her hot breath fanned his ear while she guided his hand to her wetness. "I love to feel your fingers on me, *in* me." Her breath caught when he obliged. "I'm so horny when I'm with you I'd welcome anything! Tie me up, come on me, bite me, suck me. I love it all!

"Dang," she said and then chuckled and squirmed against his rock-hard erection. "I'm turning myself on just thinking about the ways I want you to, um—shoot, why can't I even say the word? It's not like you can understand what I'm saying." She took a deep breath. "Fuck me. Fuck me hard and long and all night." She traced the pulsing tip of his erection with her fingernail. "Make me forget every other man I've ever been with or seen. I want to come until I can't walk or talk."

She pushed him to his back and grinned down as she lowered onto his more-than-ready-willing-and-able cock.

He arched his back, driving higher, eliciting a squeak out of her.

"Yikes," she murmured and then grinned. "I forgot 'fuck' is the same in any language."

He grinned back at her and said, "Fuck?"

And they did.

Cool. A strange coolness oozed between her legs. Swimming toward wakefulness, Ryan felt the bed dip with Jean's weight. What was the coolness? Now it was on her breasts, Jean's hot breath immediately warming her while he suckled and licked.

Finally her eyelids opened. She struggled to sit up. *My god, is that blood?*

He pushed her back against the sheet, gently plucking her nipples. The smell of cherries wafted to her. Between her legs, the coolness drew her attention. She watched as he massaged what appeared to be Jell-O into her genitals. Coolness within told her he'd filled her vaginal canal.

She was dying to see what he did next. She didn't have to wait long.

Sitting between her legs, he dragged his slick hands down her eager body. At her groin, his thumbs massaged her legs to their widest position. Sliding back, he bent down and began lapping the Jell-O from her external area and then swirled his tongue in and around her vagina and sucked on the sweet goop until she came, bowing off the mattress.

Petting her back down, he grinned at her, his lips red from the food coloring, blue eyes slumberous.

His warm breath fanned her cool folds right before he closed his mouth over her semifrozen clit and sucked it to screaming life.

Orgasm number two left her wrung out, lying spent and limp on the messy sheet.

Jean gathered her close to his chest, murmuring against her ear French words she was too exhausted to translate. She tried to rally, thinking about another session of hide-the-soap in the big tub, but found it required too much energy.

Through her lashes, she noted he'd lit several candles at some point. He hauled her against him and stripped the bed and then threw another sheet over the mattress before lowering her to its welcoming softness.

Heated oil dribbled across her breasts. Jean's busy hands followed, doing a thorough job of massaging the oil in. The smell of almonds filled the warm air. Her head lolled to one side, then the other as he rubbed the oil into her neck and shoulders. His sensuous path made its way down her rib cage to her hips. She noticed he paid special attention to the genital area, and she tried not to squirm. On downward, his talented hands went until they finished with a to-die-for foot massage.

Wait. Apparently he wasn't finished, because he turned her to her stomach and began again, this time from the feet up. Once again, her genitals received special attention, his oiled fingers sliding up and down and in and out until she moved restlessly on the sheet, aching for his touch.

He slid his arm under her stomach, urging her to her knees, legs together.

Rubbing her breasts against the sheet in an effort to appease her frustration, she was about to beg when she felt the first lap of his tongue.

5

Jean stood, absently rubbing his oiled palms over the soft globes of Ryan's ass while he tried to calm his raging lust. Within his chest, his heart slammed against his ribs, its beats echoing in his ears.

Clamped between her legs, her pink feminine lips pouted prettily at him. Daring him, taunting him . . . begging him to take them. Take them as she'd suggested when she thought he didn't understand.

On bended knee, he dragged the tip of his tongue over her sweetness. So responsive, she gasped at his touch, her folds immediately glistening with moisture.

But he wanted more. Much more.

He played with her nub until it darkened to a deep rose, her wetness dripping from his hand, her intimate flesh quivering at his slightest touch. He circled her opening with the tip of his finger, smiling at her whimper of need. But he wanted her to need him more. He dipped his finger in her heat, careful not to let her push him deeper. It was important to make her want, need him to the point of madness. To the point where she would welcome anything and everything.

With great reluctance, he withdrew his finger and then immediately slapped her upturned bottom, careful to cup his hand in just such a way as to let her feel only a pleasurable sting.

Immediately he knelt and sipped her nectar, bathing the sting away with his tongue.

His cock was going to explode if he didn't bury it deep within her.

Praying she told the truth about her lust for him, he dragged her to the edge of the bed and spread her legs wide before slamming into her from behind.

She went wild, her cum gushing around him to bathe his sacs and trickle down his legs. Wrapping her legs behind him, her heels digging into his butt, she ground her wetness against him, all the while making primal sounds. He braced his feet to keep from falling backward with their combined weight.

Too soon, it was over. Damn. He'd never had a problem sustaining the pleasure before. Yet, with Ryan, he was like a junkyard dog. Randy and eager to hump her at any and all given opportunities. His polished finesse deserted him around her. As Roman was so fond of saying, he could only think with his little head.

Before he completely deflated, he had to hear her scream once more.

Insinuating his hand beneath her, he located her swollen clit and began stimulating it. He rubbed, enjoying her renewed slickness.

All it took was a well-placed squeeze once, twice, to have her screaming her passion, the evidence wetting his hand, streaming around his cock.

After a quick shower, he cooked for her.

Wrapped in a towel, her mouth salivating with the aroma of

the omelets, she watched his hands. Hands that only a short time ago had stroked and petted every millimeter of her eager body. Long, thin fingers stroked melted butter around the pan before heating it. They caressed the eggs before cracking them into a bowl.

With growing arousal, she shifted and watched him whip the egg mixture with a wire whisk, those talented fingers gripping the shaftlike handle like a lover.

He poured the eggs into a second heated skillet and then turned to the first and checked the filling he'd added earlier. A flip of his wrist folded the omelet into the perfect shape. He prodded the puffy creation with his fingertip.

"Almost," he said with a smile before turning to the second skillet to repeat the process.

Almost. He had no idea, she thought, shifting with renewed arousal. Moments before she'd been almost faint with hunger. Now her hunger was for something entirely different.

Talk, Ryan. Say something to take your mind off stripping the towel from his gorgeous hips and licking him all over.

"You do that really well. Were you ever a chef?"

"*Non.*" He grinned and winked before flipping both omelets onto a serving platter. "Do you know the best thing about a well-made omelet?" He set the platter aside and walked to her, his smile entirely too sexy for the early hour.

She shook her head, hoping his thoughts were heading in the same direction as her own.

"They reheat." He ran his hands beneath her towel and parted it from the inside. "Wait."

He turned and picked up the crockery bowl of remaining melted butter from the stove and then dipped his hands in it.

The combined warmth of his hands, where they cupped her breasts, and the fragrant slickness of the butter put her senses on immediate alert.

He laved off the butter with his talented tongue and then

dribbled more to trickle between her breasts, streak down her abdomen and puddle between her legs. His hungry mouth followed.

He grabbed a large pastry brush and painted between her legs, bathing her in the butter's oily warmth.

Her breath lodged. "No fair," she finally managed to wheeze out.

Hands shaking, she picked up the bowl and then finger-painted his torso with melted butter. Before she could decide where to lick first, he growled and lifted her from the counter to allow her to slide down his slickness until her bare feet touched the cool tile.

She dipped her hand and then clasped his erection, loving the feel of the slickness on hardness.

Sliding down his slippery length, she knelt and took him into her mouth.

Jean locked his knees and touched any part of the woman before him he could reach. Her hungry mouth on his cock felt incredible. Especially when she swirled her tongue around it from head to base and back.

When she took his balls in her hot little mouth, he could stand it no more.

He urged her to her feet, grabbed the bowl and woman and half dragged her to his bedroom.

"Stay." He pointed at her and then strode to the bathroom and ripped his new shower liner from its hooks.

Back in the bedroom, he tossed the vinyl over the sheets and followed her down on it. Picking up the bowl, he poured a generous amount over her luscious body, smearing it around to his satisfaction.

Next he rolled onto her, sharing the butter until they were both slick.

She relieved him of the bowl and poured a generous amount

over him, quickly scooting her butter-slicked body around and over him until he thought he might be the next one to scream.

"Look what I brought," she said, holding up the pastry brush.

He gasped at the feel of the melted butter being brushed all around and on his testicles then held his breath while she licked it off.

Vibrating with need, he made quick work of commandeering the brush and bowl. Between her spread legs—her feet resting on his knees—he used the remaining butter to paint her pussy, loving the way it glistened with oil and her own excitement.

Ryan held her breath, anticipating the touch of his talented tongue, her well-oiled body more excited than it had ever been in her entire life.

His hot hand covered her, holding in her heat, massaging in the butter. Soon it was replaced by a hard yet incredible smoothness.

She opened her eyes.

Jean knelt between her legs, head thrown back, eyes closed, rubbing his erection back and forth over her slick skin.

It was the sexiest thing she'd ever seen.

Her sex wept to share the experience.

"Now," she whispered, totally forgetting French in her need, spreading her legs wide due to the language barrier. "I want to feel it, too."

Jean's eyes opened languorously, his heated gaze meeting hers.

Without words, he slid his hands down her thighs, parting her wider still, and then massaged her nub with the well-oiled pads of his thumb.

The action brought her to the brink. As she teetered he

pushed his hard length deep inside, his thumbs manipulating her swollen sex. He glided in and out, slowly, ever so slowly, while his thumbs continued to hold her suspended in a constant preclimax state.

Spread so wide, with his forearms holding them apart, she couldn't get her legs up around his hips to pull him close or force him to increase the tempo.

Inspiration struck.

Getting her elbows under her, she pushed up to a semisitting position. Close enough to touch.

Abdominal muscles quivering with the effort, she caressed his pectorals, drawing little downward circles until her hand closed around the base of his shaft.

Gazes locked.

She licked her lips, loving the way his eyes flared as he followed the movement of her tongue.

Two of her fingers dipped downward to pet his testicles. They immediately puckered.

"Do it," she whispered, "do it now. I want it hard and deep." She gave a little tug, enjoying how his breath caught. "I know you have to understand what I'm saying. Sex like this needs no translation. Especially when it's this hot. This urgent."

With strength she had no idea she possessed, she pulled herself closer until she was able to move her legs. Pushing hard against his erection, burying it deeper, she stretched her legs up his chest and flicked his earlobe with the tip of her toe.

Deep within, his penis stirred.

Her smile was wicked, she knew, but she couldn't help it. "That's what I thought," she said, wiggling her bottom and purring at his strangled response. "Sex is the universal language."

She wiggled against him again, petting everywhere she could reach.

"Yesss!" She arched her back, bowing up to meet his increased tempo.

Her nipples tightened; her muscles clenched.

Jean gripped her knees and pounded into her, his excitingly bare sacs slapping her with each powerful thrust.

The gentle slapping of his balls against the smooth skin of Ryan's ass heightened Jean's excitement. His climax was violent, wringing him out.

She tumbled after him, her scream echoing in his ears.

Spent, he collapsed on her, barely able to roll his weight to the side.

She said something, but it was drowned out by the thundering beat of his heart.

It was the perfect opportunity to convince her to marry him. In the heated aftermath of passion, she would be vulnerable. He was a skilled lover. Surely she would want to continue to experience earth-shattering orgasms and would leap at the chance to be his bride.

Even temporarily.

Yes, he would bring it up—and also possibly the part of his anatomy that was reeling from the last experience—to help her make up her mind.

Air wheezed in and out of his taxed lungs.

He'd open the discussion. As soon as he could find the strength to open his eyes. Or move his hand.

6

Ryan rolled away from Jean and edged toward the side of the bed. In the weak light, she was able to sidestep the wadded-up shower curtain by the bed.

Gathering her clothes, she dressed without panties because they were MIA.

Jean had moved across the bed in her absence. She wasn't going to read anything into it. Probably seeking body heat. And the heat from any body, from what she'd heard, would do.

"Thanks," she whispered and then let herself out.

Walking down the deserted streets, the incredible sex from the night before replaying in her mind, she almost missed the turn for her rented room.

Memories of Jean's lushly furnished home contrasted sharply with the austere abode she called home.

Dropping her backpack on the sofa bed, she again cursed Bill. What had started as an adventure had turned into a nightmare. She glanced around her single room at the icebox and hot plate, the shower curtain that served as a wall to separate the living area from the miniscule bathroom. A roach skittered across the floor and disappeared beneath the baseboard. The smell of old grease and stale smoke permeated the air, no matter how much she cleaned. The place was a dump, no two ways about it.

She pulled a Coke from the icebox and popped the top. If Roman ever discovered a shortage of soda, she would starve. Saving every dime, she ate most meals at the restaurant, sometimes taking any leftovers home for breakfast the next day.

Mentally counting her meager savings—if she was able to save at her current rate—she should have enough in her Kill Bill fund to get back to the States by early fall, Thanksgiving at the latest. Plenty of time to hunt down the scum-sucking bastard and kill him yet still enjoy the holidays.

She shoved away any slight twinge of guilt. Bilious Bill deserved whatever she chose to do to him. In spades.

One foot tucked beneath her on the end of the couch, she sipped her Coke and thought of the humiliation suffered at Bill's hands. Softening, she compared it to the utter bliss she'd experienced the night before.

For the first time in months, Bill had not so much as crossed her mind for literally hours.

Did that mean anything?

A glance at the smiley-face clock hanging on a nail over the hot plate had her finishing the soda in a giant gulp. Barely time for a quick shower before she had to head to work. It had taken months to earn the coveted day shift, and she knew there were other employees waiting in the wings to snatch it away if she screwed up.

Sam gave a low whistle and stretched to lean over the bar. Jean paused from folding napkins to follow the bartender's gaze.

Ryan. Paused by the door, she was bent over to tie her shoe, the sweet curves of her shapely butt like a siren's call to any heterosexual male in a five-mile radius. The ribbon of her thong panties, exposed by the low-slung uniform pants, made Jean's mouth go dry.

Stand up, he mentally urged. For some reason, the thought of other men seeing Ryan's underwear or ogling her ass made him want to punch something.

Finally she stood, slinging her backpack over her shoulder. The woman was guileless. Didn't she know the effect she had on men? He frowned at her, irritated with the way the burden of the backpack pulled the thin fabric of the cheap uniform shirt taut across her spectacular breasts.

Good Lord. He wanted her. Now. How was he ever going to make it through their shift?

"Bogart!" Roman's irritating voice bellowed from the stockroom.

Setting aside the napkins, he sighed and strolled to the employee entrance.

"*Oui?*" He leaned against the open stockroom door and crossed his arms over his chest.

"Get in here, and sort this order." Roman shifted the ever-present cigar to the other side of his mouth. "And grab someone to help you check the invoice." He tossed the papers onto an open box and grumbled, "Bastards are always trying to cheat me."

"I was folding the napkins for the lunch crowd," Jean pointed out. It was a menial task, but Roman loved to rub Jean's nose in the fact that Jean was nothing more than a servant, insisting he be the one to perform the napkin task every day.

Roman waved the smelly stub of his cigar. "Screw the napkins. Let Sam do 'em."

Without waiting for a response, the repugnant rodent waddled out of the room.

From the bar, Jean heard Ryan laugh. Sam was being his charming self, no doubt. The thought pissed Jean off.

Stalking to the door of the stockroom, he said, "Roman said for us to check in the shipment of supplies, Ry-an. Bring in some Cokes, will you?"

Back in the stockroom, waiting for her, he glanced down at the obnoxious bulge in his uniform pants. "Behave," he whispered.

Minutes later, Ryan walked in, carrying two Cokes and glasses, two bags of chips clutched in her teeth.

Her cheeks were flushed, and he noticed she avoided looking him in the eye.

When he'd relieved her of her burdens, she flashed a smile and said, "Thanks. I'll go grab some ice. Be right back."

He'd opened the sodas by the time she returned. Ice clinked in the barware, followed by the distinct fizz of the sodas.

"Do you miss America?" He took a casual sip.

She swallowed and ran the tip of her pink tongue over her upper lip. "Sure. I guess. Pogo-Doo is beautiful, but I can't live on this island forever. I need to get back to my real life in the States."

"And kill your boyfriend?"

"Ex-boyfriend," she corrected. "And yes. That's the plan."

They went through the first box in silence, Jean unpacking and Ryan checking the items off the invoice.

The room seemed to get smaller with each passing minute. Jean could practically smell the sexual attraction.

He dropped the package of spaghetti back in the box and reached for her.

She came willingly into his arms, her mouth meeting his with a rivaling hunger.

He ground his hardness into her, showing her his need without words.

Instead of reciprocating, she broke the kiss and stepped back, her breasts rising and falling with her labored breathing.

Eyes locked on her lush curves, he salivated, wild to touch and taste her again.

"Jean! I'm up here. Read my lips."

When he reluctantly dragged his covetous gaze to her face, she continued. "We can't do stuff like that here. When we kiss, I want more." She glanced down at the proof of his obvious interest at the front of his pants. "I know you do, too. But we can't. Not here. Sometimes I think Roman is just looking for an excuse to fire me. I don't want to give him a reason."

She stepped close, the hardened tips of her breasts burning into his chest. "Understand?"

He nodded but placed his hands on her waist to hold her in place when she began to step away.

When she didn't resist, he shoved up her shirt and pushed aside the scrap of lace masquerading as a bra and feasted on her.

Immediately pliant in his arms, a little moan escaped her.

She stiffened and stepped away, pulling her clothing back in place. "Jean, we can't. You know that as well as I do."

He stared, waiting for her to stumble into a translation. When it didn't come, he asked in a hopeful voice, "Fuck?"

To his shocked delight, she glanced around and nodded.

"But it will have to be a quickie. Fast. *Vite!*"

She went to the partially closed door and peeked out.

Vite he could do.

Pulling a rubber from his pocket, he sheathed himself, walked behind her and jerked her pants and panties down in one smooth movement.

She gasped.

"Shhh," he said against her ear, shoving his hands beneath her shirt to push up under her bra and fill his palms with her breasts.

* * *

Ryan stiffened when Jean pulled her pants down. The cooler air of the stockroom didn't feel unpleasant against her heated skin.

His hot erection bumped her back, the feel of a condom an odd reassurance.

"*Vite*," he whispered in her ear, pushing into her eager flesh from behind.

One of his hands left her breast to trace her slit then rub her clitoris. Behind her, he increased the tempo of his thrusts, timing them to his squeezing of her breast and aching nub.

He nibbled her neck, murmuring French against her skin while his penis and hands did exciting, naughty things to her.

Her heart pounded; her breath caught.

"Shhh," he warned again, his breath hot and panting against her ear. "Come quietly for me, *ma chérie*."

His movements increased. Harder, faster, he pounded into her.

Her head quietly bumped the doorjamb with each thrust.

Excitement built.

Anyone could come to the stockroom and discover them. Instead of sickening her, as her experience with Bill had done, she was shocked to find it excited her beyond belief.

Moisture gushed. Her breath caught as she topped the crest and tumbled over.

Behind her, Jean pumped faster, and then with a strangled sound he ground into her and stilled.

Beneath her shirt, he petted her nipples and then pulled her bra in place and smoothed down her shirt.

In slow, erotic motion, she felt him withdraw. Coolness seared her bare backside.

Jean's warm hands smoothed down her legs and then pulled up her panties. He reached around and patted her mound and then caressed each buttock before bending again and dragging her uniform pants up to her waist.

The sound of him righting his clothing rustled behind her. The doorjamb cooled her heated forehead.

Paper rustled. She turned in time to see Jean disposing of the condom in a packing slip and tossing it in the trash.

"Yo, Jean! Ryan!" Sam's voice was near, but she hoped he hadn't left the bar. "Customers."

"Be right out," she managed to call and then turned to Jean. "*Ça va?*"

He nodded, and she let out a relieved sigh then left.

Jean watched her go directly to a couple the hostess had seated in Ryan's section. Ryan was poised, beautiful and had impeccable posture.

Good genes.

That thought brought him up short. Good genes? What did he care? He wasn't planning to stay around long enough to father children with Ryan.

But he did need a wife.

As a U.S. citizen, it would be so much easier to accept the lucrative job offer within the allotted time.

If the activities of last night—and today—were any indication, his temporary marriage would be no hardship.

All he had to do was keep her hot and willing in his bed for as long as it took to convince her to marry him.

7

Ryan leaned back against the bar and sipped yet another drink Jean had handed her. Was this the third or fourth? It didn't matter. Business had been brisk all day, the heat making tourists thirsty. Thirsty tourists were good tippers.

A rivulet of sweat trickled behind her ear. She tucked back an errant strand of hair and watched the busboys clear tables.

"Dang, it's hot in here." She picked up a bar napkin and swiped her forehead. "What is this?" she asked Sam over her shoulder. "It's good. Refreshing." She drained the glass and pushed it toward him. "Gimme another."

She saw the look that passed between Sam and Jean and rolled her eyes. "I'm a big girl. I can handle it. See?" She closed her eyes and brought her finger up to touch her nose. And poked her eye. "Ow!" She shot a *don't mess with me* look at Jean and the bartender, who were obvious in their attempt not to laugh. "I slipped; it doesn't mean a thing."

"Here, Ry-an, drink mine."

"Thank you, Jean." She picked up the glass and shot Sam a dirty look. "It's nice to know there are still gentlemen around."

She ignored Sam's snicker, tossed back the drink and walked to meet the next guests.

"I don't know what you're planning, old man, with the lovey-dovey looks and cooing French to each other," Sam said close to Jean's ear to keep the conversation private, "but Ryan's got enough antifreeze in her to light up half the dock. Have you lost your touch? You think you need to get your women liquored up before they'll spread their legs for you now?"

"Do not be crude," Jean snarled.

Sam held up his hand in surrender. "Hey, it's your business." He leaned closer again. "But I like Ry. She's a good kid. Didn't deserve the stuff that went down with her slimeball boyfriend." He shone the bar next to Jean industriously when Roman walked by. "I'm just saying, if you're only looking for a good time, I suggest you look somewhere else."

"I will take your suggestion under advisement."

"Yeah, right." Sam made his way to the other end of the bar to tend to business.

Jean watched Ryan maneuver from table to table, checking on her customers. There was no one else for him. Time was running out.

If keeping her half drunk got her to the justice of the peace in an expedient manner, he had to do it.

Toward the end of their shift, Sam served them hamburgers and fries. Seated at the bar, eating in companionable silence, Ryan wondered if she'd get lucky with Jean again after work.

If the looks Jean kept sending her were any indication, her dry spell was definitely over. Tonight she had a few ideas of her own.

She squirmed on the bar stool, anxious for their evening to begin.

Walking toward the exit after turning in her money, her heart did a funny twitter when she saw Jean standing by the door. He had to be waiting for her, because everyone else was gone.

The blistering-hot sex of the night before flashed through her mind. As intense and enjoyable as it had been, she couldn't keep fooling herself. It would kill her to be just another conquest. Their relationship, if you could call it that, had moved at warp speed. Cruising level was more her speed. She took another peek at Jean leaning against the doorway, devouring her with his eyes. Dang, the guy had *hot* written all over him.

Forcing her mind into *français* mode, she searched for the words a second before they came to her. "Do you like to dance? A club." She motioned in the general direction with her hand, urging him to walk with her. "It's not far. You know, dance?" She made a little mambo motion. What was the word—got it. "*Si on allait danser!*"

Jean beamed at her. "*Très bien! Oui, si on allait danser.*"

Let's go dancing. She nodded and returned his grin. Dancing she could do. Dancing she could handle. She just hoped dancing wouldn't lead to the horizontal mambo. Jean consumed too many of her waking thoughts as it was, and a few of her dreams, too.

But she needed to be in his arms. Actually ached for it. Dancing was the safest alternative.

Jean walked beside Ryan, a steadying hand on her back. The feel of her firm back beneath the fabric of the sweater she'd changed into after work telegraphed sensation up his arm and directly to his groin. He'd love to let his hand slip lower and walk with it cupping her ass. But it was a possessive gesture he had no business making. Not yet, anyway.

The Jazz Club was hot, packed to capacity with gyrating bodies. They ordered drinks and stood by the end of the bar because all tables were occupied. There were booths upstairs, Jean knew, but he also knew what would happen if he took

Ryan up there. And he was determined to keep his cock in his pants tonight.

He turned to see Ryan stripping off her sweater. The silk tank she wore beneath was practically transparent from perspiration. *Mon dieu!* He prayed for the silk to dry quickly. While he was at it, he prayed for his survival. He'd never been so hot for a woman.

Yet another reason she was the perfect candidate to be his wife.

"Let's dance!" Ryan yelled, her voice barely audible over the band. Tossing back another drink—who was buying them for her?—she grabbed his hand and made her way toward the dance floor.

Dancing was only dancing in the sense that they were swaying and shifting a step here and there to the beat. The crowd precluded any actual footwork.

He spotted an empty table next to the dance floor as the music stopped.

"Ry-an! Let's sit." Shoving her in the direction of the tiny table, he motioned to the waitress.

Seconds after they were seated, his heart sank. He'd dated the cocktail waitress a few times. Getting rid of her hadn't been pretty.

"Jean!" She hugged him close, pushing his face into her augmented bosom. Leaning back, she jiggled one barely covered breast close to his mouth. "Have you been a good boy? My shift ends in an hour. Want to come play with us?"

He glanced meaningfully at Ryan, wishing she'd do something to cause the female barracuda to back off. What that might be, he wasn't sure. Anything was better than the way her suspicious gaze darted from Holly the waitress to him to Holly's cleavage and then back. Not that it was any of Ryan's business, but he wanted to tell her there was nothing going on between him and Holly. Hadn't been anything for several months.

Never would be again, he thought as Holly reached past him to collect a tip and managed to drag her breast across his face. The thought that he'd ever had sex with her turned his stomach. As soon as he'd learned her gang-bang reputation, he'd dropped her. Although, truthfully, he'd wanted to be rid of her long before he found out.

He inclined his head toward Ryan and ordered another round of drinks.

"What is this?" Ryan leaned close, her fragrance wrapping him in sexual longing. "It's wonderful! *C'est formidable!*"

He nodded and clinked his glass to hers. Strawberry Blonde was an innocuous name for a drink that packed such a lethal punch. Strawberries blended with whipping cream and rum— heavy on the rum—topped with a dollop of whipping cream and a fat strawberry, the Blonde could sneak up on a person and knock them to their knees before they finished the second drink.

It was Ryan's fourth. Probably his as well. The sweet concoction went down smoothly in the stifling room.

When Ryan got up, gyrating her hips and tugging on his hand, he shook his head. After running his tongue over the topping of his drink, thinking of how he'd love to spread it over Ryan, to his embarrassment he sported a monster hard-on.

He would not, could not leave his chair.

Ryan snatched his drink and downed it, her hips moving to the heavy beat. She ran her hands around and up her torso, cupping her breasts through the thin silk of her tank top.

Jean groaned.

Ryan licked the last trace of whipped cream from her upper lip and moved with the music. Woo-wee, it was hot in there. A glance at Jean and his heated gaze on her rapidly hardening nipples increased the already sweltering atmosphere.

Dance. Just think of dancing. She half rubbed against Jean, writhing to the beat, feeling it in every cell of her body.

The waitress set down four more drinks, leaning close to speak to Jean.

Ryan frowned. The waitress was extremely well endowed and very pretty. She practically oozed sex appeal. But if Jean so much as touched the cocktail waitress, he'd be in such a world of pain. She glanced at the little tent on his lap and saw red.

Picking up two of the new drinks, Ryan downed them, never missing a beat.

She danced closer to Jean until she straddled his legs. Leaning close, she said in his ear, "I'm not wearing any panties."

The look on his face was priceless. She grinned and cupped her aching breasts, taunting him.

Dang, it was hot. She tossed back another drink, this time shimmying her breasts against Jean's face. In hindsight, she guessed she asked for it.

Jean grasped her waist, drawing her closer. His tongue left a hot trail where he dragged it across her cheek. "You are playing with fire," he said on a growl, his breath ruffling the hair that had escaped from her ponytail.

At least, that's what she thought he said. It was so loud, and after so many drinks, her French was shakier than normal.

He could've said she was hot. The thought pleased her, so she inched forward until she sat on his lap while she danced.

A giggle escaped her. Lap dancing. She was lap dancing. The thought struck her as hilarious.

The next few minutes passed in a blur. Sound blurred. The lights and patrons blurred. Everything except Jean blurred to fade into the background.

Their gazes locked, she continued her sexy little dance. Her skirt hiked up, exposing her thong-clad flesh to the rough texture of Jean's trousers and the very interesting hard ridge bisecting his hip area.

She squeezed her legs together, pushing her weeping flesh against his hardness, loving the way heat flared in his eyes.

Downing another drink, her boldness got the better of her.

She grasped Jean's wrists and placed his hot hands over her breasts, squirming at the tactile pleasure.

She leaned down and kissed him. Kissed him with all the desire she felt and with the longing to be alone with him where they could both act on their passion.

He returned the kiss.

Emboldened, she dragged his hand down to her crotch, pushing aside the fabric and nudging his fingers close to her heat.

His eyes widened. Before he could withdraw his hand, she pushed forward, capturing his fingers just inside her.

With a grin, she ground against his hand until his fingers were where she wanted them.

Her lap dance took on a whole new level of sensuality until she gave up any pretext of dancing and rode his hand faster, harder, the elusive release she sought just out of her reach.

Jean's eyes glazed over, and she wondered if anyone would notice if he unzipped and finished what they started, right here, right now.

She ached for him, for his touch, his—

"*Mademoiselle! Vous êtes en état d'arrestation!*" A small man in a tan uniform of some kind, socks pulled up to his knobby knees, stood next to them, his face grim. He looked at Jean with a dour expression. "*Vous êtes en état d'arrestation, aussi.*"

Ryan and Jean exchanged glances. A sick feeling invaded the pit of her stomach.

It could not be happening.

They were being arrested?

8

Ryan leaned, naked, against the hard stone wall of the interrogation room, the rough edges cutting into her hands.

The policewoman slapped Ryan's legs to a broadened stance and then proceeded to violate her with a rubber gloved hand.

Humiliation stung Ryan's cheeks. She blinked back tears and willed her stomach not to recoil.

When the cavity search was over, the woman silently handed Ryan a stained gray jumpsuit and her panties.

"Do you speak English?" Ryan asked, turning her back in a vain effort to protect her modesty.

"*Oui*," the woman answered.

"Why were we arrested?" It took a few tries to negotiate the tin buttons.

"Lewd and lascivious conduct in a public place. It is a misdemeanor." The woman waved her hand. "You pay the fine, you leave."

Ryan noted the chewed-off fingernails and bloody cuticles and thought about giving the woman the name of the nail salon she'd found. Then her words sank in.

"Lewd and lascivious! We were just dancing! Well, actually, I ws just dancing. Jean was sitting down." There was no way anyone could have seen her place his hand beneath her panties . . . could they?

"One of the employees called it in." The matron held open the door for Ryan to go back to her cell. "If you hadn't made such a scene, *le policier* would most likely have given you a warning. Of course, there was the evidence, so maybe not."

"Evidence? What evidence?"

"Your boyfriend's hand was slick with your fluid, and your panties were soaking wet."

Ryan's cheeks heated. Having no defense against that statement, she dropped glumly to the hard little cot and examined her options.

A few minutes later, the cell door creaked open, and Jean walked in.

"They're putting us in the same cell?" Ryan glanced around and found that hers appeared to be the only cell. "Men and women aren't supposed to be in the same cell. That's just not right."

Jean slumped next to her and ran a hand through his hair. "I suspect, in our case, they didn't think it mattered."

"Jean, I'm so sorry I got us into this!" She threw her arms around him and breathed easier when he pulled her close and kissed her hair.

"It's entirely my fault," he said, brushing her hair from her face. "I knew how strong the drinks were, yet I did nothing to stop you."

"What are we going to do?"

"Sleep." He snuggled her closer and slumped against the wall. "We can't get out before the banks open in the morning."

Ryan calculated the money in her Kill Bill fund. "I'll bail us out. I have the money set back."

"I could not allow you to spend the money you've saved for your return."

She took his face in her hands. "Listen to me. I want to do this. I have the money. If it hadn't been for me and my stupid jealousy, we wouldn't be here in the first place." She shrugged. "Besides, I still haven't come up with a solid plan to use to kill Bill, so it's not like I would be going back to the States right away anyway." She snuggled back against his shoulder. "What do you know about poisons?"

"You're late!" Roman yelled when they trekked into the employee lounge several hours later. "Suit up, and get out there!"

As soon as the door whooshed shut behind the little man, Jean drew Ryan into his arms and kissed her. "Stay with me tonight?"

She nodded. Not only did she owe him after their little foray into crime the night before, she'd had a realization as they had lain on the stained cot in the dismal cell.

She was falling in love with him.

And the desire burned hotter than ever at the thought. It also answered a lot of questions about why Jean could do things to her she'd have felt repugnant about with anyone else. And why she was on fire to jump his bones at every opportunity. Duh. What else could it be but love?

With each hour, the tension grew. Her panties grew damper, her skin more sensitive, senses on alert.

Finally it was quitting time. Ryan turned in her till and hurried to change into street clothes. Maybe she and Jean would have a nice, quiet dinner before she went home with him and had her wicked way with him all night long.

The scarf she'd found hung in her little locker, its golden and silver threads reflecting the weak light from the overhead bulb. She ran an appreciative hand over it and then tied it around her hips. It had driven Jean wild their first night. Maybe he'd be up for a repeat performance.

* * *

"Jean, I don't know what you're planning, but if you don't tell her you can speak English as good as anyone, I will."

Ryan stopped behind the edge of the bar, listening to Sam's words.

"I never told her differently," Jean argued. "She chose to believe it, and I just never bothered to correct her."

One of them laughed.

Ryan's teeth ached from clenching her jaw.

She stepped around the edge of the bar. Jean smiled at her. She blinked back tears. Obviously, her burgeoning love was one-sided. Although for the life of her she couldn't think of a reason why Jean would keep the secret from her she would still go with him. She would still make love. She would still spend the night, welcoming him into her body all night long.

Then she would walk away and never see him again.

After a quiet dinner that ended too soon, they went back to Jean's cabana. It was his idea to take a horse-drawn carriage ride from the restaurant. Along the way, he nibbled her neck and touched her intimately whenever he thought their driver was not looking. Despite her determination to remain aloof, by the time they stepped through the door, she was on fire for him.

"Ry-an," he said on a breath, pulling her tight against his aroused body.

She silenced his lying lips with a scorching kiss designed to make him beg for more.

Only, she was the one who felt the overwhelming urge to beg.

In the blink of an eye, they were naked, moonlight from the open draperies their only light.

He lifted her midkiss and laid her on the kitchen table, located just inside his front door.

Standing at the end of the table, between her legs, he whispered, *"Belle."*

Yeah, if you thought I was so beautiful, so belle, *why don't you say it in English?* She averted her gaze and blinked back treacherous tears, trying to concentrate on the feel of the cool planks at her back, the warmth of his tongue as it circled her nub, the act itself. Anything but the feeling of being used. And the feeling of betrayal.

Jean plunged his finger into her wetness, causing her to bow off the table, her legs spread wide in begrudging supplication.

He whispered softly to her while he pleasured her with his fingers, flicking his thumb against her clitoris and rubbing her slick folds while his other hand squeezed her breast and nipple in perfect sync to the movement of his fingers buried deep within her.

She wanted to resist, to be immune to his touch.

Instead she writhed on the hard table, her cries echoing from the exposed rafters as she begged with guttural sounds for completion.

When it finally came, nearly drowning her in sensation, she may have passed out from the pleasure. Did modern women actually swoon anymore?

Regardless, Jean picked up her pliant body and carried her through the kitchen to his bedroom, where he deposited her on his clean-smelling sheets and then lit candles.

Through a sensual haze, she watched his graceful movements as he walked around the room and then undressed, all in a leisurely manner that left her hot and bothered.

At last, he joined her on the bed, pulling her against his naked warmth.

"Let me love you properly," he said in a low voice, rolling onto her.

His lips took hers, his tongue invading her mouth while at the same time he pushed his erection into her once-more-eager body.

He talked the entire time he thrust into her, exciting her beyond belief. For all she knew, he could have been telling her his grocery list. She didn't care. It was sexy as hell, just hearing his enunciation.

His tempo increased. If she didn't do something, he would be finished before she got off.

Pushing his shoulders, she was finally able to get him onto his back, still deeply embedded.

She grinned down at him. If this was their last night together, she didn't want to waste it.

She moved her hips in a tight little circle and was rewarded by his moan.

He grasped her breasts, and she lost her train of thought for a second or two. What was she about to do? Oh, yeah, that felt wonderful.

Wait. She was the aggressor.

She hooked her heels behind his knees and began her ride.

By the time they shouted their completion, they were glistening in sweat, gasping for breath.

She collapsed against his chest, smiling at the pounding of his heart against her ear.

Rolling to his side, she severed their connection and cuddled close. As soon as she caught her breath, she'd ride him again. She'd come four times before it finally came to an end.

Woman dominant was her new favorite position.

She awoke to coolness being stroked over her skin. With a satisfied grin, she opened her eyes.

Still naked, Jean knelt on the bed beside her, gently bathing her heated skin with a wet washcloth. He paused when he saw her watching him.

"Don't stop," she whispered. How did she say "Don't ever stop" without sounding pathetic?

After her impromptu sponge bath, Jean rubbed cinnamon-scented lotion onto her skin from head to toe and then licked most of it off.

"*Je t'aime*, Ry-an," he said, coming up to her level and pulling her into his embrace.

I love you. Say it in English, Jean, and I might believe you. I want to believe you. Instead, she just whispered, "*Je t'aime.*"

He clutched her to his chest and said something, but their collective heartbeats drowned it out.

"*En anglais, s'il te plait.*" It had to be said, had to be brought into the open. If he really loved her, truly loved her, she wanted him to say it in English.

He stiffened and then drew back to look down at her. "*En anglais?*"

"*Oui.*" She nodded her encouragement. "I know you can speak it," she said in English, her voice low. Tears burned her eyes. "I heard you," she said around the lump in her throat.

In response, he brushed his lips across her cheeks, her eyelids, her forehead, her nose and finally settled on her mouth.

The gentleness of his sweet kiss almost had her collapsing against him, crying like a fool and begging him to forget everything and just stay in bed with her forever. Almost.

With great difficulty and as much dignity as she could muster, she pulled away and looked at him. Waiting.

"How long have you known?" he finally asked, his English sounding rusty and stilted. And oh, so sexy.

"I heard you talking to Sam." She didn't add it was only tonight. Let him think she'd played him the way he'd played her.

His hands fell from her, leaving her cold and alone even though he still sat, naked, less than two feet away.

"I did not set out to mistreat you. You assumed I did not speak *anglais;* I merely allowed you to continue in your assumption." He touched her knee, drawing his finger in lazy circles along the edge of her thigh.

Just the simple action made her wet. Was she pathetic or what?

"I'd planned tonight. I wanted it to be special. For you. For us." His shoulders slumped. "Now, because of my foolish action, all is lost." He shook his head, looking incredibly sexy in the mussed sheets, the candlelight reflected from his hair. "I cannot ask you what is in my heart."

Huh? What did that mean? "Ask," she urged.

He took her hand, moving close again, his rapidly recovering erection bumping her hip. "Ry-an, will you marry me?"

"What! Are you out of your mind?" She hopped out of bed so fast she tripped in her haste and knocked over a candle. "Jean! The rug is on fire!"

He ran around to her side and beat the flames into submission with his shirt.

"Ry-an," he said, taking her hands again, once the crisis was averted. "Please marry me."

She pulled out of his grasp. "No!" She walked backward toward the bathroom, rubbing her arms. "I can't marry you, I— no! That's nuts!"

"But you said you loved me." He took a step. Then stopped when she held up her hand.

"It was said in the heat of the moment. Neither of us meant it." She picked up her clothes from the table and walked into the bathroom. "Would you please call a cab? I need to go home."

9

Jean watched Ryan get into the cab and waved good-bye. It was the only polite thing to do.

Despite her protests, she loved him. He knew it. Now all he had to do was convince her to marry him so he could get to America to accept the job he was born to do.

He'd worry about the fact that he was using her later, after they divorced.

He wasn't asking for much, actually. They enjoyed each other's bodies; the sex was mind-blowing. He wouldn't be a burden. He had saved enough to support himself until he was collecting a regular paycheck. Once that was accomplished, they could quietly divorce.

That was his plan. It had always been his plan. Why now did it feel selfish and shallow, almost cruel?

So what if he told her he loved her. People said that every day without truly meaning it. It was expected if one proposed.

But what if Ryan's feelings were genuine? Could he stand the look of disappointment or hurt on her face when she discovered the truth?

* * *

At work the next day, they avoided each other. Ryan avoided him, anyway. Whenever he approached her, she refused to look at him and made an excuse to walk away.

Seeing her go into the stockroom, he knew it was time to make his move.

Her delectable derriere had its usual effect on his libido. Her posture while bent over a box of chips gave him the perfect view.

He could not, would not let his raging lust take control. He needed a wife. Soon. She was the only candidate. Lust had nothing to do with it.

At that moment, she leaned farther into the box, the thin fabric of her slacks stretched taut over her sweet ass.

The hell it didn't. He took a deep breath and adjusted his suddenly tight pants. But that didn't mean he was going to act on the lust.

"*Pardon*," he said to let her know he was there.

She spun around, eyes wide, cheeks flushed from her efforts.

Damn, he wanted her. Wanted to touch her, kiss her, bury himself in her heat.

"Jean. I didn't hear you come in." She straightened her shirt and looked everywhere but at him.

He stepped close, blocking her escape, should she attempt it. "Please. Do not avoid me." In times of stress, his English came out strangled-sounding. He ran a shaking finger down the soft skin of her cheek. "I cannot bear it."

"Look, Jean, I don't know what kind of games you're playing, but I—"

"I play no games." He backed her into the corner between a stack of boxes and a rack of cans and then placed his arms on either side of her. "I meant what I said. I want you to marry me."

"And you love me, right?" Arms crossed, she waited for his answer.

He paused. He could lie. He should lie. He wanted to lie. But looking into her sweet face, lying was not an option.

"Never mind." She shoved him back and tried to walk around him. "That's my answer, isn't it?" Shaking her head, ponytail swaying from side to side, she gave a sad laugh. "I should have seen that one coming."

"Wait!" He grabbed her arm, halting her progress.

"Let go or I'll scream," she said between clenched teeth, eyes glittering—were those tears?

"I love you, Ry-an." Reality slammed him with the grace of a sledgehammer to the head. It was the truth. "I'm telling the truth, *chérie*." He rubbed her upper arm with his thumb, willing her to believe him. "I may have fallen in love with you the first time I saw you."

"Horsefeathers."

He frowned. "Horses do not have feathers."

"Exactly." She pulled from his grasp. "I have to get back to work."

"How can I prove my love?" Inspiration struck. "I will go back to the States with you and kill your lying dog boyfriend."

"Ex-boyfriend," she felt compelled to remind him. "And I can kill Bill by myself, thank you very much."

"But wouldn't it be so much more fun to do it together?"

Fun? He thought killing someone was fun? What kind of a person thought that?

"Wait." He again stopped her progress. "I did not mean it as I said. It would not be fun. My *anglais* is not, ah, antique. It falls short of my intentions."

"Adequate," she said, biting back a grin.

"*Oui*, that's what I said."

"No, you said—never mind. Let go of my arm. I really need to get out here. We both do."

"We could poison him," Jean offered. "I have a friend who

handles all variety of potions. Perhaps we could speak to him after our shift."

"Perhaps not!" She lowered her voice and shoved him back into the storage room. "Are you crazy? Do you have any idea what would happen to us if customs found stuff like that in our suitcase?"

Us. Our. Referring to them as a unit had to be a positive thing.

He pulled her close and ground his arousal against her.

She shivered. And returned the pelvic caress.

"I love you," he said against her ear, kissing his way down her neck. "And I plan to continue telling you until you believe it."

"Stop." She pushed away, and this time he let her go. "Look, we're both going to get fired. Can we discuss this later?"

He nodded and watched her walk away, admiring the curve of her cute little behind, the provocative sway of her hips. Perhaps when they were naked and had slaked their lust, she would believe him.

Ryan glanced over her shoulder. All night long, whenever she looked up, Jean was watching her. If he wasn't so hot, and if she wasn't so horny, it would be creepy. As it was, it was kind of a turn-on.

Her shift crawled by. When she walked out of Roman's office, Jean was waiting for her.

She paused, once again struck by how gorgeous he was. Beyond handsome, he was almost pretty. What did he see in her?

His smoldering gaze devoured her. Without a word, he tucked her close to his side and walked her out of the restaurant, down the street and to his front door.

At the touch of her lips to his, he went wild. They both did.

Hands roamed restlessly, eager to expose skin.

With a growl, Jean wedged his hands between them and shoved her pants and underwear down past her hips. Immediately he plunged his finger into her.

Her breath caught at the rough intimacy. Loving it. Loving him.

Insinuating his leg between hers, he pushed her clothing the rest of the way down and lifted her free of the confining fabric.

His mouth devouring hers, holding her high against his chest, he fumbled with his zipper. His erection sprang free.

His hardness pushed into her.

They both sighed.

He rocked his hips, driving deeper into her weeping sex, his hands frenetically moving, petting, pushing aside the flimsy shirt, shoving up her lace bra.

"Take it off," he demanded, pulling at the offending garments. "All of it. I want it gone! Do not hide from me, Ry-an!"

His arms belted her, holding her securely against him while he continued to thrust.

She reached around and popped the closure on her bra, then pulled it and her shirt over her head and tossed them aside.

Grunting, Jean continued to move forcefully within her.

"You," she finally managed to gasp. "I want you naked, too." She tugged until his shirt came up high enough to pull over his head and off.

Their mutual groans echoed from the stone walls when bare chest met bare chest.

He slammed her against the wall, each thrust higher, harder. The rough stone against her back provided an almost painful counterpoint to the incredible pleasure going on at her front.

Reaching behind him, Jean grabbed a kitchen chair and pulled it around. He rested one of Ryan's feet on the cane seat, pounding into her from a different angle.

The new position touched something deep within, setting

off shards of pleasure so keen her breath hissed through her teeth.

Her knees went weak. Had Jean not held her up, she was sure she'd have wilted to hang impaled from his penis like a deflated sex toy.

"Open your eyes, Ry-an." Jean leaned back. "Look at us. We were made to give each other such great pleasure."

Opening heavy-lidded eyes, she followed his gaze. The weak light of his kitchen cast them in a bronze glow. She watched the erotic scene of his turgid, shining flesh withdrawing and then disappearing between her legs.

Pushing her back against the wall and canting her hips, she was able to actually see his penis plunging in and out of her flesh.

"Slower," she whispered, reaching down to touch him and guide him back into her wetness. There she waited, her fingers sliding around her slick opening and then closing around his penis and gently pushing it back in. The effect had her on erotic overload.

Jean's breath hissed. Where her hand rested against his chest, his heart hammered with each aroused thrust.

Balancing her against the wall and holding her with his right arm and hand, he reached his other hand down and returned the favor, flicking her swollen clit with the pad of his thumb. Occasionally sliding it along the slick folds, pushing them closer around his penis.

The effect was an immediate meltdown followed by an earth-shattering climax that left her wrung out. Clinging to him, she tried to stay awake, enjoying the rhythmic movement, the feel of hard male deeply embedded within her.

Then his thrusts touched something again and she was wide awake and riding the crest of his orgasm with him, screaming her release.

When their hearts began beating again, he staggered to his bed with her intimately wrapped around him.

He lowered to a sitting position, Ryan on his lap, her legs around his hips.

Placing a tender kiss on the tip of her nose, he brushed strands of hair from her flushed face. "You are so beautiful, *ma petite.*" Kisses brushed each eyelid. "And I love you so."

When she started to tell him she loved him, too—a fact that had hit her full force when she was being banged against the brick wall—he placed a silencing finger on her lips.

"Shhh. It's all right. You don't have to say anything. But I do love you. And to prove it, I am withdrawing my proposal of marriage."

10

"What?" She'd turned him down, but that didn't give him the right to take it back. Awkwardly scurrying backward off his lap, she pulled up the sheet to cover her nakedness. "You proposed. You can't take it back. Who takes something like that back?"

"Ry-an, do not become distressed. I will still assist in Bill's murder, if that is what you desire. I—"

"No! I mean, I need time to think about it—you know, how exactly I want it done and, well . . ." Her shoulders slumped. "If I want it done at all." She sniffed and looked at him through her lashes.

He looked kind of . . . disappointed.

Had she been screwing a killer? The thought clenched her stomach. "Um, exactly what did you have in mind? For killing Bill, I mean."

He shrugged, oblivious to his nudity. "There are ways, I'm sure. We could discuss it."

Discussing was good.

She licked suddenly dry lips. "Well, it's kind of pointless

now." She shrugged, pulling the sheet higher. "I used a big chunk of my Kill Bill fund to bail us out. I'd hoped to go back and kill him this fall, but now I need to wait a while longer, I guess. I need to save more money."

"I have money." He scooted closer, pulling the sheet from her shocked fingers. "I will share it with you," he declared and then leaned to kiss each puckering nipple.

"But not marry me?" She allowed him to slide her down on the sheet and suckle harder. Between her legs, moist tingling gathered, no doubt readying for an encore.

Against her breast, he shook his head and then licked her nipple before replying. "*Non.* It is the only way to prove my love. I will fund our voyage to prove my love and stay until I am deported."

"Deported?" she squeaked out as his finger toyed with her labia.

"*Oui.*" He met her gaze with a devilish smile. "There is only one honorable thing to do."

"Ahhh." She arched up in response to his questing finger. "W—what would that be?"

He positioned himself between her legs, his weight resting on his locked arms, and grinned down at her.

She palmed his buttocks in a vain effort to increase the intimacy. "Well . . . what?

Ever so slowly, he lowered until the hot tip of his penis probed her opening. He paused.

"Fuck me while you can."

Two weeks later, Ryan awoke to Jean dragging her scarf over her nudity.

Smiling, she stretched and reached for him. Sex with Jean was unique. Addicting. She had to have it. And because of that—and the fact that she was hopelessly in love with him— she planned to make an honest man out of him as soon as they could find a justice of the peace. No way would she allow him to be deported.

Tugging the scarf from his hand, she tickled the tip of his penis, letting the soft silk brush intimately against them both.

In response, he pulled her nipple deep within his mouth and suckled until she was breathless and aching.

Releasing her breast, he stood and pulled her to her feet. Embracing her, he walked them toward the bathroom.

"Ry-an, we have a plane to catch." He chuckled when she closed her hand around his erection. "We may have time for a very quick loving in the shower. *Vite!*" He reached to turn on the faucet. "And Ry-an? Please wear your scarf for me. I love it when you are naked with just the sexy wisp of nothing tied around your hips." He growled. "Makes me savage!"

She giggled. "You mean wild."

"*Oui!*" He slapped her bare bottom as she stepped into the shower. "That, too."

"Jean, I think the airline might object to me just wearing my scarf on the plane," she teased.

"I'd object, too! *Certainement!* Mademoiselle Holmes, no other man will ever see your beautiful pussy again. Ever. Will you live with that?"

"*Certainement!*"

Bush Intercontinental Airport was its usual madhouse. Exiting out into the bright Texas sunshine brought a lump to Ryan's throat and a tear to her eye.

"Ry-an? *Ça va?*" Jean pulled her close to his side and gave her a little hug.

She sniffed and nodded. "Sure. I'm fine." Smiling up at him, she popped open the trunk of the car her sister had left for her. "I found the love of my life, and I'm back in Texas. All is right with the world."

They lifted the bags into the trunk and closed it.

Behind them, a car started its engine.

"C'mon, Jean, let's go home. I want to show—agh!" Something pulled on her hips, jerking her from her feet. Landing with an ungraceful plop, she looked up. White fluttered from the tailgate of a departing navy-blue SUV. "My scarf!"

"*Mon dieu!* Ry-an, are you hurt?" Jean picked her up and set her on her feet, his hands running over her body.

"No." She looked at her scarf, having been snagged from her waist from the passing car and now barely a dot on the horizon, waving good-bye. She sighed. "But I really, really liked that scarf."

He cupped her face in his warm hands. "And I really, really love you." He brushed a kiss across her lips. "We will buy another scarf for you to wear for me. A sexier scarf." He leaned close and whispered, "And perhaps someday we will make babies while you wear the new scarf."

What a lovely thought.

Light My Fire

1

Something waved to Emily Mitchell in the reflection of her left side-view mirror. She pulled to the shoulder of I-45, turned on her emergency flashers and got out.

An off-white, sheer scarf hung from her tailgate. "Where did this come from?"

She popped open the door and gently removed the gossamer fabric. Sunlight caught and reflected from the little silver and gold threads accenting the delicate silk.

If she had it cleaned, it would be the perfect accessory for her upcoming trip. Maybe it was the sign she needed. Decision made, she tossed it in the car and drove toward her exit.

Two days later, she tossed the now clean scarf on her bed next to the bulging suitcase.

"I'm telling you, Amy, this week could be it." She spoke into the wireless microphone attached to her ear while she pulled out her velour robe and glared at it. It was August. Why did she pack her winter robe?

"*Em*-ily!" Her older sister's voice took on the whine guaranteed to set Emily's teeth on edge. "Think about it. You and Scott have been dating, what, a year and a half now? Wake up, and smell the coffee! If he wanted to marry you, he'd have proposed long before now."

"Oh, really?" Emily picked up and discarded pair after pair of panties from her overstocked drawer. She had to have exactly the right accessories for this trip, right down to her underwear.

Not that she planned to be wearing them much.

"Yes, really," Amy replied. "Think about it, Em. You've both graduated from college. You both have good jobs. What's he waiting for?"

"You're acting like we've never mentioned the *M* word. We have. Plenty of times." Well, she had, anyway. But Scott hadn't argued or even balked at the topic. That had to mean something. "Scott just doesn't feel he can afford to get married or even buy me an engagement ring right now. And I refuse to settle for anything less than what I've been looking at. He knows that and respects my integrity."

"Oh, gag me!" Amy made a rude sound. "Do you honestly believe all the crap he's handing you? Didn't you tell me he had over three hundred thousand in the bank? How much does he think an engagement ring will cost?"

"That money was for college—"

"He had a full-ride scholarship and graduated! What does he plan to do with it now?"

Emily looked at the sheer nightie from Victoria's Secret wadded in her hand. If that didn't make Scotty-boy sit up and beg for more, he was dead from the waist down.

"Em?"

"Oh, sorry. Well, he hopes to use it to fund college for his children."

"If he doesn't get married, or at least make a commitment of some kind, he won't be needing it. I'm sorry, baby sister, but this whole trip has disaster written all over it, if you ask me."

"I didn't." She tossed the matching sheer robe into the suitcase and sighed. "Ame, I know you love me and mean well, but you don't know Scott like I do. He's not impetuous like our family. So what if he didn't pop the question three days after we met, like Dad? That doesn't mean he's not the one."

"Yes, it *does!* Listen to yourself. You're making excuses for him. You *always* make excuses for him."

"I do not." She stuffed a pair of slippers into the side pocket of her suitcase.

"Sure you do. What about when you wanted to make love the first time?"

"He was just looking out for me. I—"

"Bull! No guy who is really into you is afraid to have sex for fear of hurting you with his . . . overly endowed 'manhood.'" Amy snickered. "I can't believe you fell for that. Did I teach you nothing?"

"I really need to go—"

"Wait! Did you find out where Mr. Romance is taking you yet?"

"A ski resort." She zipped the bulging suitcase and dragged it off the bed.

"In August?"

"Scott found a good deal."

"I rest my case." Amy sighed. "I'll keep my cell on in case you need someone to come pick you up at the airport when you come to your senses. I love you, short stuff."

"I love you, too. You and Mom and Dad are worried about nothing. You'll see. I'll call you when I get home. Bye." She pushed the disconnect button and tried to get back at least a little of her hopeful anticipation.

Scott would propose on their trip. She just knew it.

And he was right to insist they sleep apart the last night before their trip. It would make it more meaningful when they were finally together.

Scott arrived the next morning, dressed in a freshly pressed suit, promptly at six and dragged Emily out of bed.

Mittens, Emily's cat, hissed her outrage at being disturbed and promptly sank her teeth into his leg.

Ignoring the cat ankle bracelet, he half carried Emily in the direction of the bathroom.

"Hurry up, Emily," he instructed, pushing her in far enough to close the door.

He walked, dragging Mittens, to the living room. Once on the sofa, he reached down to disengage the cat from his leg.

How she managed a credible hiss with a mouthful of material was a mystery.

"You," he told the cat, "are history as soon as I buy a dog and can convince Emily you're evil."

"What?" Emily stood at the doorway to the bedroom. "Did you say something?"

"Nothing. I was just playing with your cat." He forced a smile and shot the cat a meaningful glare.

She hissed.

"Mittens Elizabeth! Behave." Emily picked up the cat and cuddled it. "Are you going to miss me, precious kitty?" She kissed the purring feline.

"Emily," Scott said, censure in his voice, "you don't kiss animals. It's embarrassing."

"But I love her." Em kissed the sleek black fur again and wished she could take the cat with her.

"She's a cat."

"So?"

He threw up his hands. "Are you ready? The plane isn't going to wait for us." He stalked toward the bedroom. "This whole thing was your idea," he grumbled. "I'd have thought you could at least be ready on time. I'll go ahead and take the suitcases down to the car." He walked past her, half dragging her baggage. "And get a move on, would you? I'll wait in the car."

"Good-bye, Mittens," she said ten minutes later, placing the cat on her favorite couch pillow. She leaned close and kissed the top of the cat's head. "Next time you see me," she whispered, "I'll be engaged."

"Scott, please," Emily said in a warning whisper, "you're making a scene." She twisted the end of her new scarf, wishing she could gag Scott with it.

"Well, someone should make a scene. I paid good money for these first-class tickets. They have no reason to be stingy with the drinks. Hey!" He stopped a flight attendant. "I asked for another Crown and Seven five minutes ago. Do you think you could talk to your friends on your own time and get me my damned drink?"

The attendant shot him an icy glare. "Yes, sir. Right away."

"See?" Scott watched the attendant's retreat. "You just have to know how to talk to these people."

"'These people' are human beings who work hard. They are not your personal slaves," Emily shot back.

"Well, cry me a river, Miss Bleeding Heart. If they don't like it, they can always find another job." He crossed his arms over his chest and closed his eyes, indicating the conversation was over.

Emily noticed he never got his drink.

Touchdown in Denver went smoothly. The train ride to baggage claim did not.

She tried to warn Scott of the need to hold on, especially during takeoff; she even pointed out the sign. He didn't listen.

The train took off at the speed of light, flinging Scott to the back of the car like a rag doll. Before he could gain his feet, it stopped, throwing him back at Emily's feet.

As soon as the doors whooshed open, fellow passengers stepped over him to depart. Just as he climbed to his knees, straightening his mud-streaked tie, the doors hissed closed and they took off again, Scott rolling between the hold rods like a human pinball.

She thought someone may have actually stepped on him a few times when they picked up passengers and once again headed to baggage claim, but it was difficult to tell with all the noise and mass of humanity.

When the train lurched to a stop again, she hurried to hold the door. Scott, by this time, didn't try to stand. He just crawled to the door and rolled out onto the shining floor.

"Don't say it," he warned, standing up, smoothing his dirty suit and straightening his tie. "I am not in the mood. Let's get our luggage and head for the rental car."

Half an hour later, they were on the road. Thanks to the GPS navigational system, their destination would be reached in seventy-two minutes.

"I can't believe they let someone else have our car." Scott signaled to get onto I-70 West and accelerated onto the ramp at warp speed.

"This car is perfectly fine."

He snorted. "That's because you don't know any different. You weren't raised with fine automobiles like I was."

"My family always had decent cars."

He made another of his condescending sounds. "Your dad always bought American cars. He wouldn't know or appreciate German engineering."

"What do my father's cars have to do with this one?" She was determined not to argue.

"Nothing." He shrugged. "I just wanted a luxury car. I reserved a luxury car. I expected a luxury car."

"Well, you didn't get one, so get over it, and let's enjoy our vacation." She settled back and closed her eyes, trying to think pleasant, upbeat thoughts.

A few minutes later, she felt as if she were being slow-roasted. Sweat trickled between her breasts. Her makeup seemed to be sliding from her face.

She took off her scarf and glanced over at Scott, who looked less than fresh.

"I think there's something wrong with the air-conditioning. I'm roasting!"

He reached out and grabbed her hand before she could check the controls.

"I turned it off. We'll get much better gas mileage in the high altitude. It's cooler in the mountains. You'll see."

Emily stood, mopping her face with a shredded tissue, while she waited for Scott to get them checked in. She looked around at the deserted lobby of the Dusty Hills Ski Resort and wondered who would ever go to a ski lodge with a name like that.

She peeked into the dark bar and saw the bartender and what looked to be one patron at the far end, slumped over his drink.

"Of course," she mumbled. "Who comes to a ski lodge in August? Must be a whole ten people."

Voices raised at the registration desk.

"Ten cheap people," Emily amended.

She strolled over to stand beside Scott. "Is there a problem?"

"They're refusing to take my coupon." Scott glared at the clerk. "I asked to speak to the manager, but he's off duty. The assistant manager says they won't take it. I told him they didn't have any problem taking my deposit."

"Did you tell the reservation operator you had a coupon?" If he did, the hotel didn't have a leg to stand on.

"Well . . . not exactly. I knew if I told them, they wouldn't give me the best deal."

"Let me see that." She wrestled the wrinkled slip of paper from his iron grip. "It says 'Not valid with any other discount.' If they gave you a discount from their regular price, the coupon isn't any good."

"Thank you," the clerk said with a smile. "That's what we've been trying to tell him."

"But—"

"Scott. I'm hot. And sweaty. Give the man your card so we can get our room." Their current situation was not conducive to the proposal she knew was to come.

After all the time she'd invested in their relationship, it darn well had better happen.

2

Emily put away her clothes, smoothing the beautiful scarf on top, and took a shower. She'd invited Scott to join her—it was one of those showers designed for two—but he refused, saying he had a little work to do.

She spritzed head to toe with body spray. Her nipples tingled from the misting. She slipped into her sheer peignoir set with matching mules and walked to the doorway to strike a pose.

Room service had been delivered. The cart stood next to the couch. A fire burned merrily in the fireplace. At first glance, the room looked set for seduction.

Then she noticed a light in the corner. Beneath the light, Scott sat in a recliner, his laptop on his knees, furiously typing.

"Scott?" She walked into the room and placed herself strategically between him and the fire, the better to let him see what he was missing.

"Hmmm?" He didn't look up.

"Supper's here. Why don't you stop what you're doing and eat?" She dropped her robe.

He glanced up. "I already ate. You go on. I need to take care of this."

She smoothed her hands over her nipples. *You need to take care of this, too,* she wanted to say. But, of course, she didn't.

The shrimp was delicious. So was the wine.

"How about a glass of wine?" she asked, pouring her second . . . or third.

"How about you drink the wine and leave me alone?" He stood, laptop clutched beneath his arm. "Emily, I don't want to sound rude, but if I wanted a glass of wine, I'd have had one. And don't pout, it's childish. And selfish. I really need to get this stuff done. I'm going to work in the bedroom. I'll be busy most of the night. You might want to order pay-per-view."

She stuck out her tongue at the closed door.

When the wine was gone, she stared at her empty glass. "How childish and selfish of me to drink the entire bottle all by myself."

She wandered around the suite, bored and restless.

She flipped through the hotel brochure. According to the brochure, each suite had a hot tub on the balcony. She could go for a soak under the stars.

Scott didn't answer her timid knock. She turned the knob to find him engrossed in whatever business deal he had going. If he found out she'd consumed the entire bottle of wine, he would not approve. She decided against asking him to join her.

A few minutes later, she stepped onto the balcony, wrapped in the plush white hotel robe. Beneath it, she went commando.

Heck, it was a private balcony, who would see her? And if Scott decided to join her, she'd be ready for action. Assuming the sight of her naked body distracted him from the smell of wine on her breath. She sighed. Sometimes he could be such a prude.

The sound of bubbling water drew her attention. To the left, a set of cement stairs led to a box hedge. The sound came from the other side of the hedge.

Odd place to put a hot tub. She shrugged out of her robe and climbed the steps, stepping through an opening in the scratchy foliage onto a ledge.

Watching her step, she stuck her toe into the bubbling hot water.

"Hello," a deep voice said.

She screamed. The slick wet surface beneath her foot slid away, and she toppled into the tub to slide beneath the churning water.

Spa jets were a lot louder, she noticed, when they were amplified by water.

Strong hands gripped her shoulders, yanking her above the surface.

Gagging and coughing up water, and most likely a little wine, she tried to keep her back to the man, shielding her breasts with her arms. Not an easy feat, with hands grasping her shoulders in an iron grip.

His hold loosened when her coughing fit stopped.

"What are you doing here?" she finally managed to ask in a raspy voice. She wheezed a few much needed breaths while she waited for his answer.

"I was thinking the same thing." His voice could have been termed whiskey smooth. Warm, modulated with just the hint of a Southern drawl.

A familiar drawl.

"Where are you from?" Cowering against the side of the tub, she wiped her eyes with the back of her hand.

He grinned, his teeth white in the darkness. "Probably the same place as you."

"Texas," they said at the same time and then laughed.

"I'm from Austin," he volunteered a heartbeat later.

"Houston."

He nodded. "I've been thinking about moving there."

It was the truth. He'd made up his mind about thirty seconds ago. He picked up her bare left hand. "Damn, you're gorgeous. You're not married, are you?"

Something flickered across her face.

"No." She glanced toward the neighboring deck. "But I sort of have a boyfriend."

Boyfriends were expendable. Especially the "sort of" variety.

He *tsked* and moved closer. "Must not be much of a boyfriend, to leave you all alone on a night like this." *Naked.* His trunks grew a size smaller. "Would you like a drink?" He motioned toward the cooler on his patio table. "There's all kinds of beer, bottled water. I think there may even be a wine cooler or two.

She shook her head. Several strands had escaped her loose ponytail. In the semidarkness, it was difficult to tell if it was brown or blond. It looked silky. So did her skin.

He clasped his hands behind his back. The heavy scent of wine filled the moist air, telling him she'd already been drinking. His grandmother would skin him alive if he took advantage of an inebriated woman.

"Well, maybe a wine cooler," she said in a small voice. But, he amended, he could still get to know her and enjoy her company.

"Stay right there," he said, hopping to the edge of the tub and getting out. "I was going to get another beer for me, so I may as well get yours while I'm there."

As though she'd even think about getting above water level. Emily found a bench at the far end of the tub where the jets frothed the water and sat down. If she didn't hold her head as high as possible, water slapped her in the face and spurted up her nose.

She should probably go back to her room. But the night really was lovely and the frothing water not only felt interesting where it teased her femininity, it hid her nudity.

The man bent over the ice chest.

Emily wasn't the type of woman who ogled men's derrieres, but his was a particularly fine specimen. A real work of art. It wasn't a crime to admire art.

He turned and walked toward her, his smile glowing in the darkness. The light from what she supposed was his room bathed his broad shoulders and firm chest in a golden glow. His chest tapered into a trim waist and lean hips. Even knee-length trunks, when wet, left little to the imagination.

No imagination required.

And walking toward her was the living, breathing embodiment of her every fantasy.

3

He stepped back into the tub without spilling a drop, the muscles in his legs flexing.

"Here you go," he said, handing her an iced margarita glass filled with a peachy-smelling concoction. "It's a Fuzzy Navel. It was that or sangria." He looked hesitant. "I can get you the sangria if you'd rather have it. It's no problem."

"No, I love peaches. This is fine." She took a sip of the sweet drink. "Mmm. Thank you."

He held out a square hand. "Jason Quartermaine."

They shook. She ignored the tingle that zinged down her arm to her nipples. "Emily Mitchell."

They drank in companionable silence.

"So, Emily Mitchell," he said, stretching his arm along the edge of the spa, "you fall nekked into strange hot tubs regularly?"

Her Fuzzy Navel went down the wrong way, resulting in a coughing fit. She held up a hand to keep him on the other side of the tub when he made a move toward her. "I'm okay. I'm fine," she gasped out. "No, I usually wear a bathing suit, but since I thought it was a private tub"—she shot him an accusing glare—"I decided not to. For the first time in my life, I might add." And probably the last. Was it possible to die of embarrassment?

"Just check in?" He drew designs in the condensation on his beer bottle.

Fascinated, she watched, imagining his touch on her heated skin. No, that wasn't right. She couldn't be thinking that. Darn wine. It muddled her thought processes.

"Ah, yes. A few hours ago." She tore her gaze away from his hands. "Have you been here long?" And, more important, when was he leaving so she could get out of there before she turned to a prune?

"Checked in this morning." He shifted and looked across the steaming water, his gaze doing funny things to the pit of her stomach.

"If you brought a date, would you leave her alone on the first night after you checked in?" she blurted out.

His light eyes widened. A slow smile transformed his face from handsome to breathtaking. "No, ma'am. I was brought up better. If I cared enough about a woman to bring her on vacation, I'd make sure she knew it."

She nodded, worrying her lower lip with her teeth. So she was partially right—if Scott hadn't cared about her, if he truly wasn't that into her, he'd never have agreed to the trip. Why didn't the thought thrill her?

"Any particular reason you asked?" He broke into her thoughts, reaching over the rim of the tub and retrieving another wine cooler to refill her glass.

"Um, no. Just wondering." She frowned at her empty glass. When did she drink it? After consuming an entire bottle of wine and then the wine cooler, her eyelids were having a difficult time remaining open. She blinked, ordering her lids to go back up.

"Would you like to go to breakfast tomorrow morning?"

When had Jason moved closer? Beneath the water, his toes brushed hers, sending an unwelcome jolt of awareness streaking up her legs to a place that had no business being aware.

"They're supposed to have a great breakfast buffet," he went on, oblivious to her libidinous thoughts. "I hate to eat alone."

"I do, too. I'd love to go." Shoot. She totally forgot about Scott for a second. She chewed on her lip, the heat of guilt burning her cheeks. "But I can't. My boyfriend will want me to eat with him." She hoped. "But thanks for asking."

With a nod, he stood.

She meant to look away. She really did. But with all that gorgeous skin and flexing muscle . . . well, what was a red-blooded, in-her-sexual-prime woman supposed to do?

"It was a pleasure meeting you, Miss Emily Mitchell." Smiling, he stepped out onto the platform and reached for a towel. "I think I'll turn in. All this fresh air made me tired." He walked toward the sliding glass door and then looked back over his shoulder. "Unless you need some help getting out of there?"

"No! I mean, I'm fine. Really." Hefting her glass, she added, "Thanks for the drink. Drinks. It was nice meeting you, too."

He waved, not looking back, and closed the door behind him.

She sank as low as she dared without danger of drowning and watched the air currents in the steam. Now that the sun was down, the air had turned cold.

Shivering, she took a final glance at the closed door and drapes and stood, careful to set her drink on the ledge before climbing out of the water.

Jason stared through the opening in the curtains and watched the goddess emerge from his hot tub while he adjusted his erection. Had she not been slightly drunk already, they could have had a high old time in all that steam and hot water. When a woman fell at his feet, he wanted it to be from lust, not wine.

As it was, he was just hot and bothered. And horny. And alone. He watched until she disappeared from view.

Wrapped securely in her robe, Emily stood staring at the hot tub she hadn't noticed bubbling merrily on her side of the deck. Obviously the hot tub that belonged to her room because it was on her side of the hedge. Duh. Heat crept from her chest to her face and ears.

Talk about feeling like a blundering idiot.

She was fortunate Jason had been a gentleman. So why did she feel so . . . disappointed?

Creeping into the suite, she slid the door shut and bolted it. Darkness surrounded her.

No light shone from beneath the bedroom door. Scott was obviously asleep, but it would've been nice to leave a light on for her.

Her toe hit the leg of an end table. Tears came to her eyes while she bit back a cuss word. Scott hated to hear her cuss. She'd been really good the last week or so, but after the night she'd had, she could easily fall off the wagon.

Hands on the wall, she felt her way to the bathroom, not turning on the light until the door was shut. It was the polite thing to do.

Besides, she didn't want to answer any questions Scott might ask. Not now, anyway.

Turned out to be a moot point. When she came out, she saw by the light of the bathroom that Scott was not in the bed. Neither was he in the bedroom nor anywhere in the suite, for that matter. He also had not left a note.

It's okay, she thought, pulling on the T-shirt he'd tossed on the floor and crawling into the big empty bed. She was too tired for sex anyway. Must've been the fresh air combined with the relaxing effect of the hot tub. Not to mention all the wine she'd consumed.

Knowing Scott's reaction if he'd known she'd drank so much, it was definitely a good idea not to mention it.

Or their hunky neighbor.

Too soon, sunlight blinded her. Rubbing gritty eyes, she sat up and tried to focus on the whirlwind of humanity whizzing around the bedroom.

Was Scott actually wearing another suit?

"What are you doing?" She yawned. "What time is it?" She ran her tongue over her dry lips and winced. Her mouth tasted like an army had marched through it. After they'd marched through the local dump. If even that good.

Her teeth were wearing little sweaters.

"Seven," Scott answered, tying his tie in front of the mirror.

Why was he so anal? He didn't need a mirror to tie his tie. She'd seen him do it many times.

Stop, Em. You're just a little hung over. That's the reason you're thinking such unkind thoughts about Scott. You need to be pleasant and loving if you expect him to pop the question.

"I'm awake." She smiled and threw aside the covers and then gave her legs a pep talk to get them to stand. "Give me a few minutes, and I'll go to breakfast with you."

"Don't rush. I already ate." He straightened his already straight tie. "An hour ago." His gaze met her guilty one in the mirror. "How late did you stay out last night?"

"Well, I was just—wait a minute! You were gone when I came in! Where were you?"

"I had some international calls I needed to make so I went downstairs to the conference center."

"Did you fall asleep there?" She pulled on the robe and hugged it around her.

He shot her a condescending look if she'd ever seen one. "Don't be ridiculous. Of course I didn't sleep there. That would be embarrassing, don't you think?" He picked up some papers from his open briefcase and straightened them and then put them back and closed the case with a snap. "I decided to use the conference room today, so I won't bother you. I can't believe no one utilizes it! What a waste."

"Gee, you think? Why would people bypass a perfectly good opportunity to conduct business at a resort?" She slapped her forehead. "Hey! Maybe it's because they are on *vacation* and therefore not working! You think?"

Scott shook his head. "Don't be facetious. It's embarrassing." He picked up his laptop. "See you later."

Emily watched the door close and resisted the urge to throw something at it.

Instead she stomped her foot. Unfortunately one of her high-heeled mules connected with the tender arch of her foot.

"Son of a bitch!" she yelled. Hopping on one foot, she threw the shoe at the door as hard as she could. It hit the wood with a satisfying thud.

The only sound that could have been more satisfying would have been if it had hit the back of Scott's hard head.

Now that would be "embarrassing," she thought with a smile. Her smile faded when she realized he'd never told her where he'd spent the night.

The breakfast bar was extensive. Fresh fruit, eggs, bacon, sausage, waffles, gravy, biscuits, dry cereal and muffins. Because she was alone, Emily chose two of everything except the sausage and cereal.

Thinking unkind thoughts about Scott, she scarfed down her breakfast in record time. Drawing circles in the leftover gravy with the tip of her fork, she debated the wisdom of a second helping of biscuits and gravy.

Scott would not approve. Despite her size-2 body, he constantly reminded her how easy it was for short women to pack on weight.

She knew he was right, but it still stung when he mentioned the "junk in her trunk."

"Hey, there, good morning," a smooth voice said close to her ear. "No boyfriend this morning?"

Glum, she shook her head.

"Mind if I join you?" He smiled down at her. If possible, his perfect teeth were even more dazzling by light of day. "I brought you a present."

He took his hand from behind his back with a flourish.

Biscuits smothered in milk gravy wafted their delicious aroma her way.

Strong. She had to be strong. "I already ate some, but thanks." All she needed was one good reason and she'd cave.

"Aw, come on. I saw the way you eyed them. You want 'em." He sat down next to her, his plate loaded. "And I really do hate to eat alone." He shoved the plate of biscuits and gravy in front of her and handed her a fork. "Go ahead. You're too skinny. You could use a little meat on your bones."

That was one good reason.

4

"So," Jason said when they'd polished off their breakfast, "I'm fixing to check out the nature trail. Want to join me?"

Depends how much nature you can take, hot stuff. She shifted on the hard dining chair. What was wrong with her? She was practically engaged. She had no business thinking impure thoughts about the man sitting next to her, the heat from his denim-encased thigh warming her leg. Shoot! What was she doing even noticing his heat, much less his thigh?

"Forget I asked." Jason took a sip of coffee, breaking eye contact. "I forgot. You have a boyfriend."

"No, it's not that. Scott wants me to have fun and enjoy myself. It's just that, well, I'm not much of a hiker."

"We could go golfing." He inclined his head toward the back of the lodge. "Or there's a miniature course, if that's more your speed."

"You think I can't golf?" She blotted her lips and folded her napkin, mind racing. She really didn't want to be stuck in the lodge all day and be bored out of her mind. Golf was innocent enough.

She glanced at the miniature course just outside the lobby. What if Scott saw her?

"Why don't you get us a tee time while I run up and change?"

A slow smile crept over Jason's face, all but taking her breath away.

"Yes, ma'am." He patted her shoulder as he stood. "I'll give you a call to let you know when we tee off."

She managed a feeble smile. "I'm in room—"

"I know what room you're in."

His departing wink caused a full-body flush. Dang, the guy oozed sex appeal.

Not that she was remotely interested.

The subtle sway that stopped just short of a swagger, encased in well-worn denim, drew the attention of more than a few female guests. How rude, she thought, for the women to be eyeing Jason's backside like that.

She watched the play of muscle under denim and sighed. The guy was definitely hot. Hotter than anyone she'd ever dated, that was for sure. Was he out of her league?

Wait. It didn't matter. She had Scott.

Scott never filled out a pair of jeans like that, her mind argued. But Scott had other fine attributes. None came immediately to mind, but she knew they existed.

So what if Scott didn't make her blood thunder through her veins and her heart pound? That would change. Eventually. Once they were married.

In the meantime, would it really hurt to keep herself occupied while Scott worked for their future?

Decision made, she hurried up to her room to change.

Down, boy. Jason took a deep breath and watched Emily stride from the elevator. For such a little person, she had mile-long legs. Lean and fit, they ate up the distance. In the blink of an eye, she stood before him, a smile lighting her gorgeous face, her blue eyes sparkling.

"Hi," she said, looking up at him.

"You have really long eyelashes." Smooth, Quartermaine, smooth.

Color blossomed in her cheeks. "I never know what to say when people say that."

"Let me help you." He leaned closer, subtly enjoying the light floral scent surrounding her. "You have incredibly long, beautiful eyelashes. They go with your incredibly long, beautiful legs."

She grinned. "Thanks. I think."

Hand on the small of her T-shirt–covered back, he directed her toward the door. "Do you have clubs?"

She nodded. "They're at the desk."

Her clubs were a lot like Emily, Jason mused, carrying both sets to the rented cart. Small and cute. The pink bag held only a few clubs. He'd seen them before. They were called a power set of clubs.

"Do you like your power clubs?" He helped her into the cart and then went around to get behind the wheel. When she nodded, he asked, "Am I about to get my butt kicked?"

She just grinned, and he found it really didn't matter. If she kept smiling like that, he might just let her win.

As it turned out, he didn't have to do that. She royally kicked his ass.

"You didn't tell me you were a pro," he kidded when they stopped for a drink after the ninth hole.

"You didn't ask," she said primly, grinning over the paper cup. "I'm not even close to pro, and you know it. You're probably letting me win."

He wished.

"Hey! Em!" A tall man loped across the fairway, heedless of the vocal reprimands of other golfers.

Beside him, Emily's smile faltered, her back straightening. "Scott."

"You know that guy?" Jason resettled his Astros cap, his gaze going from the man to Emily and back. Neither looked especially happy to see the other.

The boyfriend walked up and Emily introduced him to Jason.

Jason might have squeezed a bit harder than usual. It's what the guy got for wearing a suit on the golf course.

If Scott had a problem with his girl spending the day with another guy, he didn't show it. In fact, he seemed almost grateful.

"—so I need to go back to Houston for the day. A few days, tops." He told Emily and then glanced over at Jason. "Help me out here. Tell her it's okay for her to stay here without me. Hell, the room's paid for, why not? Right?"

Jason nodded. Emily alone. In the room right next door to his. It was more than all right. It was damn near perfect.

"But what am I going to do all alone?"

Scott waved an encompassing hand toward the course. "Same as you're doing right now, Em." He turned. "Jason, you can take care of her, can't you?"

Absodamnlutely. "Sure." He hoped his shrug looked casual.

"See?" Scott turned back to Emily. "It's all set. I'll be back before you know it." He pulled her into a hug, and Jason couldn't help but notice how ridiculous the height difference made them look.

"I have to go now." Scott patted her head like she was his obedient puppy and then gave Jason a salute. "Thanks, man. I owe you."

"No, you don't." Really. "It's my pleasure."

They watched Scott until he disappeared over the next hill.

Emily looked decidedly less perky.

"Hey." Jason tipped her chin with his finger. "What's wrong?"

Tears sparkled in her big eyes. "I don't need a babysitter. He shouldn't have asked you to—"

"I meant what I said. It's my pleasure. To be honest, you're doing me a favor by keeping me company." He winked, earning a small smile. "I've already heard all my jokes."

"Do you mind if I quit for the day?" She picked up her clubs. "I'm not in the mood to kick your butt anymore." Dang. She shouldn't have mentioned his butt. Now all she could think about was how sexy it was. "I mean, I'm kind of tired."

Grinning, he took her hand and tugged her toward the cart. "No problem. I'm kind of tired myself. Why don't I give you a ride back to the hotel?"

After Jason walked her to her door, an act she really didn't need but that also gave her a little thrill she couldn't tamp down, she took a quick shower and curled into a fetal ball between the crisp sheets of the big empty bed.

Could her friends and family be right about Scott? Was he really not that into her? Maybe she really was wasting her time.

She certainly couldn't picture Jason leaving the woman he loved alone on vacation.

Jason. She gave a little sigh and tried to clear her mind. Maybe if she took a little nap, things would look brighter.

A breeze blew over her skin, beading her nipples. She opened her eyes to find herself lying naked on the eighteenth green, legs spread around the hole. Scott and Jason stood by her feet. Scott laughed and slapped Jason on the back. "If that doesn't stiffen your putter, I don't know what will! Take care of her for me, will you?" Humiliation burned her cheeks. She closed her eyes.

When she opened them again, Jason was lying next to her naked. She glanced down. And he was very much aroused.

Wow, was he hung. Hey, it was a dream, she could think stuff like that.

His hot mouth trailed kisses over every inch of her skin, setting her on fire from the inside out. Restless, she shifted, the grass tickling her back.

Next thing she knew, he'd entered her, taking her with fierce thrusts. The sun went down; the moon came out. The sprinklers came on. Still he pounded into her eager body.

All the while, he played with her breasts, squeezing her nipples, and flicked her engorged nub. How many hands did he have? How was he staying upright without crushing her? It was a dream, so she went with it, she didn't really care. She just knew she wanted the lovely sensations to go on and on.

The sun came up, and still they copulated. Dang, the guy was a real stud! Her heart tripped, breath caught. Close, she was so close. Hovering on the precipice, her heart hammered. . . .

Bam, bam, bam!

With a wheezing gasp, she jackknifed to a sitting position, sheet pooling at her hips. The cool air of the suite bathed her sweaty skin.

Bam, bam, bam! Someone was banging on the patio door.

Weak with lingering desire, she fought through the sensual haze of her dream and staggered on wobbly legs to the sliding door.

The sunlight temporarily blinding her, she threw her hand over her eyes. "What?" she asked the shadowed shape.

Silence.

"You're not dressed," Jason's strangled voice said a nanosecond before she realized the same thing.

With a squeak, she grabbed a magazine and shielded her breasts, her other hand hiding her femininity.

Jason turned his back. "I'll wait out here while you throw something on."

She bumped into something and swore.

He turned to glance over his shoulder in time to admire the sweet curve of her bare ass as she disappeared from the room.

This is nuts, Quartermaine, leave her alone, his voice of reason warned.

He sat on the overstuffed chair just inside the door. He never had been one to listen to the voice of reason.

Emily's scent entered the room before she did.

She was worth the wait.

"Hi," she said, stopping a few feet in front of him.

He did a quick visual scan of her tanned legs, flowered miniskirt and purple halter top that made him instantly hard. No amount of calculations could come up with a way to get her out of the outfit and into his bed.

Not yet, anyway.

"I thought you might be getting hungry," he said instead. "They just have the salad bar out now. Dinner isn't for another couple of hours, but I thought if you were hungry, a salad might help hold you until then."

When he turned, she was right behind him, her breasts burning into his chest.

"Sorry," they both muttered.

"I am kind of hungry," Emily said.

"Yes, ma'am. Let's go then." He held the door for her.

Emily stood next to Jason in the elevator and took little greedy breaths of his mouthwatering aftershave. The dampness between her legs told her it wasn't just his scent that drove her to distraction.

Stupid dream. Get a grip.

The elevator stopped, and he held open the doors, waiting for her to exit. She liked that he was such a gentleman. She frowned, trying to remember when she'd last had a date who held doors for her.

Wait. It wasn't a date. Darn. Well, not really darn, because she was practically engaged to Scott. Well, she was at least in a committed relationship. At least *she* was. Committed, that is. She inhaled again. Then again, she and Scott should probably take a break.

Oh, for pity's sake. She and Jason were nothing to each other. They weren't dating. They were just two people who happened to be going to get something to eat at the same time. Plain and simple.

He chose that moment to lightly rest his hand on the small of her back, his fingers idly rubbing her skin, guiding her toward the salad bar.

Maybe not so simple.

5

Emily filled her salad plate, surreptitiously watching Jason talk to Doug, his friend who owned the lodge.

Doug, with his dark hair and semiscowling expression, was a distinct contrast to Jason's tanned, blond good looks.

Stop. You're practically engaged. So what if Jason was good-looking. So was Scott. Sort of. It was just a different kind of good looks.

A plump strawberry rolled off the fruit already piled high on her plate. She picked it up and tossed it into the trash and then turned to look for a table.

And walked straight into Jason, her fruit salad smushing all over his pale yellow polo shirt.

His breath hissed, and he bowed back, but the fruit had already made its crash landing.

"Oh!" Emily set her plate on the edge of the bar and grabbed a handful of napkins in an attempt to sop off some of the goopy mess. "I'm so sorry! I didn't see you!"

He grasped her wrist as her hand followed the dripping trail of fruit past his waistband onto the fly of his khakis.

"Stop. It's okay. I'll take care of it." At her crestfallen look, he added, "But thank you anyway." He winked.

Heat seared Emily's cheeks. What had she been thinking? Well, that was a no-brainer. She'd been thinking of nothing but sopping up the mess she'd made before it totally ruined Jason's clothes. The fact that she was industriously rubbing the front of his pants hadn't occurred to her until she felt the hard ridge beneath his zipper—which was about same time he grabbed her wrist and told her to stop. Could she be any more clueless?

She peeked up through her lashes. To her surprise, he just stood there, grinning at her. Scott would have been furious.

He glanced down at the mess on his clothes and laughed. "If you'll excuse me, I'll go up to change." He brushed a quick kiss on the end of her nose. "I'll be right back."

The tip of her nose tingled as if he'd touched a live wire to it. She absently rubbed it while she watched him stride to the elevator. Dang, she loved watching him walk away. She sighed. When he walked toward her, it wasn't too shabby either. It made her a little breathless. Should she be concerned about that?

Sitting on the big couch in front of the fireplace in the rear lobby later, having an Irish coffee, she didn't hear Jason approach.

"Hi," he said, dropping to sit close to her. Too close for comfort, if her heart rate was anything to go by. "Miss me?"

"Was I supposed to?" she fired back with a smile.

"Hmmm." He took her cup and placed his mouth where hers had been and then took a sip. "That's good." He signaled a waiter. "Could I get one of these, please?"

He put the cup back in her limp hand. "I owe you a sip of mine when it comes."

The thought of sharing his coffee made her breathing shallow. *Get a grip, girl, it's just coffee. He probably does stuff like that all the time.*

While she reasoned with herself, he reached out and took her cup for another pirated sip, then licked his lips and smiled.

She swallowed and forced a little smile. His smile made her damp in places that had no business getting damp.

"It always tastes better when it's from someone else's cup, don't you think?"

Like an idiot, all she could do was nod.

After his next sip, he placed the cup to her mouth. Positioning it, she noted, exactly where his lips had touched.

Without thinking, her tongue darted out to lick the spot before taking a sip.

Jason sucked in air, his gaze heating. Eyes locked with hers, he pulled away the cup and ran his tongue over the same area on the rim and then took another sip.

Good Lord, that was a sexy move. She struggled to regulate her breathing. How embarrassing it would be to have an orgasm from just watching a guy drink a cup of coffee. Pathetic.

Too soon, the coffee was gone. By a happy coincidence, sometime during their sensual encounter, the waiter had left Jason's cup.

He inched closer, put his arm around her and pulled her legs up to lie over his lap.

She snuggled against his side, amazed at how comfortable the position was and sipped the sweet coffee.

"You have a little speck of whipped cream." He stopped her hand. "No, let me." He leaned close, his breath fanning her heated face, and swiped the tip of his tongue over her upper lip.

It happened so quickly, yet she felt it to the soles of her feet. Before she could stop it, a little half whimper escaped.

Jason set down the now empty cup, gave a low growl and half pulled her onto his lap. She'd never been one for public displays and was shocked to realize she didn't mind at all.

His lips dipped to sweep hers in a butterfly of a kiss. So light, so fleeting, she didn't have time to protest. Even if she'd thought about it.

With a sigh, she leaned in and touched the tip of her tongue to his mouth. It was warm and tasted faintly of Irish cream. She licked her lips, enjoying the shared flavor.

He groaned and gathered her closer, taking nibbling kisses from her mouth. Sweet and soft, never taking possession, frustrating her.

Now pretty much completely on his lap, she put her palms on his cheeks and pulled him to her for a genuine full-frontal assault—an open-mouth, tongue-engaged kiss.

They both groaned.

Against his firm chest, her breasts ached. Moisture surged. She barely avoided the temptation to squirm on his arousal, evident where it pressed against her hip.

He broke the connection to trail a string of kisses down her neck to the spot where her pulse beat wildly.

She let out a shuddering breath. "I think I'd better go back to my room until dinner."

"Want me to join you?" he asked, his warm breath ruffling the hair next to her ear.

Man, did she ever! But she shouldn't. She couldn't. She wouldn't.

She sighed and extricated herself from his lap to stand before him. "I don't think that would be a good idea."

He stood and took her hands in his. "Because of the 'sort of' boyfriend?"

She nodded and swallowed past the lump in her throat. If Scott ever found out what she'd done—or, worse, thought of doing—he would never propose.

"I understand." He stood, rubbing the pads of his thumbs on the backs of her hands, sending sparks streaking through her body to her womb. "The least I can do, though, is walk you to your room." At her arched brow, he assured her, "Don't worry. I'm just seeing you safely to your door."

She nodded, and they walked in silence to the elevator.

They had the shining brass elevator to themselves.

Jason pushed the button for their floor. "Doug has a nice place."

Doug? Oh, his friend who owned the lodge. "Yes." Without realizing it, she must've closed the distance between them because suddenly she stood with her breasts—still aching, by the way—against his chest.

He placed his warm palms on her shoulders and gently rubbed, gaze locked with hers. "Call you when it's time to go down?"

Oh, mother of—wait, he meant go downstairs to eat. *Get your mind out of the gutter!* She nodded, not trusting what she might say in her current state of lust. The liquor in the coffee had had more of a kick to it than she expected. That had to be the reason she felt so restless, so . . . well, horny.

He dipped his head and brushed a kiss across her mouth, making her knees go weak.

She grabbed his hair and pulled him back, deepening the kiss. What the heck—she was going for it.

Tongues dueled. His hands pushed her skirt up to her hips, finding her wet and more than ready.

She whimpered her need into his mouth, grinding her aching femininity against his hard ridge, legs now around his narrow hips.

Jason reached back, slapping his hand against the wall until the elevator ground to a halt with an annoying buzz of the alarm. Luckily it was mercifully short.

A few fumbling minutes later, the sound of his metal zipper echoed in the quiet elevator, mingling with their labored breathing.

"Ooh!" She couldn't help it; she moaned when he shoved her damp panties aside and pushed into her, and she wiggled to drive him deeper. If she'd ever been this hot, this needy, she couldn't remember when.

They staggered to the opposite wall, mouths joined, teeth clicking, tongues mimicking the thrusts of their lower bodies.

Too soon, ecstasy rose to meet them, their earthy expletives a counterpoint to their labored breathing.

Jason lifted her off, holding her waist until he was sure she was steady on her feet, and then straightened his clothing while she did the same.

He pressed the button to continue their ascent, hating the silence but finding his mind totally empty of anything constructive to say.

The sex had been mind-blowing. Earth shaking. Words were inadequate. And he wanted—had to have—more. Much more. God, if she left him now, how would he ever survive?

He had to say something. Anything. But it had to be meaningful. Maybe the best sex of his life had killed off some brain cells.

The elevator dinged its stop, and the shining doors whooshed open.

Emily stepped out. He hurried to follow her, noting how she keep her eyes straight ahead.

She paused at her door, fumbling with her card key.

Pleased to see her hand shaking, he took the card from her. "Allow me." The green light came on, followed by the distinct click.

She stepped into the open doorway and looked at him.

That look almost brought him to his knees.

"What just happened . . ." she said, pausing and chewing on her lower lip.

"What about it?" *Please don't say it was a mistake or mention your soon-to-be-ex-I-hope-boyfriend.*

"It doesn't change anything," she said and swallowed.

He stopped her from shutting the door.

"Wrong," he said, holding her gaze. "It changes everything."

6

Emily stood staring at the closed door. She lusted, big time, after a guy she'd just met. She'd cuddled with him. She'd kissed him.

She'd had wild elevator sex with him.

And she wanted to do it again. And again. It had taken a monumental amount of willpower not to drag him into her room and have her way with him. To forget dinner and feast on his hard body all night long.

She was a slut.

Wait. It hadn't been her idea. Well, not entirely. Jason shared the blame. He came on to her. Followed her. After all, everywhere she went, there he was. She was only human. And because she was only human and followed a basic human instinct, she hadn't technically cheated on Scott. It wasn't her fault, it was just plain biology. Biological urges were danged hard to resist. They were hardwired into a person's DNA. Given the right trigger, anyone would have had a lapse in judgment. The thought cheered her.

It was all Jason's fault.

* * *

Jason stood beneath the icy shower spray with his eyes closed. Had he any strength left, he'd have pounded his hard head against the tile until he bashed it in.

Emily's effect on him was intense and immediate. He'd known she was "the one" from first sight. Their chemistry was hot enough to singe his hair. It felt like a knife to his heart, hearing she had a boyfriend.

Then he'd met the alleged boyfriend. Either the guy was totally clueless or didn't give a rat's ass about Emily. Possibly both. When Scott asked him to take care of his girlfriend, Jason had heard a distinctive sound . . . it was opportunity knocking. Ignoring opportunity would be plain stupid.

And Jason was not stupid.

Well, not until the incident in the elevator. He frowned and twisted off the controls before grabbing a towel. He and Emily were both more than half turned on before they stepped into the elevator. Kissing her was heaven and hell. Things heated up way too fast, and before he knew it, he'd been buried deep inside her heat, fucking like a porno star.

He smacked his forehead with his palm. Why couldn't he have kept his cock in his pants? Damn, he'd deserve it if he lost her.

Closing his eyes, he said a little prayer that it wasn't too late and began his damage-control plan while he dressed for dinner.

Not trusting Jason, or herself, Emily convinced him to meet her in the dining room.

Taking cautious glances up and down the hall, she made her way to the elevator. Inside, she imagined she smelled their activity from the hour before. It made her knees instantly weak, heated her cheeks and increased her respiration.

By the time she exited on the lobby floor, she was in full-blown sexual flush, complete with damp panties.

Jason waited by the door of the dining room, his smile bright. Her step faltered. Could she do this? Could she have a sexual encounter with a man she barely knew and then sit and calmly share a meal and have small talk with him?

He stepped forward as she approached, offering his arm. She took it, determined to ignore the heat blazing through the sleeve of his jacket.

His scent enveloped her, warmed her in places that had no business warming.

Helping her with her chair, his hand brushed the side of her breast. It could have been an accident. She narrowed her eyes and contemplated his handsome face. If he had intentionally copped a feel, he had the best poker face she'd ever seen.

All she saw was a devastatingly handsome man seated across the table, devouring her with his eyes. It was at once thrilling and terrifying. What if Scott came back early and saw them?

She thought of Scott palming her off on Jason and decided Scott wouldn't notice or care. He also had not answered his cell either time she'd tried to call him. Of course, he had gone back to attend to a business matter, so it wasn't all that unusual for him to not answer his phone. He'd call when he could.

The wine steward brought their wine, and the waiter placed leather-bound menus in front of them.

"When did you order wine?" Emily took a sip, pleased to find it was the sweeter, light kind she preferred, as opposed to the strong, dry swill Scott insisted was superior. "I approve."

He winked and lifted his glass to hers. "Thanks. I hoped you'd like it." After taking a sip, he set the glass down. "I ordered when we first sat down." He smiled. "I guess you weren't paying attention."

Heat climbed up her neck. "I'm sorry. I was—"

He shook his head, placing his warm hand over hers on the table. "It's okay, Emily. I don't need your constant attention or expect you to hang on every word."

He didn't? Wow. That was unusual.

Dinner was ordered, served and eaten. Emily had no idea what they ate but was certain it was delicious. Throughout the meal, she peeked through her lashes at Jason. Every single time, he was looking at her.

She watched his hands break apart a roll, his fingers casually caressing the handle of the knife while he stroked butter across the tender flesh of the bread.

Her breathing became shallow.

He bit into the roll, his tongue flicking out to swipe any telltale remnant of butter from his upper lip. Her nub swelled, pressing against the silk of her thong. She stifled a groan, intent on ignoring the dampness.

Too soon, he finished, and the plates were removed.

"Dessert?" he asked, nodding toward the dessert cart.

Not unless I can smear it over your hot body and lick it off. Instead she shook her head and mumbled, "No, thanks. But you go ahead, if you want."

"How about another cup of Irish coffee?" he asked as she took a final sip of wine.

She must've inhaled because the wine got as far as the back of her throat before it decided to make a return appearance.

Jason was out of his chair and at her side before she took her second gasping breath, pounding her on the back. That's when she knew she wasn't in imminent danger of choking to death because the pounding caused her nipples to rub against the inside of her cocktail dress in a very interesting manner. They responded by puckering into tight, almost painful little beads.

His gaze dropped to the front of her dress.

She looked down, horrified to see she'd dribbled wine onto the silk bodice. That was going to leave a mark. Even more horrified, she saw her traitorous nipples standing at attention through the fabric.

Dabbing frantically at the spot, she pushed a little harder in the hope of pushing them down. It didn't work. In fact, if anything, they got harder.

Jason watched Emily pushing and rubbing her nipples and swallowed a groan. If they didn't get out of the dining room, he was going to embarrass them both.

He pulled her chair back, steadying her and then helping her to her feet. "Let's get you back to your room so you can change." Grasping her elbow, he strode toward the bank of elevators.

A man could only take so much.

In the elevator, she pulled her arm from his hand and stepped back toward the far corner, folding her arms across the stain.

He knew she remembered what they'd done earlier in the same elevator. He sure as hell did. But this time he was determined to be a gentleman.

Even if it killed him not to take her silk-covered nipples into his mouth and suck away the wine. Damn. Why did he have to think about that?

The elevator dinged, and the doors slid open. He held the doors for her and then walked silently beside her to her room.

Without a word, he took her card key from her hand and opened her door, then followed her in.

She turned so quickly, she slammed into his chest, her hair tickling his nose.

"Sorry," she said, stepping back just as fast. "I was going to tell you I think I'll turn in." She yawned, but it wasn't fooling him. "Thanks for dinner."

He nodded but didn't move. He should go, he knew, but he also knew if he left he might never get the opportunity to regain their easy intimacy of the afternoon.

"Why don't you go change into something comfortable," he suggested, walking past her, "while I light a fire and see what movies they have? Do you like romantic comedies?" Most women did, and from the way her face lit up, Emily was no exception. "Great. I'll see what's available and then let you make the final decision."

He forced his gaze to the list of pay-per-view movies on the menu screen rather than at the wine stain that made his mouth water.

Emily stood in the bedroom looking at her meager choices. She'd packed with the idea of seducing Scott not a casual movie date with the hottest guy she'd ever seen.

Wait. First, it was not a date. Second, he wasn't hotter than Scott. Her shoulders fell. Like heck he wasn't. Compared to what sat out there on her couch, Scott was a Neanderthal.

She eyed her filmy nightgowns and robes. The question was, what did she intend to do about it? Should she play it safe and hide out in the hotel robe or a pair of Scott's sweats? Or should she just consider it a final . . . final what? Fling? It didn't feel like a fling.

Adventure. Yes, that's what it was. An adventure. Maybe even sort of a test to solidify her belief Scott was the right choice.

She nodded and compromised by slipping naked into the plush hotel robe. Right. A test. If she could sit naked beneath the robe next to Jason and watch a movie, Scott was the right one.

She could do it. She was woman, hear her roar.

She paused at the doorway, struck by the perfection of Jason's profile. He'd taken off his sports coat and tie and opened a couple of buttons on his starched white shirt. He'd also taken off his shoes. The sight of his black socks sent a bolt of heat through her. Who would have guessed socks could be so sexy.

Tightening the belt, she walked to the couch and sat next to him. "What are our choices?"

He turned, his gaze raking her, making her question the reasoning behind wearing a robe. The exposed skin on her chest burned. Finally his gaze met hers. Eyes she'd first thought blue turned out to be more turquoise, so clear it was as though she could see clear through to his soul. Her mouth went dry while other places gained moisture.

So close—his wine-scented breath bathed her face—he said, "*One Fine Day, The Wedding Planner.*" He leaned closer and brushed his lips over hers. "*Monster-in-Law,*" he whispered against her lips. "Pretty much all the newer releases. And some old standbys like *Romancing the Stone* and—"

"Do it again."

He frowned and then returned her heated gaze. "No, I don't remember that one."

"Kiss me," she demanded in a strained whisper, "That's what I want you to do again."

"Yes, ma'am," he said with a smile against her lips.

His arms went around her, his mouth covering hers in a kiss so carnal, so passionate it was probably illegal in some states.

Her bones melted. She clung to his broad shoulders, ordering her lungs to keep working, her heart to keep beating.

By the time he came up for air, the belt to her robe was loosened and Jason's hand warmed her left breast. He dragged the pad of his thumb over the distended tip, causing a hitch in her breathing.

"I swore I wouldn't do this tonight," he said, drawing little patterns on the sensitized skin.

Why? But she didn't really want to know. She just wanted the feel of his hands on her to go on and on, so all she could manage to push out of her constricted throat was, "You did?"

He nodded, a lock of silky hair falling onto his forehead. She reached to push it back and was rewarded by a flare of heat in his eyes. "I love it when you touch me."

She arched her back, pushing her breasts against his palm, and all but purred, "And I love it when you touch me."

"I wanted you to change because I knew if I had to look at the wine mark much longer I'd be forced to take you into my mouth and suck it out of the fabric." He looked down at her exposed breast, covered so possessively by his hand. "And now this. You really know how to test a guy's resistance."

She slid her hand lower, thrilled to feel the hard evidence beneath his zipper. After giving his erection a little squeeze, she reached up and drew his head down until his breath tickled her breast. "Who's asking you to resist?"

His hot mouth clamped onto her nipple, tugging with a suction she felt to her toes and every spot in between.

What if Scott walked in? Her brief moment of lucidity—and panic—left her when Jason's other hand covered her now totally exposed chest, squeezing her other nipple while he suckled.

Good Lord, how could something that felt so right be wrong? She let her legs fall apart, encouraging his questing hand.

Moisture surged at the first touch of his fingers on her already swollen labia. All it took was one finger inserted just so to push her over the brink.

Colored lights flashed behind her closed eyelids while her body convulsed in pleasure so intense her heart skipped a beat or two.

As soon as she could move her hands, she tugged and pulled at his clothing until he was totally naked. She stared at the proof of his arousal and swallowed. Dang, how had all that fit into her? Instant recall of their time in the elevator had her more eager than ever to experience the exquisite fullness again.

"This time, slow and easy," Jason whispered against her neck before taking her mouth in another bone-melting kiss.

Her thoughts exactly.

7

Emily closed her eyes and sighed as Jason slid into her. Right. It felt so right.

He slipped his hand between their bodies and found her aching nub, flicking it with the pad of his finger.

She moaned into his mouth, slick with desire, and attempted to shimmy closer. The effect was added friction on the spot that needed it most.

Why hadn't Scott ever found that spot?

Heart pounding, breath now coming in shallow pants, she was close. So close . . .

Jason's talented fingers abruptly left her. Hard on the heels of that, she realized his hips had stopped their lovely pumping action.

Cool air drifted across her puckered nipples, still wet from his tongue.

She opened her eyes to find him staring down at her, his eyes chips of turquoise ice.

Before she could register the meaning, he pulled his glorious hot length out of her needy body and stood.

208 / P. J. Mellor

He stepped into his underwear and pants and pulled them up together.

"Jason?" What happened? One second he was filling her with his heat—and more joy than she'd ever known. The next he was looking at her as if she were something that just crawled out from under a rock.

His cool gaze flicked over her as he reached for his shirt.

Exposed, she closed her legs and pulled the robe tightly around her. Sitting up, she said in a low voice, "I don't understand."

"You don't?" His voice was tight sounding. He looped his tie around his neck and picked up his jacket. His eyes met hers. "I heard what you said."

"What I said?" What had she said?

He nodded and walked to the door and then paused with his hand on the knob.

"When I'm buried deep inside you, I expect you to know whose cock it is," he said in a hard voice.

"Wait!" She jumped up and ran to the door as it was closing. "What did I say?" She grabbed the edge of the door to prevent him from closing it.

His nostrils flared. His gaze swept her from head to bare feet and then back up. "You said *Scott*."

Numb, she watched him stride to his door without a backward glance.

Why on earth would she have said that?

After tossing and turning all night, Emily gave up and took a shower, then sat on her balcony to drink a cup of coffee before going down to breakfast.

The brisk air on the balcony was nothing compared to the coldness in Jason's eyes the night before.

She shivered and willed away the knot in her stomach. Today, room service was not an option. For some reason, it was important he know she was not a coward.

Plus, she really wanted to see him again, to let him know his was the only *cock* she was interested in. She'd already called Scott and told him. Well, she'd left a voice message, anyway, telling him as of right now, they were on a break.

She had to admit, Jason turned her on. Turned her on in ways she'd never imagined. She owed it to herself—and Scott—to get Jason out of her system.

Or see where their mutual passion might lead.

Jason sat brooding in the corner, looking at the congealed gravy on his plate. He should just cut his losses and head back to Austin.

"This seat taken?" Emily said close to his ear.

Closing his eyes briefly, savoring her scent, he gathered his courage. "You can have both of them. I was just leaving."

He looked at her sunny smile, intent on ignoring her bright yellow sundress that displayed her lush curves, curves that had haunted his dreams. How he longed to untie the silky scarf from her neck and drag it slowly over her bare skin. But he couldn't. He needed to remember that.

Her face fell. Damn, why did she have wear her emotions on her beautiful face? It made him feel like an even bigger jerk.

"I hate to eat alone," she said in a soft voice. "Please stay."

Her strained look told him it took a lot for her to ask. A part of him softened. She brushed against him as she sat down and another part of him hardened.

"Is that all you're eating?" He eyed her plate, bare except for half of a partially burned English muffin.

She nodded, sniffed and took a sip of coffee.

Pitiful. His heart twisted.

"I'll go get you something." He stood. "You need more than that."

"It's okay. Really. I don't like to eat alone."

His breath whooshed out. "How about I fill plates for us

both?" He grinned for the first time since the night before. Maybe there was hope after all. He gave a quick wink. "I don't like eating alone either."

After they'd eaten, conversation became easier. They talked and laughed until Jason looked around and noticed breakfast was finished, the buffet cleaned up.

Shoring up his courage, he asked, "Got anything planned for the day?"

She shook her head, the action brushing the silken strands of her golden-brown hair against her oh-so-kissable neck.

"I thought I might take advantage of the stable and go for a ride. Care to join me?"

"I haven't ridden a horse in a long time." She gnawed on her lip again and looked down at her shoes.

He tilted her chin up with the tip of his finger until their eyes met. "It's something you never forget. You'll do just fine."

Compressing her lips, she nodded. "Okay. What time?"

He glanced at his watch. "About an hour work for you?" When she nodded again, he told her, "Great, I'll go set it up. Meet me at the stable, okay?"

"Okay," she said. "And Jason?"

He paused and looked back over his shoulder.

"About last night . . ." She walked closer to him and whispered, "If I said Scott's name when we were, you know, it was only because I was thinking how much better it was with you than anything I've ever experienced with him. Or anyone."

Despite telling himself to keep walking, he pulled her into his arms for a brief hug. Inside his jeans, his cock did a little happy dance. "Thanks for telling me." He stepped back and did his best to shoot her a hard look, only to have it spoiled by the smile threatening to break free. "But, for future reference, I don't want you thinking about 'how it was' with anyone else when you're with me."

Pink colored her cheeks, but she flashed a shy smile.

It was all he could do, walking away and knowing she was watching him, not to leap in the air and click his heels.

Emily chewed her lip and looked dubiously at the huge specimen of horseflesh standing before her. Besides being huge, the thing didn't smell fresh.

"Do you need help getting in the saddle?" Jason walked toward her, leading his own monster horse.

"No, of course not." She placed her left foot in the stirrup and jumped, grabbing for the pummel. Twice. "I mean, yes, please."

He chuckled and put his warm hands beneath her armpits, his fingers moving against the sides of her breasts. Her gaze flew to his. He winked. Nope, not an accidental brush. For some reason, the thought thrilled her.

Lifting her as though she weighed nothing—Scott would've been moaning and groaning—Jason smoothly patted her butt before she settled in the saddle. The gesture was so quick, so intimate and familiar, it took her breath for a moment.

He swung into his saddle and clicked his tongue. Both animals began walking toward the gate.

Emily held the saddle horn in a white-knuckled grip, her tender behind bouncing in the hard saddle with each loping step. If she wasn't careful, she'd bite her tongue. How did cowboys do it? They must have buns of steel—literally.

"Em?" Jason's tone told her it wasn't the first time he'd said her name.

"What?" she ground out, eyes glued to the path.

"It's easier if you try to relax."

She went to a carefree laugh but suspected it sounded more hysterical. "I'm relaxed." She hunched over the horse's neck, her knees pushing against its sides.

"What are you doing?"

"I'm fixing my pant leg."

"Sit up, Emily, sit up. The horse will think you want to do something you really don't want it to do!"

Too late.

With a snort, the mare took off like a shot, Emily bouncing in the saddle, her screams echoing in the trees.

8

"Yah!" Jason nudged the side of his horse, tightening his knees. The horse took off in hot pursuit of Emily's horse, hoofbeats vibrating the earth. "Hang on!" he yelled, wondering if she could hear above her own shrieks.

Her horse disappeared behind a clump of trees and then reappeared. He leaned low over the saddle, closing the distance between the two animals.

That's when he noticed Emily was not in the saddle.

He reined to a stop. The other horse disappeared. "Em?" Frantic, he dismounted and searched the tall grass.

Panic began to set in when he failed to locate her within a few minutes.

The grass rustled to his left, and Emily stood up, brushing dead grass from her pants.

With a shout, he pulled her to him, nearly crushing her in his enthusiasm.

She clung to him for a moment, basking in the warmth and safety of his embrace, then pulled back and looked around.

Docile, Jason's horse stood to the side, munching on weeds. Meanwhile, her horse was nowhere to be seen.

"Where's my horse?" Shielding her eyes, she scanned the area.

Jason gave her a quick hug from behind and brushed a kiss on the top of her head. "My guess is headed back to the stable."

Emily brushed at the stain on the knee of her new jeans. "Good thing. I'd have been tempted to kick some horse butt." She turned to Jason when he snickered. "That horse was evil. It deserved to have its butt kicked." Despite her words, a smile threatened. "Don't laugh."

He did, drawing her into his arms for another hug. She didn't mind. In fact, since meeting Jason, she'd discovered she actually liked being touched. A lot. Especially by him. Was that significant?

"I can't remember laughing as much as I have since I met you." His lips brushed her nose. "Thanks," he said in a low voice. "I didn't realize what I've been missing."

She leaned back within his embrace. "Don't laugh much, huh? What do you do that makes you so unhappy?"

"I'm a financial adviser."

Emily cringed inwardly. Her personal finances were a disaster. Maybe they weren't so alike after all.

"It's not that I've been unhappy . . ." Jason continued. "I guess I just haven't realized how happy feels for a long time." He gave her a squeeze. "When I'm with you, I'm happy. Simple as that."

She licked her lips and watched his mouth descend. He was wrong: It wasn't simple. She had issues.

Those issues were quickly forgotten, though, in the heat of his kiss.

She slid her arms up around his neck, grasping his silky hair, and met his tongue, stroking, parrying and thrusting. He tasted of sunshine and vaguely of mint.

He pulled her tighter against his hard body . . . and another, more thrilling, hard thing.

Her breath caught; her breasts ached where they pressed against him.

He palmed her denim-covered butt, sending heat surging through her, and then growled when she did a little answering shimmy against his erection.

Just when she was ready to topple him to the ground and rip off his clothes, he broke the kiss and stepped back, severing the hot contact.

His heated gaze singed her from her boots to her face, pausing along the way at strategic spots. Spots that were screaming for his touch. Finally his gaze met hers.

"We'd better head back. You can ride with me."

Oh, yeah, baby—wait, he meant on the horse. Shoot. Do something. She reached out and grabbed his belt buckle, pulling him back to her. When he came closer, she slid her other hand around to gently grasp his tight butt.

His eyes flared.

"Not yet," she said in what she hoped was a sexy purr.

"Emily, I don't think you know what you're doing—"

"Wanna bet?" She dragged her palm down his bulging zipper and then gave a little squeeze.

"Em, listen to me." He gripped her shoulders, putting some distance between their bodies. "If we let nature take its course, we might end up spending the night in the grass with me buried so deep inside you I never want to come out."

And that would be bad because . . . ?

"You deserve better," he said in a ragged whisper, lifting her to his saddle.

She reached down to cup his face, halting his progress. "I deserve you," she whispered back, awed to realize it was the truth.

He swung up behind her, his heated length nudging her, sending streaks of need flaring through her.

"And you'll have me," he assured her, his voice rumbling in her ear. "But we've already lost control in the elevator. I want to make love to you in a bed where I can savor you." His hand, at her waist, slid up to cup her breast, making her jeans moist. "All," he whispered, gently squeezing her flesh, "night," through her thin T-shirt and sheer bra, he rolled her distended nipple between his thumb and forefinger, "long." He gave the ripe nipple a little tug, sending streaks of desire straight to her womb.

Holy crap. Couldn't the horse go any faster? Did horses have passing gears?

After a few minutes that had her squirming against him, they stopped near a ledge. Below them grasses waved in the hot breeze, their dry sage color disrupted here and there by brilliant splashes of red and purple.

"It's beautiful, isn't it?" Emily tilted her head for easier access to her neck, closing her eyes as he blazed a trail of kisses to her collarbone.

Sometime during their ride, he'd popped open the front closure of her bra, holding her breasts in possessive hands.

"Gorgeous," he agreed against the skin of her neck.

She purred and arched her back, thrusting her breasts higher against his palms.

In the blink of an eye, he lifted her and turned her until she was seated in the saddle, facing him, her legs wrapped around his hips.

"I have to see you," he said in a low, growling voice.

"Yes," she whispered, wanting it too, and crossed her arms to pull the shirt over her head.

He took it from her and tucked it securely beneath his belt, then removed her bra and hung it from the pummel.

She grinned at the slash of pink against the dark brown, gleaming horseflesh, then gasped when Jason lifted her higher to feast on her breasts.

Each pull from his mouth sent a thrill shooting straight to her groin. Arms around his neck, she tightened her legs around him and ground against his erection.

Wild for him, she pulled his shirt from his waistband and tugged until it joined hers. Both now naked from the waist up, she rubbed against his hard chest, loving the way his skin felt against her breasts.

"You're killing me," he muttered, fumbling with her zipper, saying a prayer of thanks for the low-rise style. Easier access.

Beneath his questing fingers, she was wet and slick. Cock protesting against the confines of his jeans, he ran his finger up and down her slick folds before dipping the tip into her heat.

With a strangled cry, she all but climbed his torso, allowing him greater access to her weeping flesh.

She rode his finger, now buried deep within her wet heat, making sexy little cries and bucking with her need for release.

He lifted her higher and feasted on her sweet nipple, pulling it deep into his mouth.

Making little halting whimpers, she pumped against him faster, harder, finally stiffening, her internal muscles clamping around his finger. Moisture gushed over his hand. He made a vow to be deep inside her the next time she did that.

She shuddered and cuddled closer, her heart pounding against his.

Her breathing slowed, but she whimpered when he removed his finger.

His heart swelled along with his cock.

Her small hand delved into the front of his jeans to close around his erection.

He jerked in her grasp.

"Em, baby, I don't think that's a good idea." He tugged on her forearm, but she maintained her grip. "I can wait."

In response, she moved her hand up and down his erection and then swirled the pad of her thumb around the head until it gave up a pearly bead. His breath caught when she spread it over the head of his penis. Slick and hot, it made his cock jerk in her hand.

"I don't think you can," she replied, a knowing smile on her sassy mouth.

The horse chose that moment to shift its weight. Emily gasped but maintained her hold.

Gaze locked with his, she began moving her hand. Slowly it traveled up and down his rock-hard shaft, giving an occasional erotic swivel. He grew impossibly harder, his hips moving in involuntary thrusts against her smooth skin.

His hands dropped from her waist to her open fly where he shoved aside the thin scrap of silk and fondled her swollen labia.

She wiggled against his hand and increased the up-and-down movement of hers.

Trying not to come all over her hands—they were both now in his pants, one burrowed deep to caress his balls while the other milked him harder and faster—he tried to concentrate on the creamy substance his fingers coaxed from her wet folds. He smeared it over her feminine lips and then swirled it around her engorged nub where it peeked from her hood.

"Pretty," he said through his rapidly increasing shallow breaths. "So pretty and pink. Wet and swollen, all for me." He glanced up at her passion-glazed eyes. "You have no idea what seeing this does to me. I wish we were back at the lodge so I could spread you out on my bed and feast on you."

"W—what would you do . . . exactly?" He noticed her breathing was rapid and shallow, too.

"Look down, baby. See how you bloom for me, blush for me? Seeing how my touch affects you turns me on. Makes me so damn hard." He moved his hands faster, pleased to see her hips follow his lead.

"Open your eyes, Em, see what we do to each other." He watched his thumbs smear her moisture around the hard nub, now swollen totally out of its hiding place. His cock twitched within her satin grip. "So soft, so lush. All for me?"

She nodded, making his excitement edge up another notch.

"If we were somewhere else, I'd lay you down and suck on this." He flicked the nub with the tip of his thumb, enjoying the hitch in her breathing. "I'd take it deep into my mouth and suck until you came." He parted her pink, swollen lips, caressing the moisture up and down each fold. "I'd sip your cum from here and here." He slipped his finger deep, the tip searching for the elusive spot he knew existed. "And all the while I'd keep moving my finger like this." He wiggled his finger, pushing it deeper until he found the soft, wrinkled spot he sought.

With a gasping sigh, she arched, her wetness flowing around to cover his hand.

She was so beautiful, so responsive, it took his breath away. But before he could do much more than take a deep breath, her little hand got busy, pumping him, squeezing him.

He grabbed her forearm, but instead of halting her love play, he found himself guiding her, urging her on, his hips bucking to her rhythm.

Beneath the open fly of her jeans, his fingers fluttered against her wet folds, flicking her nub, daring her to come with him.

Lights exploded behind his closed lids; his breath hitched. At that moment, she shoved hard on his hand, driving his fingers into her wet heat, her muscles convulsing around them.

A few shuddering seconds later, he opened his eyes and groaned at the sight.

Emily sat facing him in the saddle, her head thrown back in the sunlight, eyes closed, a beatific smile on her lips. She still held his cock in her hand, and with the other hand, she smeared his cum over her nipples and then drew a line down to disappear in her open jeans. She pushed aside his hand and caressed herself, smearing his juice to mingle with hers.

The erotic sight was enough to make him come again. If he didn't get her back to the lodge, he'd end up howling at the moon while he fucked her all night long. Right there by the tree, in front of God and everyone.

And, while it sounded good to him about now, he doubted she'd thank him for it by morning light.

The urge to claim her, chain her to him, threatened to overwhelm him.

Damage control. He ordered his brain and hands to move.

"We made a mess." He disengaged her sperm-covered hand from his pecker and wiped it with his shirt. After cleaning up the evidence, he arranged his already recovering penis and zipped up. Taking a deep breath, he reached out and wiped the remaining mess from her delectable breasts, his mouth watering and his hand not quite steady. "Zip up, baby. I can't be trusted to touch you right now," he managed to say around the tightness in his throat.

She stared up at him for so long, he began to sweat. If she suggested an instant replay, he knew he didn't have the willpower to refuse.

Her fingers fluttered around her exposed petals until he thought he'd scream, before she covered herself and righted her clothing.

Two could play that game.

He hung his shirt from his belt loop and handed her shirt to her but held the bra high, out of her reach. At her questioning look, he slowly shook his head and tucked the undergarment in his pocket. "If I have to ride back shirtless, you can ride back braless."

Without a word, she climbed over his leg and faced the front, wiggling her sweet little ass against his already hard pecker. Maybe holding her bra hostage wasn't such a good idea.

The horse began walking, setting a sedate pace.

Emily pulled his arm from around her waist and pushed his hand up under her shirt until both of her jiggling breasts were cupped in the palm of his hand. She sighed and relaxed against his chest and then smiled up at him. "If I can't have the support of my bra, you're going to have to be the substitute."

Then again, maybe it was the best idea of his life.

Totally sated, Emily relaxed against Jason's chest and closed her eyes with a smile. She hadn't felt this good, this content, since . . . never.

Not even thoughts of Scott could ruin her bliss.

Scott. She sat a little straighter, Jason's thumb riding her nipples. Did Scott get the message they were on a break?

Jason's erection bumped her from behind, and she temporarily lost her train of thought.

His warm palm left her to straighten and smooth down her shirt. Just as she was about to protest the loss, she saw the stable ahead.

She glanced down at her pebbled nipples and bit back a groan. Following Jason's gaze, she knew he noticed, too.

"I can't ride into the corral like this," she whispered. "Everyone will be staring at my chest!"

"I know I sure will be," he said with a sexy smile.

Heat and wetness flooded her again, and she gave her body a stern lecture to stay on task.

Jason reined the horse to a stop to the left of the corral gate.

He hopped down and helped her from the saddle, managing to drag her aching breasts down the hard planes of his chest in the process. And he didn't look one bit repentant.

"Wait here," he said against her lips and then kissed her. "I'll be your shield when we walk through the lobby." He executed a quick chest rub against her hardening nipples, winked and swung back up into the saddle.

The tease.

She was still standing, mulling over the exciting and sexy evening ahead of her, when Jason returned.

"Miss me?" he asked, pulling her into his arms.

"You were only gone a few minutes," she felt compelled to point out, even though she found she had missed him.

Arm in arm, they walked to the back lodge entrance and to the elevator without incident. Just as the doors were closing, an elderly couple stepped in, nodding their greeting.

Jason pulled her tight to his chest, his body shielding her braless state from the general public. It could also possibly shield other activities.

It was sneaky and maybe a little devious, but she couldn't help herself. She slid her hand to his crotch and cupped his package. He stiffened in response. Everywhere.

She hid her smile against his chest and then took advantage again and swiped the tip of her tongue across his nipple.

He swallowed a little gasp, but not before she noticed.

The elevator stopped at their floor, and they stepped out.

"You're playing with fire, little girl," Jason warned, ushering her down the hall.

He swiped his card in the lock and pushed her into the room before she could take her next breath.

He flipped the privacy lock and pulled her toward the bedroom. Her heart gave an excited hop.

But he didn't stop at the bed. Instead he walked into the bathroom and turned on the shower. "We'll take a long bath later. Together," he said, causing the little heart hop to happen again. "Strip."

She blinked. "Excuse me?"

"We both smell like horses and dirt. We need a shower before we can move on to more enjoyable activities." He pulled her T-shirt over her head and flung it aside, his eyes devouring her. "Strip," he repeated.

"You first."

They stared at each other for a moment; then his hands reached for his belt. Within seconds, he stood before her totally naked. Totally magnificent. Totally aroused.

He advanced a step. "Strip," he said in a low, sexy voice.

Tingling with sexual excitement from head to toe, she grinned at him. "Make me."

With a growl, he lunged for her. She shrieked and ran into the bedroom, Jason hot on her heels. He caught her in less than three steps and tossed her on the bed. Before she bounced, he grabbed her waistband and unzipped her, dragging her jeans and panties off in one smooth motion.

Their gazes locked.

He flipped her over and rammed his hard length into her before she took her next breath. But breathing was overrated.

On fire for him, she squirmed, the quilted bedspread abrading her pebbled nipples. She moaned her frustration and ground back against him, desperate for more contact.

He slipped his strong arm beneath her and lifted her to her hands and knees, pounding into her doggy style. The position excited her beyond belief.

He leaned over her, thrusting deeper, reaching around to toy with her nipples.

She shoved his hand lower to her aching center. All it took was one good squeeze on her engorged nub to bring her to a screaming release.

He held her hips in an iron grip and pounded into her. Once, twice. The third time, he stiffened, driving deeper than ever, and let out a shuddering groan.

They collapsed in a pile, sweating and breathing hard.

He pulled out of her, robbing her of his heat. She moaned her protest. His response was a playful stinging slap on her bottom.

To her surprise, desire surged its return.

"Now we really need a shower," Jason said, pulling her to her feet and into his arms for a quick kiss.

Showering had never been so much fun, Emily mused as she slid her soap-slicked hand over and around every millimeter of Jason's skin.

He'd already thoroughly soaped and rinsed her until she had panted with desire and climbed up his hard body to impale herself.

After her knees recovered enough to stand upright unassisted, she'd reciprocated. If Jason's harsh breathing and iron erection were any indications, she was about to be honored with an instant replay.

She could hardly wait.

Surprise gripped her when, instead, he pushed aside her questing hands and efficiently rinsed the suds away.

Flipping the faucet to the off position, he grabbed her arm and hauled her out of the shower.

Stunned, she stood and submitted to a cursory toweling. After he'd swiped a few times at his torso, he tossed aside the towel and swept her into his arms.

"Jason!" Clinging to his neck, she felt compelled to point out, when he bypassed the bed and strode into the sitting area, "I'm naked!"

"So am I, darlin', and I intend for us to stay that way for a while." He paused by the sliding door and yanked the drapes closed until the room was shadowed from the afternoon sun;

then he walked to deposit her on the couch before lighting a fire.

He turned back, his eyes rivaling the blaze in the fireplace.

Her gaze skimmed his fit body, her heart rate increasing at the sight of his engorged penis. Anticipation prickled her skin, bare against the knobby fabric of the sofa.

He left and then returned, dragging the comforter from the bed to spread in front of the fire.

When he arranged her to his satisfaction on the fluffy spread, he produced a bottle of champagne and two glasses from behind the couch.

Maintaining eye contact, he unwrapped the foil and twisted the key until the popping cork echoed in the quiet room.

Emily shrieked, cool bubbles showering her skin, and jerked back.

"Wait," Jason said, scooting closer, tugging on her leg with his free hand. "I have an idea."

He pulled the cushion from the couch and then lifted Emily's hips and slid it under. With him now stretched out between her legs, the action elevated her almost to his eye level.

Excitement bubbled through her as surely as the cascade of champagne had bubbled across her sensitized skin.

He looked up over her mound. "Trust me?" His hot breath whispered across her damp center.

Realization dawned. Her smile slid into a more somber expression. She nodded slowly. She was so on fire for him, she trusted him to do anything to her, with her.

He grinned. The effect, given his position, was pure sex.

Lucky her.

The cool rim of the champagne bottle touched the heated flesh of her lips. He traced her swollen labia with the rigid glass a few times, making her hold her breath in anticipation. He inserted his finger, rotating it in slow, inflaming circles, and then replaced it with the tip of the bottle. One hand under her bottom, he tilted her hips and the bottle at the same time. Cool, bubbling champagne filled her.

It was far from unpleasant. She squirmed a little, opened her legs wider to allow the champagne to go deeper.

Jason growled and set the bottle aside and then grasped her cheeks, holding her angled toward his lowering mouth.

He covered her with his hot mouth, gently exhaling and then sucking the champagne from his personal human goblet, his tongue foraying occasionally to lap at the champagne.

Her orgasm hit her square between the eyes with enough force to stop her heart. Good thing she was physically fit. Otherwise the pleasure might have killed her.

On and on it went; just as she caught her breath, another wave of release would drag her down in its undertow.

Jason smiled against her pebbled nub and then swiped it with his tongue. His balls tightened, cock throbbing, just watching Emily get off.

He pulled the cushion from under her limp hips and moved up between her sprawled legs. He had to have her. Now.

He thought of the box of condoms in his duffel bag; the very thought of any barrier between him and the woman before him clenched his gut. The thought of impregnating her sent a thrill through him and made his cock twitch.

While he debated the wisdom of no protection, she rolled away and grabbed the bottle.

"My turn," she said with a bewitching smile.

When she looked at him like that, he knew he'd deny her nothing.

"Yes, ma'am," he said with a grin and lay on his back, anticipating her next move.

In one second, Emily was on her knees, the sweating champagne bottle grasped in her hands. Anticipation zinged through him. The next second, the bottle shot upward from her fingers, champagne spraying in a good five-foot radius.

They watched in horrified fascination. The bottle hung midair for a moment and then fell with an ominous *thunk* . . . on Jason's forehead.

"Shit!" He jackknifed to a sitting position, pain shooting behind his eyes, his hand over the rapidly rising bump just above his right eyebrow.

"Oh!" Emily lunged forward in an obviously ill-planned attempt to render aid.

Her head collided with the very spot the bottle crash-landed on, sending a fresh spear of agony through his brain.

He fell back on the comforter, Emily sprawled on top of him.

"Let me see," she demanded, grabbing his face.

"Ow! Watch the eye!" He jerked away, wondering if she'd poked it out.

"I'm sorry! I, well, I—" A giggle escaped, followed by an all-out laugh. "I didn't mean to h—hurt you," she said between peals of laughter. "But you look so funny sitting there!" And she was off on another fit of laughter.

Despite his pain, his mouth twitched. He bit back a chuckle. "If I wasn't mortally wounded," he said, working on controlling his laughter, "I'd turn you over my knee."

Their gazes met. Laughter stopped, replaced by a whole new level of interest.

Emily blinked, breaking the sensual spell. "I need to get going." She glanced at the mantel clock. "It's almost time to go down to dinner."

She gathered her clothes, holding them in front of her like a damn shield. Didn't she realize she didn't have to hide from him?

"I thought we were going to order room service." He propped up on his elbow and watched her flit around the suite. A wave of sadness washed over him. Damn. He'd meant to take it slow. Did his passion spook her? "We don't have to do anything. Nothing you don't want to do, anyway," he assured her in a low voice.

She looked up from stepping into her panties and then turned away from his intent gaze. Jason didn't understand. She would want to do *everything* with him. It was too soon. The fact that she didn't want to leave him had set off warning bells. The need she felt for him, wanting to be with him, having him fill her body and soul every waking second, couldn't be a good thing. She obviously had a problem.

They needed a little time apart. Otherwise she might just keep him locked in her bedroom until neither of them could walk.

If he knew what a sex fiend she was, he might run away screaming. She didn't want to risk that. After all, what if he turned out to be "the one"?

By taking a step back for a breather, maybe he'd stick around long enough for her to find out.

10

Jason kissed Emily good-bye, promising to pick her up in an hour, and then walked back to the bedroom.

After a cursory glance in the mirror at the rapidly rising bruise on his forehead, he stepped into the shower. Steam surrounded him, relaxing muscles he didn't know were clenched.

He stood beneath the stinging spray for a while after he'd finished showering and thought. Then he slowly dried off.

Meeting his gaze in the mirror, he spread shaving gel and then began his second shave of the day. If the evening ended the way he hoped it would, he didn't want Miss Emily to sport razor burn in the morning. Anywhere.

He stopped midsplash of aftershave, staring at the stunned man in the mirror.

A bark of laughter escaped.

Hot damn. He was in love.

Emily tossed the third evening dress onto the growing pile on the bed and stalked back into the walk-in closet. It was imperative she look her best.

She paused. Why was it so important? She and Jason had known each other only two days. Wow. Only two days.

"Sure seems like a lot longer," she mused, stepping into a clingy purple metallic number and then turning in front of the full-length mirror on the closet door, examining the fit from every angle. Would Jason like it?

Memories of Jason grinning down at her in the lobby, his hot gaze taking in every inch of her, his hungry touch whenever she was near cinched it.

Jason would love it.

Her cell rang just as she picked up her scarf and beaded bag, startling her. She squinted at the caller ID, not recognizing the number.

"Hello?" She kicked off the strappy sandals and slipped her feet into a pair of slides and then checked the effect in the mirror. No doubt, the slides made her butt look better.

"Emily, it's me." Scott's voice bitch-slapped her, halting her shoe inspection.

"Hi!" She hoped her voice sounded more perky than guilty. Although, on second thought, why would she be guilty? She'd left a message telling him they were taking a break.

Her heart clenched. Oh, no. What if that message was what he needed to finally make a commitment? What would she do? What would she say?

And what about Jason?

". . . so I really need reimbursement. You understand, don't you?" Scott's voice jerked her back.

"Ah . . . I'm sorry," she said, grabbing a tissue from the box on the dresser and rubbing it over the mouthpiece. "There's a lot of static. What did you say?"

She could practically see Scott's infamous eye roll.

"I said," he repeated on a put-upon sigh, "since I'm back at the office now, I won't be able to put the trip on my expense report. I'm going to have to get some reimbursement from you."

What a slime bag. What did she ever see in him?

"Excuse me? You planned to use this as a business write-off?" It was a good thing he was in the next state. She would have had to tear his heart out and feed it to him—assuming he actually had a heart.

"Of course," he replied, a definite smirk in his voice, "why wouldn't I? What do you think I brought along all my stuff for?"

"I don't know, Scott. Maybe I just thought you were anal." Unwanted tears clogged her throat. "I thought this was going to be the beginning of something special, that coming here meant something—"

"Oh, cut the crap. You're overreacting, as usual. That's so embarrassing! And, Emily, you're the one who left the message saying you thought we needed a break. I'm fine with that. I also have no problem with it being permanent, like you suggested in your last message. Now it's your turn to be a stand-up guy and pay for your fair share of the trip. A trip," he added before she could protest, "you insisted on taking, that I haven't even been there to enjoy. It makes sense for you to at least pay half. Hell, I could have just left you holding the bag."

Through a red haze, she looked at the checkout information posted on the door and forced her teeth to unclench.

"Scott?" she said in the most saccharine voice she could muster.

"You don't have to apologize. I'm just glad you see it may way."

Could she do it? Could she force out the words? Yes, she believed she could.

"Scott? Listen carefully." She held the phone away from her mouth and screamed, "Fuck you!"

She flipped the phone shut with a smile. Her grandmother was right, after all. Getting the last word was the best.

* * *

Jason paused outside Emily's door and straightened his tie and cuffs. He could do this. He'd known she was special, most likely the one, when she'd first tumbled into his hot tub. He'd controlled his baser instincts once. He could do it a while longer, especially if it meant having a future with Emily.

He knocked, shoring up his resolve.

She opened the door and stood before him in a sexy-as-hell dress that left little to the imagination—and his was in overdrive.

She flashed a little smile his whole body responded to.

One step put him within reaching distance. He pulled her into his arms.

"Hello, beautiful." He brushed her lips with his and then pulled back before he gave in to temptation and deepened the kiss. "Ready to go?"

She nodded but made no move to leave his embrace.

Desire stirred behind his zipper. He stepped back, allowing his arms to slide away, and then grasped her smaller hand in his and led her to the elevator.

During the descent, she snuggled close to his side. Her arm slid beneath his sports coat to hug his waist.

His heart soared. Good thing she held on to him or he'd fly away from pure happiness.

"You smell good," she whispered and then took another whiff. Good grief, just smelling his aftershave made her mouth water . . . and other places damp.

He absently ran his hand up and down her back, threatening to send her into a full-body orgasm.

Finally the doors whooshed open, and they walked to the dining room.

Jason sighed and put down his coffee cup. "That was great. How was your steak?"

Emily swallowed her sip of wine and nodded. "Great."

A waiter rolled the dessert cart their way.

Emily looked almost panicked.

"Dessert?" he asked, wishing her look of yearning was directed at him.

She shook her head. "Um, no." She swallowed. "Thanks."

He pushed away from the table and reached for her hand. "Then how about dancing off our meal?" He inclined his head toward the music from the adjoining room.

She stopped midstep, spine stiff. "I'm, ah, not much of a dancer."

He smiled and allowed his gaze to take a leisurely stroll over her more-than-fit body. "Honey, I've seen you move. Trust me, you can dance."

He guided her into the dimly lit room and straight onto the wooden dance floor. If he didn't take her in his arms soon, he might not survive.

She came to him with a sigh, nestling against his heart like she'd always belonged there. And she did belong there. Forever. He just had to convince her of that fact.

Emily found, to her delighted surprise, that she actually could dance. Funny, with Jason, it was easy. All she had to do was stay plastered to him. Her body picked up and followed his every move.

His hardness pressed against her hip, and she wondered if anyone else was as turned on by dancing. It was all she could do to not squirm against him.

When the band took a break and Jason leaned forward to ask if she'd like to take a drive for dessert, she eagerly followed him to his rental car.

She eyed the Lincoln Navigator and wondered if it was possible to fit two people into the big bucket seats. Hot on the heels of that thought came another: would they be able to make love in the seat?

Jason ran his hands over her behind, the fabric slipping over the skin exposed by her thong in an erotic dance. He pulled her against his erection and nuzzled her hair. "You have no idea how much I wanted to touch you like this while we were dancing."

She smiled against his starched shirt and ran her hand over the hard bulge in his pants. "I could tell."

He gave her a playful swat and stepped back to open the door. "Let's hit the road." He lifted her into the car, running his hands over her eager body a bit more than was absolutely necessary.

She loved it.

"I read about a place down the road called Just Desserts. Thought we'd check it out," Jason said, backing the big car out of the parking space.

They ordered a sampler plate and gorged themselves on chocolate and then walked to the car arm in arm.

"I'm not eating for the rest of the week," Emily declared, her hand on her nonexistent stomach.

He beeped the lock and opened the driver's door. "Sure you are. I told you, you could use a little weight. Besides," he added with a grin and a wink, "I don't like to eat alone, remember?"

He grasped her waist and lifted her into the driver's seat and then slipped in beside her.

"I guess I could climb over the console," Emily said, looking none too happy about the idea.

"No, ma'am, you cannot." He started the car and pulled her tighter to his side before putting the gearshift into drive. "I want you close." He kissed her fragrant hair. "As close as possible." He ran his thumb along the outer side of her breast, revved to notice her little shiver. "In fact, let's take the long way back to the lodge. Go for a little drive while our food digests."

"Sounds like a good idea." She snuggled closer, her leg over his thigh.

His cock liked the idea, too.

Driving one-handed, he explored her side, dipping his hand into the low neckline of her dress to squeeze her breast, stroke her hard nipple. Getting harder by the minute when she made little purring sounds and unzipped his pants, her questing hand finding him.

He shifted, allowing her freer access, stretching his foot forward, pressing on the accelerator.

Her fingers delved to find his balls, playing with them, caressing them.

The car lurched down the rod in synchronization with the increasing thrusts of his hips.

She leaned down and rubbed the tip of her now exposed breast against the engorged head of his penis.

His breath caught. He stomped on the accelerator.

Flashing lights filled the car, followed by the unmistakable sound of a siren.

Jason groaned and pulled to the side, righting himself and zipping up while Emily hastily tucked the breasts that had his mouth watering back inside her dress.

The patrolman sauntered to the car, ticket book in his leather-gloved hand. "You were going pretty fast, young man," he said when Jason buzzed down the window. He glanced in the car at Emily. "And failing to maintain a level speed." After a knowing gaze, he looked back at Jason. "License, registration and proof of insurance, please," he said around a toothpick.

Jason handed the patrolman his information. Damn. Although, it may have been a lucky thing they were stopped. A few more seconds of the action they'd been experiencing and he'd have pulled over and been inside Emily's sweet body before the car rolled to a stop. Which, given the fact the cop had obviously been following them, would have been worse.

11

Emily waited for the embarrassment to wash over her at the knowing glance of the patrolman. Didn't happen. In fact, she realized she felt only a mild disappointment at having been pulled over when she was mere seconds from taking the purple head of Jason's penis in her mouth. That had to be significant. Had to mean something.

She was either already totally committed to him or totally a slut.

Right now, she found she didn't really care which. As long as she could keep experiencing the wondrous things she'd experienced with the sexy hunk next to her.

The officer handed Jason a ticket, along with his paperwork and license, and then tipped the brim of his hat. "Watch your speed, folks. And," he said with a meaningful glance at Emily, "I'd advise you to get in your own seat, young lady, and leave your boyfriend's zipper alone." His smile shown white. "At least until you reach your destination. Have a good evening."

They sat while he got back into his patrol car and drove away.

Jason shoved the ticket onto the console along with the other papers.

"I'll pay half of your ticket," Emily said as she started to lift herself over the console. "After all, it wouldn't have happened if I hadn't had my hand in your pants."

In response, Jason laughed and pulled her back onto the seat with him. "Sweetheart, it was the best money I ever spent. Worth every penny." He took her hand and placed it over his bulging fly. "And you stay here, right where you belong."

His words shot a thrill through her, making her tingle in places that were already damp. She squirmed a little closer, loving the heat from his hard body, and gave a gentle squeeze. "Let's go back to the lodge," she whispered, "before I attack you right here."

"Yes, ma'am," Jason said on a chuckle, pushing down on the accelerator, sending the big car shooting into the night. "My thought exactly, although I'm not sure who would do the attacking first."

Backtracking, they took the shorter route to the lodge, pulling into the parking space a few long minutes later.

He turned in the seat, pulling her close, and covered her mouth with his.

She sank bonelessly against him, returning his kiss with equal passion and wonder.

Teeth clicked, tongues tangoed, breathing increased. His thumbs found her aching nipples and gave them a sensual massage that sent flares of desire to ignite in her extremities.

She was on fire. For him, only him. She couldn't get close enough. With a start, she realized he could do anything to her, even right there in the parking lot in a rental car, and she'd allow it. Welcome it.

Twisting against her growing arousal, she pushed one of his hands until it found her wet core, groaning into his mouth when his fingers pushed aside the skimpy fabric of her panties and did exactly what she needed them to do. Close. She was so close.

To her disappointment, he pulled his fingers from her eager body and smoothed her panties back in place.

"Let's go inside where we'll be more comfortable." He pulled her out of the car and into his arms in one fluid movement, shoving the door shut with his hip. After a kiss that left her weak in the knees and experiencing altered breathing, he whispered, "If I can wait that long."

The words, breathed into her ear, shot straight to her groin.

Arms entwined, they walked at a fast clip into the lobby, straight to the elevator.

As soon as the elevator doors closed, Emily jumped into Jason's arms, her legs going around his hips. "Make love to me," she demanded, covering his face with kisses, rubbing her engorged sex against his, totally frustrated with the fabric barriers. "Now. Here."

Ding!

An elderly couple got on the elevator, casting dubious glances at them.

Jason put his palm on her head, forcing her face into the crook of his neck and clutched her tighter to him, preventing her from dismounting. "Evening," he said with a smile and then patted Emily's behind. "Pardon my wife. She's had a mite too much to drink tonight."

The couple laughed politely and nodded. At their floor, the woman turned and patted Emily's back before exiting. "I hope you feel better in the morning, dear. Too bad this happened to you." She grinned at Jason. "In our prime, we'd have taken advantage of the situation and had sex in the elevator."

"Mildred!" Her husband's cheeks colored. He grasped her arm and all but dragged her from the elevator.

"What?" they heard Mildred protest as the doors closed. "I'm sure they don't think they invented sex."

Emily leaned back and returned Jason's smile and then attempted to stand.

"No, ma'am," Jason said, holding her close. "I kinda like riding in an elevator like this. With you." He leaned down to plant a tender kiss on her lips. "Only you," he whispered against her mouth before deepening the kiss.

Too soon, they reached their floor.

Emily tried telling herself the thrill she felt when Jason called her his wife was stupid. It was just a game; it meant nothing.

But it sure felt like something.

Jason's shaking hand fumbled with the card key, all the while holding Emily tightly against him, half balanced on his hip. The teeth of his zipper dug into his hard flesh, causing more tremors.

Finally the door clicked. He shoved it open and staggered into the darkened room with his precious cargo.

While he felt for the light, Emily managed to slip from his grasp and kneel before him. In the blink of an eye, he was unzipped, his hot cock throbbing in her cool hand.

Without a word, she took him into her mouth, her tongue stroking the flames higher, her hands petting his balls until he felt as if he'd burst into flames from the inside out.

He wanted to reciprocate. But his body was locked in an upright position, hands plastered against the wall of the entryway, knees locked, back arched, eyes shut. Every drop of blood congregated between his legs.

She slid her mouth down until she took him deep in the back of her throat where the head of his cock pulsed against her soft tissue. Slowly she slid him back out until her lips closed around the very tip, her tongue licking circles around his slit, taking occasional forays into it with the tip of her tongue.

His heart threatened to rip through the walls of his chest. Blood slammed through his veins like a freight train, deafening him to anything other than the hammering of his pulse.

The muscles in the backs of his legs tightened. His mind scrambled, trying to think of something, anything else to prevent his climax from occurring in any place other than Emily's welcoming body.

Exerting Herculean strength, he grasped her shoulder, pulling her greedy mouth from his cock. With a strangled cry, he shoved aside the scrap of silk and plunged into her lush, wet heat from behind.

Home. He was home.

Emily gasped and arched her back, sure she might pass out from the pleasure.

Jason flipped positions, anchoring her against the wall, the cool surface soothing her heated skin. Still pounding into her, he pulled her dress up and over her head, tossing it aside.

She wiggled closer, luxuriating in the tactile pleasure of her nipples rubbing against the skin of his hard chest.

"Harder," she whispered against his skin, the moisture of her breath reactivating his scent to waft up, enveloping her. Sensations built, tumbling over each other. Every nerve ending stood on alert. "Faster!"

The muscles tightened up the backs of his legs, his butt, on up to his neck. He'd have sworn he felt his testicles tighten and draw up. Drawing deep breaths through his nose, he concentrated on holding off his gratification. Then Emily's internal muscles began contracting around him, milking him of what little control he had left.

With a shout he pounded into her, shuddering his release.

When their heart rates returned to something resembling normal, he lifted her to stand on the tile of the entry. Just looking at her, her smooth skin flushed with sexual gratification, wearing nothing but her sexy scarf tied around her neck, made his cock stir with renewed interest.

He reached for the scarf, tugging on its end.

Her lazy smile oozed sex appeal. "What are you doing?"

His grin matched hers, he knew. "You look like a present. My present. I'm unwrapping you."

"Allow me," she said, stepping back a little and reaching for the bow. She'd never been into sexual teasing, but then, being with Jason had brought out a lot of latent instincts. With him they felt good. Better than good. Scintillating. Right.

The soft scarf slithered over the back of her neck. She smiled, loving the way Jason's eyes glazed over as he watched her drag the shimmering silk down over the pebbled tips of her nipples and then down to brush the still moist juncture of her thighs.

She pulled it through her legs and then up her back and over her shoulders again, allowing the fabric to flutter around her like a sexual matador's cape.

Feeling daring, she held it in front of her, knowing full well the sheerness only served to accentuate her nudity, making a seductive screen.

A quick peek confirmed Jason's penis had made a quick and full recovery. The sight and thought of what lay in store for her sent a hot thrill of desire spearing to her core. She slung the scarf toward him and then let it drag ever so slowly down his length to hang for a second on the bulbous tip before fluttering back to her. His quick intake of breath at the whisper-soft caress encouraged her to forge on.

Walking around him now, she allowed the silk to skim over his face, his body and then over and around her own. After a few circles, he grabbed the scarf, yanking it from her sweating hands.

"My turn," he said in a seductive, rasping voice. He looped it around her hips and drew her close, his erection bumping her abdomen.

Before she could ask what he had in mind, he scooped her into his arms and strode toward the bedroom, not stopping until he'd lain her on the satin-feeling spread of the king-size bed.

He stood looking down at her until she had to fight the instinct to cover her nudity.

"My god, you're gorgeous. Just looking at you turns me on." He gestured to the proof and shrugged with a smile. "But it's more than that. Do you feel it, too?"

Numb yet thinking if he didn't take her soon, she'd dissolve into a puddle of need right there on the spot, she nodded.

"Spread your legs for me, baby," he said in a low, gentle voice.

Why she felt no embarrassment with this man was a mystery, but she eagerly complied, and he climbed up on the bed to kneel between her thighs.

"So pretty, pink and swollen with my loving." He dragged the scarf between her legs to whisper across the moist petals begging for his touch.

Her breath caught while her heartbeat picked up, echoing in her ears.

The silky caress sent a flush of renewed moisture.

The scarf fluttered to land across her breasts. Jason's hot breath bathed her through the silk a nanosecond before drawing an aching tip into his mouth to suckle her through the fabric.

She moaned, arching her back for him to take her deeper within his mouth, moving restlessly on the bedspread, trying to tell him without words how much she needed him. All of him.

With a flex of his hips, he entered her weeping flesh, his lips releasing their silken hold on her nipple when he arched his back.

She peeled the wet silk from her suddenly cold breasts and draped it over his head, pulling to bring his lips to hers.

With a slower, more gentle and sedate rhythm, they loved each other, exchanging alternating nibbling and passionate, deep, wet kisses beneath their private silk tent.

Too soon, she felt pressure building, taking her along in a tidal wave of passion as it washed over her to leave her spent and weak, spread beneath Jason like a deflated sex toy.

His hands were everywhere, squeezing her breasts, reaching between them to fondle her swollen clitoris, dragging his fingers around and between her feminine lips and then back up her body. She wanted to smile and tell him not to worry about her; just enjoy.

Hello. A spark ignited when he nipped the tip of her breast between his white teeth. It zipped through her body, quickly spreading new flames in its path as it blazed a trail straight to her center.

Jason chose that time to pause and move his hips in little circles. Four to the left, three to the right, one in the middle and—bam!

She arched off the bed, a scream lodged in her throat, her body convulsing around him in its effort to pull him closer. He stiffened, gave another deep thrust and lowered to the mattress, pulling her to his side.

"Me, too, sweetheart," he mumbled, trailing soft kisses along her hairline.

Him, too? She would have asked, but her eyelids were too heavy, and her mouth didn't seem to work. She sighed, snuggling closer. Maybe a little nap would revive her.

Jason closed his eyes and said a prayer of thanks for the woman sleeping at his side.

The woman who had just turned his life upside down by telling him she loved him.

12

Emily propped the note she wrote on the pillow next to Jason and brushed a kiss on his hair before tiptoeing from his suite.

They'd awoken to make love throughout the night, each time better than the last.

Tears still burned her eyes three hours later when she walked through her own door back in Houston. Was the feeling she felt when she was with Jason the real deal? Did she truly, madly, deeply love him?

Yes, yes, yes and yes. Now what? She'd thought to come home and examine her feelings by light of day without the distraction of her physical attraction to Jason.

But, so far, all she'd felt was horribly alone.

Mittens padded into the room, stopped and turned around when she saw Emily.

"Great. Even the cat isn't glad to see me." She picked up her mail from the table Amy had put it on for the last few days and leafed through it. Nothing interesting or that couldn't wait.

The sun rose, and still she sat on the couch, dabbing her eyes with a soggy tissue. Mittens, evidently having endured all the hugs she could abide for one day, had left to go hide several hours ago.

Thank goodness Scott had never proposed! When she got her emotions under control, she'd call her family to tell them she was back and they were right. Scott wasn't that into her. And he was definitely not "the one."

Emily glanced at the phone, willing Jason to call. He was the one. She was not on rebound, as she'd first feared. If she couldn't have Jason, she didn't want anyone.

She sat up straighter. So what was she going to do about it?

Jason paced the living room of the suite, Emily's note clutched in his hand.

"What do you mean there are no flights out until tomorrow? I don't care how much it costs. I need to get to Houston!" His shoulders slumped. "I understand. Yes, please call me if there's a cancellation. Bye." He flipped his phone shut and tossed it onto the couch and then stared at the note again.

Jason—I'm so confused. And needy. I'm sorry if I used you. When I straighten out my thoughts, I'll call you.
Love, Emily

When she straightened out her thoughts. When would that be?

As far as he was concerned, there was nothing to straighten out. He loved her. She loved him. Enough said.

A knock sounded, echoing in the quiet suite. He growled and debated not answering the door. It could only be Doug because Jason didn't know anyone else now that Em was gone. Doug would show no compunction with using a key to get in, so Jason trudged to open the door for him.

He threw open the door to find Emily standing in the hall, eyes red-rimmed, holding a small suitcase.

"You stayed," he said around the lump in his throat.

She shook her head, tears sparkling in her eyes. "No," she finally said in a watery voice. "I'm back. If you still want me."

In response, he jerked her to him, the case falling to the floor of the entry. He kicked the door shut, hugging her close to his heart. "Only with every breath I take."

His hands ran over her curves, humbled to be able to touch her again, while he covered her face with kisses.

"Jason," she said on a laugh, pulling back, "I have to tell you something."

"I love you," they said in unison and then laughed.

His heated gaze bored into her. "Strip."

Shock was quickly replaced by the now familiar surge of arousal. Within seconds she stood naked before him.

"God, you're beautiful. What did I ever do to deserve you?"

"You're great in bed," she said with a grin, "Oh, and I love you. Totally." She took a step toward him. "Madly." Another step brought her close enough to rub her nipples against the starched fabric of his white shirt. So she did. "Now it's your turn." She yanked his belt from its loops and reached for the button fly of his jeans. "Strip."

He did, then carried her onto the patio to the hot tub. At her raised eyebrows, he explained, "I wanted you from the moment I saw you." He smiled sheepishly. "I thought maybe we could re-create it. Only, this time I plan to act on my instincts."

"Sounds like a plan," she said as he lowered her into the bubbling water; then she scooted to the other end of the spa. This time she didn't avert her gaze when he climbed into the tub with her.

Already more than halfway orgasmic, she enjoyed the bubbling effect on her breasts. She shifted and was rewarded by an interesting and powerful jet by her hip that, when she turned just so, surged into her while fluttering her labia. No doubt about it, she needed to buy a hot tub.

Head thrown back, on the cusp of a water-generated orgasm, she jumped at the sound of Jason's voice so close to her ear.

"Let me help you with that," he said in that low voice that always made her wet—even chin deep in bubbling water. His hands slid up her rib cage, grazing her breasts in a lazy manner.

She opened her eyes to find his eyes twinkling, his smile white in the darkness.

"Oops," he said, looking totally unrepentant.

He continued lifting her until he held her astride the jet of water. By happy coincidence, the position placed her breast at exactly his mouth level.

A contented sigh escaped her when he latched on to her nipple to suckle and tug rhythmically. With the water between her legs and his mouth on her breast, she went from buzzed to clear past hot and bothered to screaming release at the speed of orgasm.

He held her quaking body close, stroking her hair, kissing her neck and cheek.

"Jason Quartermaine," he said, holding out his hand.

She took it with a grin. "Emily Mitchell."

He rimmed her opening with the tip of his finger, eliciting a gasp. "I'm a financial adviser. What do you do?"

"I—I teach kindergarten," she said in gasping words, wishing he'd push his finger deeper.

"Have you ever made love in a hot tub, Miss Emily Mitchell?" he asked, now playing with her nipples.

She shook her head. "Nope." Beneath the water, she closed her hand around his erection. "I've never fucked in one either."

His gaze heated, nostrils flared. "We can take care of both of those."

And they did.

Emily woke up aroused on the king-size bed. Above her, Jason smoothed a warm cloth over her skin. "Hi," she said on a stretch, thrilled to see his eyes widen, his hungry gaze taking in her bare breasts. "What time is it?" Jason was already dressed. Of course, that didn't mean she couldn't change the situation in a heartbeat.

"I filled the tub," he said instead, lifting her from the bed and giving her butt a little pat to send her on her way to the bathroom. "Why don't you take a quick bath? By that time, our dinner will be here."

She paused at the door and struck a pose, another thrill shooting through her to see the evidence of her effect on him in the bulge in his pants. "Want to join me?"

"Absolutely," he said in the sexy, smooth voice she loved so much. "But I'm going to wait until after dinner."

"Maybe I won't need a bath then." She pouted, loving the way his eyes raked her, daring him to play in the water of the big tub with her.

"Oh, I'm sure I can talk you into it by then," he said with a definite gleam in his eye. "Go on, now, while I still have the strength to resist you. I'll lay out your clothes for you."

She hurried through the bath, not noticing the fragrant soap or decadent bubbles. She still had almost a full week of vacation before she had to go back to teaching kindergarten. She intended to make the most of every second.

Wrapped in a towel, she padded into the bedroom. Only her scarf lay on the big bed. "Jason, you just put my scarf out," she called.

"That's right," he appeared at the door, bare except for his trousers riding low on his lean hips. "I thought it might be ... interesting."

The light from the bathroom filtered to cast his smooth chest in bronze. *Interesting* was such an understatement.

Firelight reflected from the serving cart when she walked into the living room. As Jason was bare to the waist, she thought an interesting counterpoint might be for her to be bare from the waist down. Accordingly, she tied her scarf around her torso. She liked what she saw when she looked in the mirror, the darkness of her nipples playing peekaboo from beneath the silk, a promising shadow at the bottom rolled edge. By the way, Jason was devouring her with his eyes; he liked it, too.

Candles on every surface added to the romantic glow of the fire. To combat the heat, she noticed he'd opened the patio door. Its breeze flickered the candlelight, adding to the mood.

She shoved aside memories of the last room service she'd had, other than to contrast it with the beautiful, seductive scene Jason had so painstakingly set up.

"I like your 'dress,' he said with a sexy smile as he handed her a glass of wine.

"Thanks." She did a slow turn for full effect.

Jason made a low growling sound deep in his throat.

Dinner was good, she was sure, but she couldn't remember a thing they ate.

Finally Jason pushed away his plate. "I'm not sure this is such a good idea, after all."

"What do you mean?" With deliberate movement, she set her wine on the glass-topped table. *Oh, Lord, please don't let him regret inviting me to stay with him.* Had she read him wrong? Did his declaration of love have a different connotation?

He wiped his forehead with a napkin. Maybe the combined heat from all the candles and the fire bothered him.

He rose and walked to pull her, chair and all, away from the table.

"Em, it's a glass-topped table. I thought I was being sexy and clever by having you wear nothing but that sheer scarf." His bark of laughter ended on a distinct moan. "It was torture sitting across from you—I kept staring at your nipples . . . and then I made the mistake of looking down."

She followed his gaze. It really was X-rated, the way the silk parted at her hips to highlight the little patch of hair covering her femininity. Surprisingly, instead of embarrassing her, it excited her. She'd never thought of herself as a sexual being before, but all that had changed with Jason.

Confident in her allure, she smiled and leaned back, allowing her legs to fall slightly apart. "Did you like it?"

He shook his head and stepped between her thighs. "No, I loved it." He leaned with his palms on her thighs and then pushed her legs wider as his hand traveled up. At her juncture, he spread her wider, his thumbs rubbing up and down her weeping flesh. He met her gaze. "I love you," he said in a strangled whisper. "Thank you for coming back to me."

He lowered to his knees and took her screaming folds into his mouth, his thumbs worrying her nub. All it took was the addition of a few swipes of his talented tongue to bring her to a shuddering climax.

"Thank you," she whispered, tugging down his zipper when he stood. "I have a confession to make."

He paused midway through shucking out of his pants, muscles clenched. What did he think she was going to confess?

Reaching forward, she shoved his pants and boxers the rest of the way down and said, "You're the only guy I've ever had an orgasm with. . . . Is that unusual?" She traced the vein in his arousal with the tip of her finger, biting back a smile when he hissed in a breath.

"Okay, dessert's postponed." He pulled her up and out of the chair and plunged into her.

She smiled and wrapped her legs around him, rubbing her aching breasts against his firm chest and kissing him. "Fine with me. You're my dessert."

"Wear your scarf tonight," Jason whispered in her ear while she applied her makeup.

Moisture surged at the thought. She met his gaze in the mirror. "Won't that be a problem in the dining room?"

He grinned and winked. "I meant around your neck. Although, now that I think about it, maybe we should order in. I love it when you wear nothing or nothing but the scarf." His hands came forward to give her silk-covered breasts a quick squeeze. "What do you think?"

"I think," she said, pushing his hands down and regarding her nipples standing at attention through the thin silk of her halter dress, "you need to keep your hands to yourself for now or we'll get kicked out of the dining room." She stood. "Besides, we've been naked for the last three days."

"Are you complaining?" The look on his face was adorable.

Taking his hand, she pulled it under her skirt until she knew he felt her moistness. "No," she said in a husky whisper. "Never. I love being naked with you." She let his hand drop and leaned in for a light kiss. "Only you," she said against his lips.

He pulled the scarf from the pocket of his dress pants and tied it around her neck, a big droopy bow on the side. "Well, at least I can look at this, and then, when we get back to the room, make love to you in nothing but the scarf." He pulled her into a crushing hug. "God, I love you, baby."

"And I love you. Now let's go eat so we have the strength to come back here and make love all night."

A strained look passed over Jason's face, but it was gone so quickly, she couldn't really read it.

During the walk to the elevator, she fretted. Jason hadn't said a word about what would happen when they left the lodge. Since that first night, he hadn't mentioned relocating to Houston or asked her to move to Austin. Maybe he wasn't as committed to her as she was to him.

What a depressing thought.

After dinner Jason signaled the waiter, who brought and served champagne.

Emily widened eyes already droopy from all the wine. "Champagne? Are we celebrating something?"

There was that look again. Jason shifted on his chair and then lifted his glass. "Absolutely. We're celebrating our fabulous week." He clicked the rim of his glass to hers. "And us." Another click. "Our love." Click.

Tears burned her eyes. The champagne bubbles abraded the inside of her mouth, but she managed to swallow.

She blinked. Jason wasn't in his chair. He took her hand. He knelt beside her chair. Ohmigod, was that a diamond ring in his hand?

"Emily Mitchell, you are my soul mate. I can't live the rest of my life without you." He paused, the diamond of the ring sparkling in the candlelight where it hovered at the tip of the third finger of her left hand. "If you don't say yes, I'll die."

She grinned, tears streaming down her cheeks. "You haven't asked me anything yet."

He grinned and wiped a tear from his eye. "Will you marry me?"

In answer, she reached down and pushed the ring the rest of the way onto the finger that had waited her entire life for that moment. "Yes," she said in a ragged whisper.

He stood, pulling her out of her chair into a hug and swinging her around before kissing her with all the passion and promise she could ask for.

Around them applause broke out, several people offering congratulations. They sat back down, smiling at each other.

The waiter refilled their glasses.

Jason raised his in a toast. "To us." He leaned over the table. "Kiss me, future Mrs. Quartermaine," he said, love shining in his eyes.

She sighed. "Mrs. Quartermaine. I love the sound of that." She leaned to meet him halfway.

Light flared to her right, followed by stinging.

"The scarf!" They both yelled. Jason ripped it from her neck and threw it to the floor, stomping until the flames subsided.

He pulled her close. "Are you all right?" He ran his hands up and down her arms. "Did you get burned?"

"No." She looked down at the charred remains of her scarf, smoldering on the hardwood floor. "But my scarf didn't survive."

He pulled her tight against him. "I'll buy you another scarf. A hundred scarves. All I want is you."

"What a coincidence. . . ." With a smile, she pulled him toward the elevator.

Strong, brave and hotter than hot. Meet three gorgeous heroes, ready to come to your rescue. . . .

Hot Down Under, Susan Lyons
Australian men are just plain sexy. And Mick Donovan, Australian firefighter, has to be the sexiest of them all. Tash McKendrick is far from home and ready to party in the land down under. Sex on the beach. Sex in the air. Mick knows just how to rock her world . . . all night long.

All Fired Up, P. J. Mellor
Firefighter Nick Howard transferred from Houston to a tiny Texas town expecting peace and quiet . . . not a steamy tryst with the unbelievably sexy Tricia Lundsford. Their bedroom chemistry is combustible, and every mind-blowing encounter has Nick fantasizing about the next. . . .

Fighting Fire, Alyssa Brooks
Fire chief Brent Sommers stopped by the Lucky Hart to safety-check the place. Just his luck that Carmen Harte, the club's new owner and his former flame, is looking dangerously beautiful. And when a faulty door latch leaves them locked in Carmen's office for hours, there's only one way to pass the time—surrendering to burning lust. . . .

**Please turn the page for an exciting sneak peek of
The Firefighter,
now on sale at bookstores everywhere!**

"I what?" Nick looked so shocked she would have laughed, had she not been on the edge of hysteria.

Instead, she pulled the old afghan closer and pushed him out the door onto the little landing. "Never mind. Bye."

He stopped the closing of the door with his hand. "I'll be back. Seven."

She nodded, fighting back tears, and then quietly closed the door.

Reaching under the throw, she maneuvered the bra until she had Her Highness off and then slung it across the room.

It hit the wall of the kitchen with a soft thud and then slid down, leaving a wet trail on the powder-blue wall.

What a waste of money. She dropped the afghan, unzipped her jeans and shoved them down and off. Her boots, socks and thong followed until she stood completely naked in the sunshine that streamed into the cozy living room. Maybe a shower would give her some energy.

The click of the door caught her attention.

Nick stood in the open doorway and swallowed, his gaze searing her from head to bare toes and back again.

She snatched the afghan from the floor and held it in front of her.

"Sorry," he said, biting back a smile and looking anything but, "I wanted to ask if I needed to dress up for dinner."

"Ah—no. Everything is pretty casual around here." She scanned his lean, jean-clad and oxford-cloth-shirted frame as though she didn't already have it memorized. "What you're wearing is fine—without the gel of course—just about anywhere we decide to go."

He nodded. "Okay. See you." Before the door closed, he stuck his head back in and said, "This time you'd better lock the door behind me. If I come back in, I won't want to leave again."

Promises, promises. But she walked to the door and slid the bolt home anyway.

After Alex the Aggressively Unfaithful had used and dumped her, she'd taken a vow of celibacy. Being home again, at the original scene of the crime, so to speak, just made her more vulnerable. She could handle it. Ooh, bad choice of words. She was celibate. She wasn't going to handle anything.

She thought ahead to her dinner date, how sexy Nick was and the heated gleam in his eyes. Where were chastity belts when you needed them?

Nick tilted back in the metal chair of his new office and regarded the man leaning against the doorway. "What, exactly, are you telling me?"

Jack, his second in command, stepped in and lowered his booming voice a decibel or two. "I just thought you should know. All through school she wasn't called Hurricane Lundsford for nothing. She just has a habit of. . . Well, she attracts trouble." He chuckled and shook his head. "Hell, I give her credit for having the balls to come back, even after all these years. Small towns have memories like elephants."

"Sounds to me like she had too many critics in Harper's Grove. No wonder she bolted." He tried hard not to let his irritation show, but what right did Jack have to try to warn him away from the first woman he'd been even remotely attracted to in almost two years?

"That may be, but—aw, hell, do what you want." Jack raked his hand through his spiked blond hair. "You're gonna anyway. I thought you might stop thinking with your little head for a minute and realize it's not a good situation to have the town see you aligned with Hurricane Lundsford before you even get settled." He turned to leave.

"Jack?"

Jack paused, his hand on the doorknob.

"Thanks, anyway," Nick said quietly. "I'll take it under advisement."

Jack nodded and let himself out.

Nick glanced at the industrial looking clock on the white wall. If he hurried, he'd have time to shave again and shower before he picked up Tricia.

He rubbed the stubble on his chin as he walked to the truck. He was only shaving again because it wasn't polite to go on a first date with five-o'clock shadow.

The thought of Tricia's fair skin marred by razor burn had not a damn thing to do with it.

The scented lotion glided over her shower-warm skin like liquid silk. Her body heat activated the cherry scent to waft over her, making her achy and restless.

She circled her areolae, watching the dark skin pucker, budding her nipples into stiff peaks, and bit back a groan.

Celibacy wasn't all it was cracked up to be. It was darn hard work.

Her lotion-slicked hand skimmed down to the neatly trimmed pubis, and she couldn't help wondering if Nick would appreciate the little heart she'd painstakingly crafted.

Wait. Nick would never see it. She was celibate. She needed to remember that.

Her reflection in the wardrobe mirror of her bedroom snagged her attention, and she studied her body with a scrutiny usually reserved for laboratory rats.

In hindsight, purchasing the Her Highness bra wasn't one of her brighter moves. She hefted her breasts and decided they weren't all that small, and if she really wanted cleavage, she could always duct tape them together. Remembering the rash from the last time she did that, she winced and scratched. Then again, maybe not.

She turned and glanced critically at her rear end. Too much junk in the trunk. She thought of the way she'd caught Nick gazing at it and decided maybe she'd overcompensated when she bought the Her Highness in her effort to draw attention away from her hips and butt. It had seemed like a good idea at the time.

Heat flashed through her at the thought of Nick's hands on her breasts, his erection pressed firmly against her mound.

The last time she'd had sex was . . . way too long ago to count. That had to be the reason that just the thought of Nick made her wet and empty-feeling.

Wait.

No one knew she was home, other than the few patrons of Cup Half Full. She could do pretty much what she wanted for at least a day or two.

She brushed her fingertips across the now swollen lips protruding from the close-cropped heart of sandy curls and gasped at the intimate feel.

Opening her eyes, she looked at her flushed reflection. Did she dare? Nick was practically a stranger.

All her teenage boyfriends passed through her mind, a blur of humiliation.

A stranger might be a welcome change.

She could ride him all night, slake her lust, and no one would be the wiser. If she kept the lights off and lit enough candles to appear romantic, he might not even notice her less than perfect body.

Tomorrow she could begin her celibacy again.

* * *

Nick turned off the porn movie and finished shaving. He'd thought to watch the flick and whack off before his shower to take the edge off. He was as horny as his granddad's hound dogs. Weird. Just the thought of Tricia gave him an instant hard-on, yet watching the graphic movie had left him cold. What was it about the little blonde that had his dick twitching with eager anticipation?

He shrugged and stepped into a less than warm shower that caused a hitch in his breath and forced his mind to the evening ahead. Slow and easy. He'd take it slow and easy if it killed him.

Tricia lit another candle and coughed. They were more potently scented than she remembered. A glance at the clock on the microwave confirmed that Nick would arrive in less than ten minutes.

She wiped her sweaty palms on the side of her terry robe and said a little prayer that she'd read the handsome firefighter correctly.

A knock sounded in the quiet apartment. Her heartbeat echoed in her ears.

"Who is it?" she called, even though she had a pretty good idea. It wouldn't do to open the door, primed for lust, and find anyone other than Nick. Like her grandmother.

"Nick," came the deep voiced answer.

"Just a sec!" She met her semipanicked gaze in the decorative mirror over the fireplace mantel, took a deep breath and tossed the terry robe into the closet. On wobbly legs, she walked to the door.

No retreat. "Take no prisoners," she whispered before opening the door.

Nick stood in the doorway, clutching the neck of the bottle of chardonnay in a death grip.

He was a dead man.

Tricia stood before him, the candlelight behind her playing a wicked game of peekaboo through one of the sheerest scraps of lingerie he'd ever had the privilege to encounter.

"Hi." She motioned him in. "I thought we could either have dinner here or have an appetizer here and eat later," she said, stepping back for him to enter.

So dead. "I brought some wine," he said inanely.

She took the bottle and set it on the side table next to the door. "Maybe a little later." She smoothed the gossamer fabric over her lush hips and then met his hungry gaze. "You asked, earlier, what I made." She put her arms out to her side and turned in a slow circle. "I thought I'd show you."

He may be a dead man, but one part of his anatomy was leaping to life at the sight. Her nipples were dark shadows beneath the elaborately embroidered red and hot-pink hearts shielding them. When she turned, the sheer fabric swept against her hips in a sensuous rustle of silk. Beneath the sheerness, a red ribbon bisected a trophy ass if he'd ever seen one.

His eager cock pressed against the button fly of his jeans.

She rose on bare tiptoes to brush her lips over his, her pebbled nipples poking his chest through the layers of their respective clothing.

"This is from my Valentine Lovers Collection." Her voice was low, seductive, wrapping around his cock and squeezing from within. She ran a red-polished fingernail along the embroidery until she came to the top of one nipple. "I call this pattern Secret Bliss." A crackling sound came from her chest before she flipped down the heart shape to reveal a pebbled nipple. "What do you think?" She flipped open the other little secret door.

He locked his knees to keep from falling at her feet in a pile of lust-crazed hormones. Praying his voice wouldn't crack, he said, "Looks like a winner to me." He took a hesitant step closer. "But maybe we should do some product testing."

She closed the distance between them, looping her arms around his neck. "I couldn't agree more." She leaned back, her nipples jutting toward him. Begging him to take them.

It would be ungentlemanly to let a lady beg.

* * *

Tricia closed her eyes and clamped her thighs together to keep from rubbing against the man in her arms when he closed his hot mouth firmly over her nipple and suckled her.

Moisture saturated the crotch of the scanty thong.

He reached up to palm her other breast, squeezing rhythmically with his suckling.

One of them moaned. It may have been her. Thank goodness the guy was strong, or else she'd have been on the floor. Her knees had taken on the consistency of overcooked spaghetti with the first strong draw of his mouth. When he added the tongue action, she all but swooned.

He gave a final lick to each well-tested nipple, his breath fanning the wet tips. "We need to check out the entire ensemble." His breath came in shallow pants, his eyes fever bright. "Where can we do more thorough testing?"

Hot damn. Her grandmother was right about the effectiveness of advertising after all.

She pointed to the couch. She'd have chosen the bedroom, but her bed was still a work in progress, piled high with clothing. Besides, with all the candlelight, the lighting was more flattering in the living room.

Just as she was thinking how romantic it would be if he swept her up in his arms and carried her to the couch, he came up with a much more interesting variation.

Behind her, he hugged her around her waist, his lips trailing kisses up and down the side of her neck, setting off tingles in places that hadn't tingled in a very long time.

One of his hot hands smoothed down her stomach and then pushed on her pubic bone while he ground his hardness into her buttocks.

Before she could react or decide if she wanted more, he pushed both hands up her rib cage to cup her breasts.

Oh, yeah. She definitely liked this. To encourage him, she pushed back hard against his erection, eliciting a sound somewhere between a growl and a groan. It made her exposed nipples bead impossibly harder. She was sure her thong would literally drip if she tried to move.

He squeezed her breasts to the point of near pain, thrust his hips against her butt and lifted her from her feet to carry her to the couch.

Unconventional, maybe. Erotic . . . definitely.

He set her on her feet next to the couch and leaned around to lick her lips.

"Show me more," he whispered, his breath hot against her cheek.

Did she dare? Oh, who was she kidding? If she thought she felt wicked designing and making the prototype she wore, it was nothing compared to the way she felt at that moment.

"I plan on it." She turned and pushed him to sit on the couch and then stood straddling his knees. "This number is multipurpose." She ran her hands up his steel-like thighs to barely brush her thumbs against the hardness beneath his fly. "Designed to be used by one," she said, licking her flavored lip gloss, "or more lovers at a time."

"Do tell," he said, eyebrows arched.

She nodded, emboldened by the heat in his gaze that made her nipples tingle. "For instance," she explained, taking his hands and placing them on her exposed nipples, "You could play here." Her breath caught when he lightly pinched the hardened tips and then brushed the pads of his thumbs over the points. "And, um . . ." She licked her lips. What the heck. "Someone else could play here." Before she lost her nerve, she placed one bare foot next to his thigh and canted her hips for him to better view the heart shaped opening in the crotch of her matching thong.

His eyes widened, along with his smile. "I don't think so, baby." Pressure on her nipples drew her closer.

He released one nipple and cupped her buttock to pull her up onto his lap until she was stretched along his length.

"I can multitask," he said, drawing her abandoned nipple into his hot mouth. At the next heartbeat, his fingers played with her slick folds, making them impossibly wetter before inserting one talented finger after the other.

The ribbon bow on her hip slipped, the thong falling away. His fingers left her for less than a second to drag off the wet fabric. On sensory overload, she could only whimper, unable to even move her hips in counterpoint to the renewed thrusting of his fingers.

Ripe sensation filled her until the dam burst. It was beyond the big O. Until that moment, she'd never experienced an all-over orgasm. Every pore gushed.

She gasped for air, her entire body one giant orgasmic contraction.

Sometime during her attempted recovery from her in-body experience, Nick had shed his pants. The feel of hot male flesh against her ribs barely registered before he lifted her from his blast furnace body.

Before she could form a protest—yeah, like that was going to happen—he brought her down on his more than impressive erection. The tip of his penis kissed her uterus. Again and again she slammed down on him until she was screaming her need.

She may have even passed out for a few seconds.

When her mind could put more than gasps and grunts into her thoughts, she tilted her head from his chest to tell him how spectacular he was, only to be silenced with another rock-her-world kiss.

One of his fingers slid between them to draw lazy circles around her opening where his penis was still deeply embedded. His fingertip found her nub and began playing with it until it swelled with renewed lust.

She sighed.

Celibacy was so overrated.

*For a taste of sheer, sensual bliss, the adventurous women
in these sizzling stories are willing to do anything,
risk everything, and break all the rules . . .*

"Checkmate"
Courtesan Cora Durand longs to find a man to satisfy her
own hidden desires. Rupert Roland has dreamed of having
beautiful, defiant Elsa at his carnal mercy, and when each gets
their wish, the outcome is pure ecstasy . . .

"Lust's Vow"
Hannah Rosworth's late husband claimed that she was too
sexually inexperienced for his tastes. But Kenneth Walker, an
infamous rake, can see the fire beneath her sedate exterior.
And at the season's most decadent orgy he'll show her how to
give—and receive—the ultimate pleasure . . .

"Night of the Taking"
At the Festival of Catus in a small English village, local virgins
take part in a mysterious, erotic ritual. Jessica can hardly believe she's been chosen, but the irresistible green-eyed male
who claims her will use any wickedly seductive means to
prove that she is his mate—and his queen . . .

**Here's an exciting sneak peak of
Lacy Danes'
WHAT SHE CRAVES
coming next month from Aphrodisia!**

1

LONGING

Surry England 1815

"Come on, Emma, hit him harder."

W-A-A-CK.

"Uhhh."

"Oh . . . God . . . good girl, Emma, good girl. . . . Again."

She shouldn't listen to this. Hannah's brows drew together as she strained to hear the voices coming from Lord Brummelton's secluded summerhouse.

What were they up to?

The tone of their voices . . . intrigued her. She stepped forward to continue on her daily ritual to the mill—blast—she couldn't get her feet to move. She needed to know what mischief was about.

Her maid, Gertie, said Mr. Roland arrived back from the war with friends but—

W-A-A-CK.

Another pleasure-filled groan filtered on the fall breeze.

She started at the octagon-shaped structure. Floor to ceiling windows that faced the river reflected the dappled light of the late afternoon sun, marring the view within. Nothing, she couldn't see a thing.

"Oh, God, Emma, his arse is so red. Reach around and touch his prick."

Hannah's eyes widened. *Oh, my.* They engaged in a sexual act.

"He's not ready, Rupert." Emma said in a exasperated voice. "Even though you could spend, I want this to last." Emma's squeaky voice paused. "Isn't Kenneth supposed to join us?"

"Who cares about Kenneth? Get on with it, woman!"

Biting her lip, Hannah hesitated. Maybe at a different angle she could see . . . something. Her heart pounded in her chest as she stepped forward.

C-R-U-N-C-H

She stopped. Blast. Fallen leaves. The sound so loud to her ears in the silence of the woods. They would surely hear.

The leaves scattered in a thick carpet all around the structure. She frowned. There was no way she could approach silently, but if they were engrossed in the love act, they might not notice.

A pleasure-filled groan came from a man with a baritone voice, and shivers cascaded down her arms. Hannah closed her eyes. Good lord, she longed for that sensation.

She didn't care if they heard. She needed to learn how to pleasure a man. At least two men were in that summerhouse engaged in wicked futter, and thoroughly enjoying it. Enjoying the act as her husband never had with her. Surely she would learn to pleasure a man if she could see them, and if by chance they saw her . . . Well, she didn't give a damn.

Hairs on her arms and neck stood in anticipation as she determinedly crept forward, shuffling her feet to not make a sound. She would finally understand what made Simon leave her bed.

The path that followed the river went directly in front of the summerhouse. *Please let there be no reflection on the glass at a different angle.* Her heart sped in her chest as another groan filtered through the trees.

Once in front of the structure, she scooted behind a birch tree. The width was a bit narrow but she could hide her face if she needed to. She inhaled the crisp fall air, and closed her eyes—*please let me learn*—then peeked at the windows of the cottage. Oh . . . my . . . Her eyes bulged in shock.

A man with pale skin knelt on the floor, his breeches pushed down past his knees. A blond woman, younger than herself, stood behind him, a long thin switch in hand. She held the birch out to the side and *swoosh*, the twig hit his bottom with a loud crack. Ouch. That's not what she expected.

The kneeling man flinched from the impact and groaned. Another deep groan came from a man who stood farther back in the structure.

He watched them as she did.

While giving orders to Emma, his penis jutted out of his pants. His long fingers stroked the length, settled at the tip, and then rolled. Hannah bit her lip. His well-proportioned hands stroked in a musical rhythm. Beautiful. His hands held an artistic quality.

In her mind, those big graceful hands slid down her body, working their magic on her bare skin. She trembled and her eyelids fluttered. Oh my! His fingers caressed her breasts, her inner thighs, and the swell of her bum. What would lying with this man be like? She groaned. Amazing. His expertise in this act shone in every motion. Her skin tingled with dew. What a sensation he would create in her and such a shocking thought.

The man on the floor did not cry out in pain as the switch hit him again, but moaned in pleasure.

How could anyone find pleasure from a spank? Her eyes narrowed, and she tilted her head to the side. Surely she missed something. She blinked again. Yes, he found pleasure. His breath puffed in and out, and his bluish-red penis stood stiff as whalebone between his legs. Amazing. And . . . strangely the sight aroused her. Her eyes widened. How could she like watching such an act?

She tried to take in the whole scene but she couldn't stop staring at both men's sex. The man who knelt possessed a long narrow phallus, much narrower than the two of her experience, but a good thumb longer than Simon's.

The other of her comparison was a vague memory of beauty and satiny skin, to which neither of these could compare. Her heart sped and her skin heated with dew as her youthful hand trembled, rubbing down the hot skin and plum shaped head. She shook herself, and pushed the pleasant memory from her mind.

W-A-A-CK

Hannah flinched. She couldn't imagine Simon finding pleasure from a spank, but then again nothing she did pleased him, so maybe she was wrong. He only found excitement in his whores and at his clubs.

The man moved from the back of the cottage into a better view. Hannah ducked behind the old birch tree and closed her eyes.

God, she was mad. She gasped for air.

The five lonely years since Simon's death had made her crazy with the urge to learn to please a man. First she lowered herself to purchasing all sorts of bawdy books. . . . Books that talked of things such as this. And now . . . Now she ogled Mr. Roland and invaded his privacy.

Her chest tightened. The reality was she would never hold the skill to master . . . such pleasure. God, this was agony. She needed to leave before one of them noticed her. Indeed . . . her shoulders slumped. Oh, poppiedust. She turned and stepped in the direction of Huntington cottage.

"Emma, dear, I want to feel your hot cunt while you frig Kit with your mouth."

Hannah flung around. This she couldn't resist. She read about kissing a man's sex in the *Perfumed Garden* and wondered if men and women truly found pleasure that way.

Emma knelt on cushions on the floor. Kit lay in front of her, his phallus standing straight as the trees that surrounded her.

Hannah's hands brushed the smooth trunk of the large birch tree that stood by her. Imagining the hotness of smooth male flesh as her hands ran across rough cool bark, she slid her hands out to the edges, then up and down. In her mind her hands explored every ridge and vein of his sex. Her pulse increased, and her chest tightened. God, she needed to feel a man again. Her hands trembled. With all the books she read, the next time a man joined her in bed she hoped she would have an idea what to do.

Emma leaned down and her tongue traced the head of the man's penis. Kit groaned.

"Umm..." Hannah's tongue slid out and traced her lips. She imagined the salty flavor of skin and the tapered shape of a prick head as an erection pressed into her mouth. Her nipples peaked hard beneath her corset.

The other man, Rupert, knelt behind Emma. Flipping up her skirt and petticoat so they lay on her back, he ran his hands down the swell of her creamy bottom. "Good girl, Emma, take Kit in," he murmured, then slid his hand between her spheres. Hannah whimpered. Oh how she wanted rough male hands on her bum again.

"No, Emma. Pleasure Kit. Concentrate on nothing but him."

Kit groaned, and thrust his hips up as Emma lowered her head down. Half his shaft slid into her mouth. As she pulled her head up to the tip, his shaft shimmered with her saliva.

Hannah's mouth watered. She wanted this... wanted to be

Emma as she slid hot male flesh into her mouth and another man caressed her. She swallowed hard. How scandalous.

Emma's tongue slid out and traced the ridge, she puckered her lips, and slid back down the length.

Hannah could feel the pressure of a phallus as the head slid into her mouth. Saliva pooled and dribbled down the length as the prick throbbed and twitched. Her lips caressed the ridge and popped to the tip. Wetness dewed her skin, and her sex pulsed as a moan caught in her throat. She crossed her legs in an attempt to control the building desire and slickness sliding down her leg.

Good lord, she should tear her gaze away. Her chest tightened and her skin tingled. Too many years . . . how she needed a man's touch. She had no prospects, no admirers. This was madness. Her lip trembled.

Kit groaned, and tears sprang to Hannah's eyes. She would never, could never, possess the ability to pleasure a man this way, but still she stood and watched. She was a fool.

Tingles slid across her body with every caress the threesome made. Her nipples strained against her corset as Rupert grasped his large stiff prick. He ran his hand along the length, then laid his prick in the crack of Emma's bum. Not between her legs, but in the crevice.

Viewing such an animalistic position caused a hunger to seep through her. She could almost feel the hot skin as the head of a penis slid between the spheres of her bum. A man's muscles shaking against her as he pumped into her like an animal in the fields.

Her sex spasmed and she arched her back in search of the imaginary prick, but there was nothing there. Oh how she wanted to diddle a man in that position. This man. Shifting her stance, she gasped, and her nubbin throbbed. His hands on the soft flesh of her bum, gripping her as his penis pushed into her sex again and again. She clamped her leg muscles tighter, and the delicious sensation spiraled. *Good Lord.*

Emma continued to devour Kit's penis. She licked and sucked until on a groan Kit thrust his hips with abandon. Her mouth slid farther down his length and he cried out in pleasure. His hands gripped Emma's curly hair as his face contorted in ecstasy.

Pain ripped at her heart and she closed her eyes. *Please let me have the chance to make a man cry out in pleasure the way this woman did.*

Her eyes fluttered open. Oh! Juices slid down her leg as Rupert slid his prick into Emma from behind. Blast it. She wanted to feel the delight they shared, but the only way to do that would be to touch herself. Trembling, she tried to restrain her hands as they slid down her dress. Her sex pounded with the beat of her heart as her face flamed with heat. What if someone saw?

Rupert pumped and flexed his ass, as he slid his penis into Emma from behind. She could hear the wetness as he slid in again and again. Her fingers found the place between her thighs and pressed her skirts between them. The fabric of her shift dampened and clung to the lips of her sex. Imagining her fingers were this man's, she caressed the swollen folds and the hard bud between. She pressed into her opening and splendid contractions weakened her knees. Oh! How she wished it were his prick.

Kenneth Walker plodded down the path toward the river. He refused to stall any longer. They needed to be ready for the members when they arrived for the masque. The masters would be excited about the event and ready for bawdy play. If they weren't there to greet them when they arrived . . . things would get out of control.

Damn Rupert for not restraining himself until the festivities for a bit of nifty. Last night finally proved to Kenneth that he preferred his loving one on one. Emma had favored him, much to Rupert's annoyance, then all but wrapped her legs around him this morning before the group could rise.

He refused to be any woman's plaything. Just the idea that Emma was Rupert's and preferred other men made his skin crawl. Out of respect for Rupert, he let this morning's flirtation pass without comment.

Cold memories of his father's sobs in his aunt's library as his mother coldly told him she would not give up her lover crept up his spine. His jaw clenched and his cheek twitched. How she reduced the powerful Duke of Deventon to a slobbering lump still puzzled him. He shook himself to rid the thought.

Never, never would he let himself fall prey to that kind of humiliation, or more precisely, to that kind of woman for more than one night.

He rounded the turn in the path, and the summerhouse lay ahead.

"Emma, dear, I want to feel your hot cunt while you frig Kit with your mouth."

Shit. He stopped in his tracks. So much for his dallying. Turning toward the river, he beheld black hair and a deep blue dress peeking out from behind a white birch tree.

Well, well . . . His lips curved up. Someone peeped on Rupert and his games. He held in a chuckle. If Rupert knew he would perform to the fullest and probably spill his seed within a second.

The woman's face slid out from behind the tree and gazed into the summerhouse. Her hands slid up and down the rough bark as if she stroked a large cock.

Damn, what a pretty thing. And oddly familiar. He glanced at her hands again as they clenched the edges of the bark. His chest tightened. Could it be? He stared back at her black hair and round face with pale, clear skin.

God, that tiny nose and those lush lips occasioned his dreams. A groan caught in this throat as he stiffened. What stood behind that tree would be just as magnificent as it had been twelve years ago. Even better, she would have matured into a woman, with soft flesh in all the right places.

Hannah Hay, the Marquess of Wolverland's eldest daughter, and the first woman to touch his cock, stood watching his friends as she stroked a tree-sized prick in her mind. Only her imagination could make such a leap. His smile grew bigger and his cock throbbed. Lulling his head back, his fingers found the ridge that pressed against his buckskins and he stroked.

Hannah's hands had been so small and soft against the tender flesh of his youthful prick. His body shook. He had longed to touch her for weeks. When she finally consented, he had been so aroused that he spent after one stroke of her silky hand.

His fingers tightened upon the ridge of his straining shaft, and he forced his eyes open to watch her as she spied on Rupert in awe and fascination. Her face was still so easy to read; curiosity, pleasure, and arousal shown clear as day on her china-doll features.

Pink tongue slid out and traced her lips, then her mouth opened as if taking a prick between their fullness. Damn, those lush lips would feel amazing on his cock. Wetness seeped into his pants and his prick strained. Closing her eyes, she sucked in the sides of her cheeks.

Good God! Without a doubt Emma sucked Kit right now, and Hannah wanted to suck someone too. Raw need flooded his body and he stepped forward. He would walk to her and offer his body like he did all those years ago.

His boyish voice came back to him. "Come now, Hannah. Let me tickle you."

She had been awkward then, just as he had. His mouth watered as he touched his boyhood tongue to the crevice at the base of her throat and tasted her skin. She would taste the same. He knew it.

The smell of her perfume and the sound of her laughter. Shaking hands, trembling bodies, and sloppy urgent kisses. His chest tightened and his throat constricted. God, the way she looked at him and gently touched his face. No woman since had been able to measure to her genuine kindness when his world shattered. This time what they shared would be different; no one would force him to leave. This time he would bed her and bed her well.

"Ahhhha!"

The cry of passion snapped him back to the sight at hand. Emma moaned and whimpered. Kit surely spent and now stroked her as Rupert had his way. They would be done soon and he wanted Hannah to know he watched her, watching them.

He cleared his throat loud enough for Rupert to hear in the cottage.

Hannah did not budge but her hands slid down the front of her dress.

He shook his head and smiled. Just like her to be so absorbed. She probably wouldn't notice if a herd of sheep wandered through. Bending down, he picked up a stick and tossed the twig at the tree she stood behind. The foot-long branch hit square against the trunk and she jumped. Her gaze flew to him as he stood in the path from the summerhouse. He grinned; *yes, dear, someone is watching you.*

The trail was the only way she could go. If she went past the summerhouse, Rupert would see. She glanced at the house, then at the path. Her face flamed a crimson shade.

Ah Hannah . . . how you flatter me. He did not know there were still people around who blushed at such things. With her head lowered, she turned on heel and cut through the trees to the riverbank.

Oh, no you don't, my sweet Hannah. In five long strides he came up behind her and clasped her arm.

She pulled but his grasp held firm. "Let go of me! You beast!"

"Sweet, sweet Hannah . . ."

Hannah's eyes widened. "Do I know you, sir? Please unhand me." Yanking her arm again, his grip eased but did not fall from her body.

Her heart pounded so hard the beat made her hands shake. How could someone have seen her? Good lord. This was the man Emma mentioned when she first spied on them. He knew what she watched. Her cheeks grew hotter. She averted her gaze to the riverbed and stepped away from him.

"Not so quickly, sweet." His hand stroked her arm and lightning slid thorough her veins straight to the place between her thighs. *Not now, blast you damn body.* She closed her eyes and tried to quell the shiver his caress caused, but failed. His muscles in return stiffened.

"Don't say you don't remember me." The man shook his head at her as she tried once again to yank her arm free.

"Damn you, sir, let go of—"

"I believe I was the first man to ever touch you."

"P—Pardon?"

He inclined his head and raised his eyebrows.

Her mouth dropped open. "Kenny . . . Kenny Walker?"

He smiled. Then laughed. "Haven't been called Kenny in ages. But yes."

Was this man truly him? The young man whom twelve years ago she spent her most memorable summer. They had run through the woods, played hide and seek, and swum in the lake with her sisters and his brother. Her first infatuation, her first kiss. Good Lord. The young man who by just saying "Hannah" had made her heart pound and heat grace her cheeks with wicked thoughts.

She searched his face. His strong, straight nose, angled cheeks, and dimpled chin were the same. His eyes, the same smoky brown that you could get lost in, stared back at her with intense heat. Her body dewed remembering all that hungry stare promised.

She studied his body. Oh my! His shoulders had broadened, and his chest—she bit her lip—encased in a tight-fitting coat, left little to the imagination. Her breath hitched at sculpted thighs encased in tight buckskin breeches. A lump formed in her throat and she swallowed hard envisioning those legs tangled in hers.

A very fit, attractive, and well-muscled man stood before her. God, he was much taller than she remembered. Her memories . . . Oh, her eyes closed. His fingers as they slid up her skirts and into the wet folds of her . . . Making her tremble in such a way she thought she would die.

Kenny gently stroked her arm and with his thumb traced circles in to the fabric of her sleeve. Her nipples ached, pebbled hard, wanting the circular motion.

His hasty departure from his aunt's after a summer of friendship and flirtation and his last words "I will bed you one day, dear sweet Hannah" slid through her mind.

She stared at his breeches where his erection bulged. He didn't even try to conceal his arousal. He journeyed to the summerhouse today to have relations with his friends. He, like her husband, was a rake, with a bad enough reputation that she heard of his adventures.

A deep rumble of a laugh came from him and his erection twitched beneath the leather of his pants. Unable to pull her stare from the bulge, her cheeks grew warm. All she wanted was to touch that ridge. God, she was mad.

"Let me tickle you, my sweet," he said as he slid his finger beneath her chin and raised her eyes.

Eyes blazing with need met hers. Her sex clenched and she groaned. His words, the same he used all those years ago. She bit her lip. Her body knew the promise in those words. But what if she was as bad as her husband claimed? Kenny had been with many women since their encounter—

"Hannah? Please . . ." His voice, filled with raspy desire, caressed her nerves. She needed to be touched and who better to touch her than the man who initiated her to the act of coitus?

"Yes. Kenny, touch me, touch me."